# CUSTOMS

# LISA ZEIDNER

# Customs

Alfred A. Knopf    New York    1981

THIS IS A BORZOI BOOK PUBLISHED BY ALFRED A. KNOPF, INC.

Copyright © 1981 by Lisa Zeidner
All rights reserved under International and Pan-American Copyright
Conventions. Published in the United States by Alfred A. Knopf, Inc.,
New York, and simultaneously in Canada by Random House of Canada
Limited, Toronto. Distributed by Random House, Inc., New York.

My grateful thanks to Alice Quinn for her help with the manuscript.

Library of Congress Cataloging in Publication Data
Zeidner, Lisa.
Customs.
I. Title.
PS3576.E37C8   1981        813'.54        80-21478
ISBN 0-394-51475-0

MANUFACTURED IN THE UNITED STATES OF AMERICA
FIRST EDITION

For Joseph,
Dorothy, Julie,
and Russell Zeidner

1

The day before I met Mildred
Howell I quit my job.

The day before that—for there's always a day before, right
back to the dinosaurs—the day before that had been Sunday.
But Sunday isn't a day, even if it smells like bacon and fresh
coffee. Sunday is an idea, like God Himself; and no matter
what you do—go to the zoo, accomplish a tan, try to relax—no
matter what, Sundays are only airbrushed onto the calendar.

But I tried. That Sunday, A. Argyle Lovett and I stayed in
bed all afternoon. We forgot where the head of the bed was; we
forgot, like sleeping children, where the door was. "Arg," I said,
which had the extra edge of being half of his middle name; and
he reciprocated with "Jennifer," which is half of my whole name
as he was half of me. When he touched my breasts, a parachute
opened over ground, miraculously, at just the right moment.
Once he touched the back of my head with the tips of two
fingers in the back of a dark movie house and I loved everyone there—including the villain in the film—just for love of him.

Still, I wanted to be happier.

Making love was non-caloric; it didn't sustain me. But what
was happy, the stage name of a stripteaser? Happy was nebulous

as Sunday. It was merely what I was not. The word *happy* sounded muffled as a suicide going over a cliff, trailing a scarf longer than the one which strangled Isadora.

It was midnight on a Sunday in the age of sexual freedom when Argyle and I finished making love, and about two o'clock when I had my vision.

In my vision, a lithe blonde woman smiled at Argyle. He smiled at her in my sleep. Argyle and I were both asleep, having decided—rather amicably—to let some wounds from recent arguments heal or gangrene as nature would have it. Her dress was red and white checked silk, like the tablecloth at an outdoor café. She smiled at Argyle, across whose sharp hipbone my arm rested. I smiled at her, as if to agree with him, as if we were both waiting for the same late train. I felt my neck as a tangle of veins on top of which no head rested, across which was taped— primitively, like a child's Halloween mask—the cardboard head of a lithe blonde woman with a smile. I sat up and woke Argyle, who muttered something and went back to sleep.

He would have said my dream was paranoia, but I knew it was prophecy. I went into the other room, opened the top drawer of his desk, and immediately found evidence of another woman I'd suspected for months, in the form of a letter from an old college friend of Argyle's now living in Seattle where he'd vacationed in December. Her handwriting—small, careful but fluid—attested to her pride in a new, open sexuality.

"Send me things," she suggested, "that smell of you."

Back in the bedroom, an erection disturbed the sheets, but not Argyle's dreams. That was my job. "This'll never work," I said, among other things, when I woke him up to argue about his infidelity. "I'm not cut out for the twentieth century. I want to get married and be good to people."

He told me not to push so hard.

In the morning, though I overslept, I spent several minutes leaning against the bathroom wall as Argyle, a real human being to whom I am not doing justice, brushed his teeth. There was his stomach to contend with, soft and relaxed; there was the touching disarray of his receding hairline; there was the fact of his aging black truck (he painted apartments to support an art habit) without me in it.

"I love you," I said, "but we're through."

On the train to work I composed a speech to explain my tardiness: "I overslept. I overslept and missed my train. I missed my train and took the wrong one. The wrong one broke down. The passengers were transferred to another train, which got lost and took us to Siberia. Siberia was hot and cold, alternately. The waves of hot and cold felt good, like the undertow in a lake. We liked Siberia and stayed a while. I'm sorry."

This rhythm so mesmerized me that I fell asleep on the train, standing up, and missed my stop. I looked at my watch, which I had had the foresight to wind and to put on my wrist. I was two hours late. There was really no point in going to work.

Crazy, where I felt I was headed, was a bordering state with only slightly different traffic regulations. Crazy was as good as love, if not better. I said "insane" very slowly: it was concrete as "in New York City," full and sexy.

But going crazy would have been going somewhere and I, an unconscionable workskipper, was clearly going nowhere. All I could do was take the train home, take a shower, and dry myself off, knowing that I was not mad on love or in love with madness, but simply a childish twenty-three-year-old with a maudlin streak that would pass as Sundays pass. That's what my mother would have said, if she'd been alive.

I slept for generations, waking only to send imaginary telegrams to Argyle.

The next morning, I took the subway from the Village to have breakfast in Grand Central Station. My jeans were smooth and reliable against my legs. I felt so much better that I didn't want to spoil the day with work. I had almost eight hundred dollars in the bank and a life ahead of me.

Mildred Howell sat down.

I didn't know she was Mildred Howell yet.

She ordered a rare English muffin.

I felt her staring at me.

She began to speak:

"The old Frenchman picked up a shoe and flourished it at the moon."

"Pardon me?" I said.

"I said, the old Frenchman picked up a shoe and flourished it at the moon. 'The story's shorter than the night,' he said. 'This story springs from the loins of an Irish sailor.' And it does, in a manner of speaking, if you call Casey French, and if you call Jim O'Brien a sailor, but I'd call him much worse myself."

Then she paused to eat her breakfast.

A quick glance had told me that this woman was not entirely in the swing of things. She hadn't bought clothes since 1962. Her darted blouse, her knee-length plaid skirt, her pointy patent leather pumps were all the Sixties rejects that crowded Salvation Army stores, now that Forties clothes were back in fashion. Even if it had been three years later, when Sixties clothes replaced Forties clothes in *Vogue*, Mildred would have looked wrong. Her blouse was untucked. Her stockings bagged at the ankle; on her calf was a run that unveiled a strip of skin, pale and bristled with dark hairs. She wore an Ellis Island babushka that clashed with a garish choker of cultured pearls. Grape jelly spackled her mouth.

"Perhaps you'd feel better about the talk we're going to have," she said, "if you looked at me more carefully."

I didn't want to look. I looked at my plate. Deformity, I was convinced, sought me out. Sometimes in the park I liked to watch the derelicts aligning themselves like amphibians with the sun, bathing in the fountain, or inspecting the trash. But I liked to watch from a distance—a long shot, with Argyle's lovely form, throwing a frisbee, in the foreground. Check-out lines often found me behind people with artificial hands, extremely lifelike, veins and brown spots painted on. Subtle changes in the pink around the knuckles. Always a little puffy, though, as if the halo from the missing limb had stuck around. An out-patient from a mental institution with a pink plastic flower nested in her hair, carrying a straw purse shaped like a monkey, so when you opened the clasp, the monkey's head lifted up, sat down next to me on the subway once and called me a slut. "I don't like you," she added. "I never liked you. You look at me like I was born in the Roaring Twenties. I was not born in the Roaring Twenties!" When she told me that 1950 was the best year of her life, I got the heartache I always get from the man with the sign on his back: DO NOT HIT ME. ONLY MY PARENTS AND GUARDIANS ARE ALLOWED TO HIT ME. I had not yet devel-oped a selective attention; I still had trouble filtering out the fundamentalists talking to themselves on the buses, the shufflers struggling with their grocery carts. But what had I exchanged my workday for, if not these experiences?

Mildred grabbed my wrist with surprising force. "Don't be a coward," she said. "I am not a monster. I don't sleep on Madi-son Avenue gratings in winter, catching the heat, carrying bags full of orange rinds, cigarette butts, and obituaries of other bag ladies. My toenails are not long, corrugated, and yellow. You will notice my handbag is a Bottega Veneta affair from Berg-dorf's. It cost almost a hundred dollars in 1960. I was one of the first women in the United States to get a doctorate. I've met J. Pierpont Morgan and Andy Warhol. A man has died for me."

I could imagine telling Argyle, over candlelit lobster, that I'd spent my afternoon with a garrulous stranger.

Mildred drew her fist across to me under the counter and pounded on my knee. "Here, take a look," she said. Whatever she released in my palm was cold and wet. "You can have it," she said.

It was a watch with a gold case. On the case, an enamel Prodigal Son, wreathed in gold, came through a red doorway. The watch was ticking oddly, syncopatically, like a jazz bass.

"Press the doorknob," she said.

The doorknob was a dab of enamel in slight relief on the case of the watch, directly underneath the outstretched hand of the son caught in indecision. The watch popped open. I could make out a tinny song that sounded like Scarlatti.

Mildred said, "That's one of my favorites. There's nothing else like it in France. That watch belonged to the king. It's the smallest music box in the world. The only other thing that small is a bomb owned by the Russians, or so Klaus told me. They could put this bomb in one can of Chicken Noodle Soup, in one button of a lady's coat, and blow up New York. That watch is probably worth about a hundred thousand."

"Where'd you get this?" I asked, turning the watch in my hands.

"From Klaus."

I held my breath and looked at her.

She was simply stunning.

Her skin was flawless. She took off the scarf and let down a shoulder-length cascade of blonde hair, only slightly thinning at the ends. Her neck, when she unbuttoned her collar, was long and tight.

"Smell my wrist," she commanded.

She shoved a hand in my face. It smelled like honeysuckle in a summer rain. The nails were shiny and perfectly shaped.

"You see?" she said. "You should always look twice. Don't be bewildered by the surfaces; in the depths all becomes law. Who said that?"

"Rilke?"

"Correct. I'm Mildred Howell—oh! I can hear thunder out there."

"It's a train underneath us," I offered.

"You're rational. That's good. At any rate, I am almost eighty. You won't believe I'm ever going to die, but that's because you think fairy godmothers materialize from the ozone for you whenever you need them. They're perpetually fifty or thereabouts, cheerful as English nannies. You don't want your fairy godmother to be a manic-depressive. But look at these gums," she said, pushing her upper lip aside with her middle finger. "Tough, healthy. Put the watch away. Be careful with it. It'll pay your tuition at Wharton; it'll buy an orthodontist for your little girl, when you have a little girl. Love preserves me in this way, remember that, not silicone and paint. Love, not art."

She tied her scarf back on.

Now that I wanted to see, I couldn't. One bare bulb in the far corner of the room created an oval of light on her forearm. The blonde hairs there all swam in the same direction, like a school of minnows. The rest of her was shrouded.

"You're interested," she leered, licking butter from a finger.

I wanted a famous film director to spy her through the glass separating the luncheonette from the station and beg her to walk through Paris in a mink coat. No one else looked. The waitress leaned against a wall, scraping dirt from her fingernails.

"You're not eighty," I accused.

She reached into her large pocketbook nonchalantly and drew out a wallet. My first thought was, she stole it. My second thought was, it's mine. She handed me a driver's license. Mildred Howell, it said. Five feet tall, green eyes. Her birthday was listed as January 1, 1901. That made her a year older than my Aunt Mara, two years older than my father. Her license expired the year I was born.

"You see?" I said. "You're not quite eighty."

"I've already surpassed the average life expectancy."

She smiled: the slightest glint of tooth, like the glint of a penny sliding into a wishing pool.

She said quite flatly, "I am magic," and nodded with pursed lips.

Grease splattered the grill. The waitress—a pretty girl, a Cinderella by Hopper—stared past us to a slim man carrying a portfolio. The color drained from her face.

The old woman could not have been as beautiful as she seemed to me. Apparently my mind had taken a train. It was the anxiety of quitting my job (if I had in fact quit my job) and of losing Argyle (if I had in fact lost Argyle), or a hallucinatory flashback. That was the second possibility, if you can hallucinate from hashish. I'd tried hashish several times at age sixteen, while I was learning *Pictures at an Exhibition*. But Mildred sat quite solidly. Her face didn't melt or swirl. She sat patiently, waiting for my attention.

"How do I smell?" she asked.

"We've been through this already."

"Let's try it again."

I sniffed. Mothballs, sour milk. Overall, not as good as her wrist—a hairshirt factory on fire.

"I'm glad you're not spellbound yet," she said. "Don't lose sight of my overall appearance."

She traced her fraying hemline and drew my attention to the run in her stockings. "Just so you know we're friends," she said, "and trust me. I am not perfect. I have hair in my nose. I have a ridge of hair in a crescent around each of my nipples. I don't use dental floss. I use no sprays, lotions, or talcs."

"Neither do I."

"But child," she admonished, "you have a toothbrush. You have a Béla Bartók record and a set of flowery mugs."

I jumped. I'd bought a record just the week before, the first one I'd bought in years. It was Bartók. The mugs I'd had since 1975. It was no fun to be so transparent.

Mildred laughed. "You're surprised I know! Dear little one, the *space* you inhabit! I could cover it with my thumb."

"You can cover the sun with your thumb, too, if you squint," I intoned.

She raised one eyebrow and told me I'd asked for it.

"You have a butcher block table, long and thick, three weeks' salary, with a centerpiece of fresh fruit that periodically rots, because you don't entertain much. You have a musical instrument—what? A violin on a stand, draped over with velvet?

The velvet looks haphazard but actually, you arrange it that way. You have a camera but you don't take pictures of your menfriends for posterity. Instead you shoot nature—artsy close-ups of shore and bark. You have a Miró print and a pastel bathrobe with a hem you need to fix. You know a little French. You fantasize about growing your hair long again. Your dream life: an English thatched house with a sun-drenched drawing room—the baby grand by the stained-glass window, Siamese cats, some big pillows hand-stitched in Turkey—need I go on?"

"Please don't."

She was right about the camera and the bathrobe. As for the violin, she was right about that too—even about the velvet. But I never played the violin; it's my father's old instrument. I play the piano.

Not only was she well-preserved. She was psychic.

Mildred leaned toward me in a mime of salaciousness. She put her palm flat on the edge of my stool and spun the stool around, until my knees were almost touching hers.

"Having problems with your boyfriend?" she grinned.

I shrugged.

"Admit it," she said. "What's his name?"

"Argyle Lovett," I said, "though it's none of your business."

"Is Argyle his middle name?"

"Yes. His first name's Arthur."

"Art!" Mildred groaned. "Does he drink his beer with an Anisette chaser? Does he listen to transistorized Mahler on the back of public buses with sunglasses and penny loafers on? Does he like to think of himself as a mixed metaphor, trying to project an image of Preppie-gone-bad?"

Relieved, I told her no. At last I could dismiss her as a crazy old woman who just happened to have a valuable watch, a nice face for her age, and an impressive vocabulary. But her face began to soften and expand until it was a wash of beauty without boundaries. When she reached out and leaned forward on her stool to cup my cheek lightly in her hand, I had no choice but to disregard the stench—to disregard, in fact, all of the evidence—and to love her.

Not even an hour had passed by my antique watch. Like every American, I expected immediate gratification. I liked fast foods, diets, painkillers, cars, and courtships. Love, I thought, was a motor that should pick up at once and soar. I wanted it to look good soaring, too—sleek and muscular as a stallion. But motors never work like that for long. Mildred Howell was going to teach me that love treated as technology entails planned obsolescence.

"Don't think about yourself so much," Mildred advised. "See that tourist over there in the umbrella hat? Think about him. Think about all the people whose lives you will never touch. My story is about tourists, in the sense that all of us are tourists. Our histories are as flat and dry as vacation snapshots. We are all maids of honor, hoping to catch the bouquet; none of us is more than an extra in the crowd scene; our most exalted moments are merely episodic. This story will take a long time to tell—weeks. Maybe months. There are eleven major characters in my story and you will have to concentrate to get their names straight, no less learn to love them—and you must love them. I want you to worship the awesome leanness of Casey's legs. You'll have to be patient. A good part of the time you'll hate me. I'll try to answer your questions and provide enough foreshadowing to keep your faith, but it's my story, not yours. Is that clear?"

I smirked. "He who would like to be a follower of mine, let him renounce himself."

"It's not a fairy tale. You can't be glib. Do you plan to listen?"

I listened. I listened because Mildred was so beautiful, and because I had nothing else to do. Later, Mildred would listen to me. We ordered more muffins, to appease the waitress, and then Mildred got on with her story.

# 2

The children of Tourisme had no parents, but they were not orphans. They had no history, but they were not without pasts. They were born on a maroon divan in the French Alps. The midwife's assistant was instructed to play piano during the deliveries, so their first impression of the world would have the maroon, velvety texture of a Chopin Ballade. Throughout their lives, they'd feel lightweight and anchored at once. Their frequent round trips from goofiness to solemnity made them peculiarly suited to love.

Tourisme, a tiny village in the Graian Alps, was settled by a group of fifty Irish immigrants in 1880. Casey O'Brien, Mildred Howell's last and most memorable lover, was among the first Tourisme generation. The town was set up by Parnell (no relation to the politician), a painter and seer who led a weekly artists' meeting in a Dublin church basement.

Parnell was a sanguine, lanky fellow who bemoaned the lack of an Irish aesthetic. How could there be great Irish art generated from a wash of unhappiness pervasive as the sea? He claimed that no Irish art would light the horizon until the Irish moved and he, for one, planned to do so.

To fund the resettlement he opened a travel agency, the

first in Ireland. Parnell would read your palm, then tell you where you ought to go. He knew the driest spots for picnics. He knew where the motley lowlife performed and what alleys you could spoon in, with a view of the bridge, disturbed only by stray cats. Parnell told his compatriots that holidays would become important. America was soon to invent the weekend, and Parnell knew that people would need to find ways to spend their time. But Ireland was hardly a tourist mecca, and the Irish themselves hadn't the time or cash for entertainment.

By 1877, however, Parnell had managed to save enough for his group's departure. He announced his plan to settle in the Alps, where he and his followers would need little money, and would not be roped for taxes or public service. In the Graian Alps, they'd interest neither France nor Switzerland. They'd be surrounded by beauty and could set up their own government (he, as chief financial backer for the trip, would naturally be president and chief banker).

Neither he nor his fifteen-year-old wife had ever even climbed a ladder. Their research into the Alps was scanty at best. Nevertheless, the fifty Irishpeople arrived after a three-year trip, spent mostly in sightseeing.

They were big-booted and skinny. Like the followers of any heavenly track, they'd left no mark on the world and, closing their eyes, spun themselves around in a dismal orgy of faith, hoping to choose fame like a party favor from a grab bag. Parnell's work with painters and travelers had given him access to a select group of talented madmen. Constrained by poverty, they'd let their minds wander on longer and longer leashes, until they couldn't find their way back to daily life. One man was expelled from medical school when he tried to perform a heart transplant on a cat. Another settler, the Aran Islands' only female carpenter, had been exiled when she burned down a house she'd coated with cellulose nitrate and sawdust in order to convert it into plastic. There was a dabbler in orthodontics and a priest turned propaganda expert. Parnell was their fairy godfather. He encouraged them, reassured them. He could have sent them to the moon with a shaving kit and a clean pair of socks, had that option been imaginable in 1880. Instead, he promised both genius and clean sheets, futuristic technology and dinner on time. His city would be an artists' colony, where people's hobbies could also be their jobs.

Fueled by Parnell's vision, everyone worked cheerfully. The men cut timber; the women baked bread. After Ireland, the Alps were a pocket of peace.

Everyone was happy but Parnell. He was almost forty and anxious for his city to prosper. For that reason, he named it Tourisme, hoping the name might inspire the trade.

But skiers chose mountains elsewhere. Americans generally preferred Paris. Prague at least had cobblestones; Lucerne had a quaint covered bridge raining spiders. America had the Liberty Bell and gold in its shallow streams. Parnell said that Tourisme would be lackluster until it found an identity.

He proposed the construction of a beach.

Not only would it be the only beach in the vicinity, but the idea of a man-made beach in Tourisme would be curious, and the publicity might attract tourists.

While some of the villagers thought the project too flashy, everyone was homesick by then for the rocky beaches of Ireland; since there was plenty of spare time, everyone agreed to help with the construction.

The sand went half a foot deep. It was Spanish sand imported from Majorca in twenty-five painstaking trips. (There were no trains in the Alps—for that matter, there weren't roads until 1884, when Tourisme's trade began to boom.) The beach was narrow and not all that large—about the size of the parking lot at a neighborhood shopping mall. The "ocean," of course, was not an ocean. The deep blue mist that the tourists saw emanated from a waterfall about a mile away on a neighboring cliff; the lighter blue was the sky itself, very pale at such an altitude, seen intermittently when the mist cleared. The two blues juxtaposed created a wavy effect, a very common form of bucolic mirage.

For three months a year, the beach served admirably, so long as you didn't try to float a raft into the water or look for sand dollars too close to the precipice. But there were advantages. You didn't have to wait for low tide to bring the seashells in. A boy got a lift with the postman to scatter shells around.

The freckled women wore white pantaloons which revealed a good stretch of calf, perfect and polished as driftwood. Hair escaped their chiffons in petulant waves. Sweat glossed their lips. The men, too, were lyrically handsome. Networks of black hair blessed their chests, but their chins were smooth as infants' bottoms. The villagers sat on blankets there, just as we do today, except that they ate banana bread painted with swirls of fresh sweet butter, anchovies, and green apples with cheddar cheese and slabs of black bread, swilled with fine dry wine from silver decanters. After they finished eating, they'd take turns serving silver fingerbowls. Through their crystal goblets, through a clump of trees, the children could be kept in check. The children! Their swaybacks, their ducky little chests! The children gathered hazelnuts in the bushes and the last of the berries that never grew larger than the children's pupils, for want of light.

The main village was a half-hour walk from the beach. All the houses one passed on the way were slightly tilted. Even the cranky goats couldn't always keep their balance. The horses were bred a mile west of town. Most of the time the slopes kept them where they belonged, the way beaded dangles in aviaries keep the birds in. But some afternoons the colts would wander down to the beach. They were all white—white colts only distinguishable from the sand by their sable shadows.

Photographs were taken of the horses frolicking, the women with manes thrown back in perpetual laughter as the children made sand castles. News of the beach appeared in papers worldwide. The tourists drove in carriages from Chamonix. The Sanity Inn was built to house them. The O'Briens, Casey and his twin sister Katey's parents, operated the inn. They were favorites at the Parnell court—for Parnell now had a court, outfitted mostly for his wife's benefit. She was with child. In preparation, Parnell hired three tutors and the gentlest pastoral nursemaid. He established an impressive library with first editions from all over the world, and purchased some first-rate artworks.

Sweet land of Tourisme! The town had its own newspaper, *The Tourisme Tattler* (Parnell, a poet at heart like many Irishmen, had a fatal attraction to assonance and alliteration). It had a cheese shop and a locksmith, although no one but the tourists locked their doors. There were no police. Despite Parnell's role as a figurehead leader, the town was basically democratic. People liked what they did, and did it even though they weren't paid. The citizens worked on a barter system; funds from the tourists were put into a kitty and used for improvements. (Parnell had a little nest egg which financed his oversize house.) Easels were nailed to the ground at the corners for public use so that the natives could paint on the streets of their city—paint, in fact, those very streets—wearing berets, giving the place a Montmartre feel.

Parnell himself didn't paint much anymore. He now preferred invention to art. One particularly fine Monday, when a sky crowded with clouds the color of used gum erasers promised a precise and studious rain, Parnell invented both the photographic postcard (in which tourists could send pictures of themselves to their relatives) and a paperweight in the form of a miniature glass dome that shook Alpine snow on the Sanity Inn. His most important invention was the ice cream cone, but he couldn't get word out before the 1904 St. Louis World's Fair, and an anonymous waffle-seller there got the credit. For the rest of his life, Parnell was in litigation for the patent.

The Parnells' daughter, Pia, was born on May 21, 1883. Mrs. Parnell died in childbirth. Parnell, anxious to dispel his grief over the loss of his good-natured wife, absorbed himself in his daughter's education.

By the time she was ten, Pia had read Petrarch and *The Symposium*. She spoke three languages, drew a likeness in ten minutes, and played Liszt by ear. Still, she had to be a teen-ager, and on a summer day in 1899, history found her relaxing on the beach, in a demure pink dress, eating grapes and polishing her toenails.

She noticed a man loitering in the bushes. He stared at her, so she stared back. She nudged her nursemaid. "Who's that?" she asked. The nursemaid shrugged. Moments later, the man was gone.

The next morning, Pia's father was dead.

Parnell had been ax-murdered in his sleep.

On the pillow beside him, written in blood, were the words: THIS WILL SELL.

Pia was overwhelmed, but it was in her blood to stay cool during disaster; she'd been primed for presidency since birth. She publicized the horrible crime and called her father's lawyers in from Paris to investigate.

We cannot let this murder take place offstage, where it belongs, for it brought fame to Tourisme briefly and increased the town's revenue. Ax murders became a trend, as hijacking did in our time. Lizzie Borden doubtless heard about the crime, as she reenacted it to the letter the very next year. The idea of an ax murder in Tourisme, like the idea of a man-made beach in the Alps, provided the right blend of whimsy and sensationalism. With all of the business around town, it was impossible to name a murderer, and the imported criminologists simply ascribed the deed to an unknown tourist.

One of the lawyers was a Sorbonne-educated Pole named Edward Maginski. His middle name was Chopin (Frédéric, he claimed, was his third cousin). Edward's big droopy eyes were lovable as a bloodhound's. He looked soft and scholarly in his wire-rims. Pia married him. The ornate wedding somewhat eased the town's grief. Maginski moved into the Parnell court, taking over most of the Tourisme paperwork, which by this time was substantial.

Pia was happy enough until Edward began to tie her up when they made love, and force her to point her toes. Sometimes he made her wear pink satin shoes with icepick heels that he'd purchased for her in Paris. Best of all he liked to suspend her from the chandelier in the master bedroom. Pia vowed never to go to Paris, if this was what they taught students at the Sorbonne. When Edward told her that her father had been crazy, that the ax murder was probably suicide, Pia immediately realized that Edward had killed her father to take over the presidency. She was frightened to death, but Edward had endeared himself to the townspeople, and she didn't want to uproot them again.

Kitsa Maginski (the name is Polish and pronounced *Keetsa*, as in para*keet* or John *Keats*), Pia and Edward's daughter, was born prematurely on December 31, 1900, twelve minutes before the new year. The baby was so small that the doctors said it wouldn't live. Pia didn't have high hopes for the offspring of sexual perversion. Sure enough, the baby's eyes were two different colors (one brown, one green) and her smile was rather simple-minded. Under the care of the nursemaid, however, the baby seemed to progress normally.

Kitsa didn't have time to know her father. Within eight months, Edward Maginski was dead—victim of another ax murder—and Pia was pregnant again, only she didn't tell anyone but her nursemaid. It was unlikely that Edward could have been the father, and, in fact, he wasn't.

A week before Edward's murder, Pia had been walking on the beach alone, as she often did, inspecting the stars and avoiding her husband. She struck up a conversation with a tourist named Jim O'Brien. Her feeling was one of tragic recognition. When the sailor squeezed her knee, she took the spark she felt as fate. They made love outside by the evergreens. When the guards found her husband dead in his study the following week and when the stranger was suddenly missing after more than several midnight trysts, during which he'd run his finger up the dark line on her stomach as she nuzzled the ticklish inside of his thigh, Pia put two and two together.

Her egg had been seeded by the man who killed her father and her husband.

Winter came like a telegram from the front. Pia had a year's mourning period, in which she refused to come out of her house or to let anyone in. The villagers were gentle with her, troubling her as little as possible.

In March, an obviously pregnant Pia sent her nursemaid to fetch the O'Briens, her father's friends at the inn. She allowed the old couple to fuss a bit over Kitsa. Then she told them the whole story.

Two murders, the childless couple advised her, did not deserve another. The baby should live. Mrs. O'Brien would walk around with a pillow in her stomach. The very idea of a pregnancy in the seventh decade would be enough to distract villagers and tourists, and to divert attention from Pia. When the child was born, the O'Briens (no relation to the stranger, although Pia was irrationally comforted by the common surname) would smuggle it out of Pia's house, and raise it lovingly at the Sanity Inn.

Pia Maginski sketched in the privacy of her garden with Kitsa and her nursemaid. She began to collect art by corresponding with gallery owners all over the world. Leaving four bedrooms, Pia converted the rest of the house into a museum to house her growing art collection. By the end of her pregnancy, only the library, with Edward's (previously Parnell's) study attached, remained intact.

There are over nine hundred buildings in France officially designated as museums, most of them established around the time that Pia decided to make her contribution. You didn't have to be a Medici to own original art back then. In Athens, a

museum was merely a ritzy villa—a sanctuary for the Muse—
where you could count on a good chat. It made sense that Pia,
accustomed to the company of intellectual men, should feel her
isolation strongly. She talked to her art. When the eyes of a
portrait followed her, she didn't take it lightly.

She had a thirteenth-century tapestry, a version of the one
now housed in La Musée de Tapisseries in Angers. This was
her first purchase and one of her favorites: an arras in which
an angel transports St. John into the desert to show him the
Great Whore seated on the Seven-Headed Beast. She had a
Giotto and a Georges de la Tour. She almost had—but refused
at the door—the mummified corpse of Cardinal LaGrange, who
died at the beginning of the fifteenth century.

The only thing that Pia didn't have was any taste.

Like her father, she befriended the underdog. She was
drawn to things which no one else could love. Had she been a
princess, she would have kissed frogs. She had six rooms full of
Wise and Foolish Virgins, a theme that enjoyed a short lifespan
on the rest of the continent (Pia had begun to think of Tourisme
as an island, much like her mythical homeland). All of the
virgins in these paintings were painfully ugly. She had a muddy
portrait of a pope who looked dumb and petty as a junior high
school vice-principal, and mechanical birds that croaked Bach
in an irritating monotone.

She was proud. Her green eyes took on the milky cast of
deep contemplation. Like most art lovers, she was slightly myopic.
She'd draw the birthmark before the shape of the face—that is, if
she could see to paint. A page of manuscript six inches away
might as well have been an aerial view of a garden. That's why
she liked art so much in the first place. Her idea of perfection
was anything that she could see. She liked to get on a stepladder
and inspect the highest angel's eardrum. Given a painting believed to be an early Bosch, she was not likely to fall over backwards gasping and cooing. She was far more likely to date the
work with a kit she'd mail-ordered from Paris, determine that

the date coincided with the time when the painter allegedly underwent a spiritual rebirth, and then, to test the painting's authenticity, see if she could interpret a small stroke in the background of the painting as a specter rising from the water. If anyone challenged her, she'd say that allegory was absolutely required of artists in Bosch's time.

Busywork delighted her. Her hope was that all of her small strokes would accrete into a pointillist masterpiece, a panoramic view.

She gave birth to twins in May 1902.

She named them Katherine and Casey. Katherine Casey had been the sailor's mother's maiden name. His mother had died young. Pia couldn't imagine Jim O'Brien hurting innocent Irish children with his mother's name. Furthermore, she still stoked a little fire in her heart for the footloose murderer. The two squealing bundles that she relinquished to the O'Briens at her back door, as if the children were unsatisfactory art she was returning to the dealer, were the twin flames in the stranger's eyes, which were, if she remembered correctly, catastrophically blue. Every time she thought about Jim, she wanted her second and third children back.

By the time Pia was twenty-one, she'd managed to block her entire late teens from her consciousness. She tried not to think about her parents or about her late husband Edward, for when she did, there was a short-circuit from their dismembered forms to the virile form of her stranger. She trained herself so that when she had to recognize her dead relations, as she often did in her executive duties, a projection of their official portraits was precipitated. The portraits hung in the State Room. The Parnells were enthroned and suitably majestic, gazing into a golden distance. Edward Maginski, with slightly wrinkled brow and outstretched hand, held a sheath of papers and looked over the top of his glasses, which shimmered seductively. These were the only pictures that Pia had of her parents, so when she tried to think of them doing anything but gazing, or of her husband

doing anything but reading, she drew a blank. The portraits were like postcards of places she'd never visited.

Pia had conditioned this response herself, in a rather Pavlovian eidetic ritual. A year after Edward's death (four months after the twins' birth), she had several local painters copy the portraits, stroke by stroke, on every wall in her house. This was common practice in Roman courts, when art collectors wanted to assure the longevity of their works against theft or decay. But Pia had her scribes use special pigments that, her research showed, would oxidize in less than a decade; though the painters warned her about the paint's life-span, she insisted on using it, praising the quality of the color. Villagers took this proliferation of family icons as a token of her devotion to the lineage and, moreover, thought that the idea of a repeated image was clever and responsive to new developments in the art world. After two years, when Pia begrudgingly allowed the peeling walls to be repainted in a cheerful blue, the villagers celebrated her release from the talons of her morbid past. The reproductions lived just long enough for Pia to engrave the images on her brain, then began to flake. She didn't have to relegate her framed relatives to the attic. She merely locked Edward's study, donated his clothes to a rummage sale at the new photography studio, and had some of his and her parents' less personal things encased in the Founders' Room in a far annex of the museum. She closed the door on her guilt forever.

An image of the stranger stepping out of a bush and bending awkwardly to kiss her hand remained with her subliminally. When the image surfaced, it was as if someone at a lecture had put the wrong slide in upside down and removed it in a millisecond. The film was reversed: Jim O'Brien backed into a bush in her mind. She didn't think about him. If she were to receive a letter from him—unlikely after all these years—she wouldn't remember the name. Conditioning had been so successful that Pia would sometimes "try" to remember her past. She only remembered that there was something she should be remembering.

During these exploratory attempts at nostalgia, she'd have hot flashes and drink gallons of tea.

There was one thing that Pia remembered: a porch attached to the upstairs window of a small white house. Long and narrow as a catwalk, the porch overlooked an undulating hill dabbed with buttercups and melting snow. It was no porch she could place, no house she'd lived in or visited; but it became emblematic of a better time, one she should like to know more about.

Citizen Kane had Rosebud and Pia had her porch.

She studied every volume on occultism in her father's library to find that some people have accurate dreams about places they've never seen. One girl in Holland had been employed by the secret police because she could dream a house down to the pattern of the curtains, the brand of cigar smoldering in the ashtray, and the number of logs in the fireplace. If she were slightly forgetful, she comforted herself with the idea that at least she had her mana. She hypothesized that the porch was Heaven and looked forward to rocking there in a rocking chair, basking in an impressionistic sunset.

Meanwhile, she tended to her administrative duties and spent evenings in bed with her hookah and her *Rapid Fact Finder*, in which she found data on the Cheeses of the World and Caves of Historical Interest, topics that recommended themselves by their lack of connection to lubricity and death. She knew by heart all of the American Festivals and the Epithets of the American Cities—from the "Town of Churches" to the "Town Opposite the Mouth of the Licking River"—all cities which she hoped to visit someday, when her responsibilities were less strenuous.

Pia would never leave Tourisme. She was bound to it as her parents had been, as her grandparents had been to Ireland. The presidency was handed to her as neatly as any serf ever inherited a plow. A mother at seventeen, Pia was an old lady by thirty—far stuffier and less flexible than the O'Briens, who were pushing ninety when Casey and Katey reached adolescence. All of the major events of Pia's life—sex, love, marriage, childbirth, widowhood—had happened within a three-year period, and this period was to her whole life as a commercial break is to a TV movie: dense, noisome, entirely forgettable.

The president spent most of her time with her hands pressed to her bosom, watery eyes cast aloft—gestures picked up from too many years spent alone in the midst of virgins, madonnas, and kings. By the time her children reached adulthood, Pia had lived in a museum for close to twenty years. The brilliant golds and vermilions of old nativities had been vitiated into the threadbare reds and greens of a dimestore Christmas. After too many four-cornered views of exaltation and despair, Pia's feelings were self-parodying. She assumed that if biblical scenarios could be distributed over the landscape of a painting, separated by a couple of trees or a brook, then she could forget and move on. She believed in moving on—she was the High Priestess of the Optative Mood.

Casey, Katey, and Kitsa would never like Pia Maginski. They wouldn't know their genealogy for a long time. They thought of the ax murders as comic relief, and indeed it was hard to think of them any other way, with the tavern at the inn called "The Ax Room," as if Parnell and Maginski were Geronimo and Wild Bill Hickok. Everything assumed the comic graininess of a daguerreotype or a science fiction dust jacket. History was something you made up to pass the time. The invention of Tourisme was a photogenic fairy tale, no more or less substantial than the towns the children liked to make from acorns, twigs, and mud.

Parnell had finally won. Even in death, his image contributed to the growth of a culture that didn't need art, because life painted itself, by spontaneous generation, in a spectrum more otherworldly than the neon blood on his pillow.

# 3

We'd moved to a bar at my suggestion before rush hour. It was Happy Hour and the drinks were cheap. I was treating. If I'd worked that day, I'd just have been feeding my cats. I drank Scotch; Mildred Howell drank Manhattans.

I yawned. The panorama of people in New York is a sundial; by the number of people passing and by their pace, I could tell that it was about nine o'clock. When I realized it was this late, I felt a flutter of panic, as if my alarm hadn't gone off.

"I was sixty-three," Mildred said. "I heard the story I've just told you from an old Frenchman at midnight. At least I thought he was French. I'd missed a wedding in Sallanches because somewhere in rural France, on my way back from an auction, my rental car spluttered to a stop, and I found myself sitting in a dump, in the rain, with a bilingual madman. The dump was behind a chicken coop. I'd taken it for a gas station when the car stalled. I could have been in Detroit."

"Excuse me," I said. "If you were sixty-three, then this was in 1964. Your driver's license expired ten years before. How did you rent a car?"

"Don't worry about the details."

"If they don't matter, then why burden me with them?"

"I might not have listened to the old man if it weren't for his art. He gave me some bourbon in a seventeenth-century gold goblet, very much like Anne of Austria's, now housed in the Louvre. I went to my car and got the magnifying glass from the glove compartment. It was dark and drizzly. On the way back I tripped over what later turned out to be bottles, tires, broken bicycles. I lowered myself on the ground to squint at the goblet. This was the position I'd used as a child for inspecting anthills, and I had the same sense of exhilaration. The feeling was so primeval that I found myself weeping into a brown sock matted with leaves.

" 'There there,' the old man said. 'I know it's pretty, with the moon so knotted up in it.' The moon, indeed, was full. 'Whenever I use it I shift so the moon becomes part of the design.' He served me a stale cheese sandwich on a small ceramic plate. The plate, blue and gold, depicted a disfigured lion trotting through a field of fleurs-de-lys, a banner in its tail. It was a faïence dish, dating from around 1450.

"The man said his name was Casey O'Brien. He said he knew more about art than any art historian, living or dead; he said he owned more art than any private collector on either side of the Atlantic. 'Sit,' he said. 'Eat. Give me a kiss, and then we'll begin.'

"I fainted. It was the first and last time in my life that I'd faint. When I awoke, I started my new life."

"Excuse me," I said. "I have to make a phone call."

Argyle's line was busy. I missed him already. When I dialed again, no one answered. Maybe he'd gone out for beer, but maybe he was late for dinner at another woman's apartment. I sat down rather drunk, rather pale.

Mildred said, "I was a phenomenal art dealer. I had a photographic memory. My brain was a phone tap that transferred everything I heard onto microfilm. I heard quite a bit—no one expected erudition back then from a five-foot-tall, ninety-pound female with a pageboy and bright red fingernails. I could plant a dagger into any discourse on art, but I planted it so slowly that no one would notice, until it was too late."

"I'm sure they noticed your modesty right off."

"Are you going to be contentious all evening?"

"Excuse me. I've got to talk to Argyle."

"A shame you're so foolish."

His line was busy again. I leaned against the wall and waited a moment before redialing. Sometimes Argyle didn't feel like answering the phone. I let the phone ring fifteen times, hung up and dialed again, watching Mildred fold several cocktail napkins into neat squares and put them in her bag. Argyle answered breathlessly on the sixth ring.

"Argyle. Where have you been?"

"Right here."

"This is Jennifer. Haven't you been answering your phone?"

"What?"

"Haven't you been answering your phone?" I said loudly.

"Jennifer, I can barely hear you. I don't think the phone's working."

"I'm in a bar with an old lady I met at Grand Central. I've been with her all day. The day before that I slept; I didn't go to work. I think I've quit."

"What?"

"I said, I think I've quit. This woman is almost eighty and looks thirty-six. She's telling me a story about art. Please meet us. Will you feed my cats on the way over?"

"Jennifer, what's going on?"

"Argyle, I wish you wouldn't preface every sentence with my name," I shouted.

"Anything else?"

"Yes. Are we done?"

"You and me?"

"That's usually what 'we' means."

"Not necessarily. Sometimes it's you and them."

"Not only are you talkative. You're illuminating!"

"Listen, Jennifer, I'm not an Assertiveness Training Therapist. I'm just a nice guy who paints houses and cows."

"I don't like your cow paintings."

"Sorry."

"And lies to women. Don't forget that. A nice guy who lies to women."

"I never lied to you."

"Here we go."

"No we don't, because I'm not going through this with you again."

"Fine," I said, and hung up with minimal guilt.

When I sat down, Mildred said, "Poor girl. I'm sorry."

"It's not your fault," I said. "Things have been tough since Adam and Eve broke their lease. The more cynical I become about the possibility of a rewarding relationship, the more romantic I get on the sly. I'm not alone. The age of marriage is over for all of us. Still, I want to be a pilot and marry a pilot. I want to specialize in animal husbandry, so an attractive zoo administrator can hire me to mate the lions on the first day of spring and fire me on the last, preferring my vast talents as a wife. In like a lion, out like a lamb. We'll collaborate on a children's book defining love once and for all, with only one line per page, so there's a monogamous relationship between word and illustration. Maybe I'll have to marry the vice-president of an insurance company and get bored, so when my husband is murdered on the elevator one night, I can properly appreciate the rough love of the detective on the case. It doesn't much matter, since I'm still rendered breathless by the curve of a man's kneecap. I'd settle for a man who would slap me playfully in public and let me wear his hat. We'd both still be individuals."

"Are you through?" Mildred asked. "My, are you overwrought! As I was saying, I was terribly ambitious. When I woke up from the faint, I was determined to befriend this man with art. My vision was bad by then and without my glasses on, Casey was in front of me like the beating wings of Leda's swan. Can you visualize that?"

"He was raping you."

Mildred rapped me on the arm. "Of course not!"

"But that's the myth. Zeus dresses up as a swan and descends upon the pubescent girl—"

"I know the myth! Don't exasperate me. Casey had white hair. I didn't see well, and it was dark. He was sitting before me with his white hair. I couldn't focus. It's hard enough to create a vivid picture for you of something that happened a long time ago to people you don't know. Please try to use your imagination. Dote on yourself less and listen better."

"You should work for a greeting card company."

"If you don't button your lip," Mildred warned, "I'm going to embarrass you."

"How could I be more embarrassed?"

Mildred called the bartender.

He was a young, moon-faced fellow with high cheekbones and one gold earring. Mildred looked at me like a child at the pool ready to demonstrate a dive for her parents. She turned to the bartender and began to unbutton her shirt. The bartender and I exchanged horrified looks.

"I don't know her," I said.

She cupped her hands under her breasts and cocked her head. The bartender leaned forward with a bottle in one hand and a glass of water in the other.

"What do you know," he said thoughtfully.

I had my elbows around my face.

"Will you look at that," the bartender said.

I cowered as Mildred turned to me. She held her shirt open by drawing it back with her hands and planting her fists firmly on her waist, like Superman with his cape.

Her breasts were small and firm as a girl's. The nipples were hot pink; the promised hairs were fine, long, and curly.

But that wasn't all. Over each nipple there was a tattoo in Gothic letters:

K L A U S         C A S E Y

"The men in my life," she said.

I yelped, and anyone at the bar who hadn't already been gaping or guffawing at this demonstration did so then. She buttoned her shirt distractedly, as if she were in front of a vanity mirror in a house all alone, dreaming of a husband off at sea. She smiled, though not directly at anyone; she asked the bartender for another round. People turned back to their drinks.

"You made me do that," she said. "It's not my style. As I was saying, I woke up from the faint. I couldn't focus. Casey was hovering over me like an angel with his white hair. He looked like an angel—a mean, street-wise angel. He looked like Brando or the young Yeats. He asked if I felt better; he began to kiss me. I hadn't been kissed in more than a decade. I opened my eyes and I swear to God, he looked like Klaus."

"Klaus on your nipple?"

"Correct. There was something going on."

"Apparently."

"But not what you think. Of course we made love, but that wasn't the significant part. Casey would never have left Tourisme and I would never have stayed. Neither of us would budge an inch. That drew us together. I loved Casey. What does love mean? What part of love is language, what part of love is history?"

I was thinking that people in the bar could have easily mistaken us for student and mad professor, if Mildred hadn't done the number with her breasts.

"When I slept beside Casey, I felt as if I had fallen into a place where my dreams were public property and that, of course, is what the ancient Greeks believed. Even in sleep, Casey linked me to the pulse of history. I don't think you could have cut through any part of his body with a power saw. He was slim; but he had an incredible compactness, like the world had been pressed into him. I was aware at the time that I was doing something historically significant, and, like anyone involved in anything significant, I was aware of nothing but my passion for the work, the moment and my presence in it. Every sexual act is historically significant. Language went through my head. I didn't have to pay much attention to know that each scrap of language was just how I felt at that second. First just words. *Speleology* went by and the word *Lausanne*, which is also a place. Then the names started. *Nicolo Renieri* went through my head. Not Renieri himself, mind you—just the name Renieri. Renieri was a forger, the best, and here we were in a dump, a place with unloved objects; then *Madame Bonelli* went through my head on tiptoe, just a picture of her name rushing into the museum to rescue Galileo's telescope as Florence was washed away by floods, just as the old man rushed into my life and, at least for the moment, saved me, even if he himself was the danger. And then, of all things, I saw Albrecht Dürer! I saw Dürer's betrothed curled up on a chaise longue (on the curvy word *chaise longue*) as he painted his self-portrait, his wedding gift to her; I saw her and I saw Dürer, then I came. That's the word you use now, right? Wrong. I was already there. But Albrecht Dürer's wife! Had she existed, she would have been an ordinary thing, known only by her connection with her famous husband. A modern equivalent would be, say, Margaret Trudeau. No. Wait a minute. I can't think of anyone."

"Okay, I get the point."

"Don't be jealous. It may happen to you someday. We were in a dump. I want you to understand that. I'm sure that you and your little friend Argyle—"

"Cut that out!"

"—have made love outdoors once or twice, with a grandiose display of self-conscious ease. But this was more than outside. Is this clear?"

"Yes, this is painstakingly clear."

Mildred gave me a steady pitying look. "Shall I go on?"

"Only if you get right on with your story," I threatened.

"You want me to skip Casey? You want me to delve right into Casey's past, the story he told me?"

"You got it."

"But what's the point of Tourisme without Casey? It's like the albatross without the Ancient Mariner!"

I rolled my eyes.

Mildred suggested a deal. "Put your watch on the counter. The watch I gave you. That's it. So pretty!"

The watch glistened against the fake grain of the counter.

Mildred agreed to tell the story of Tourisme as expediently as possible. We'd see how far we got in a shorthand form by midnight, at which point we'd call it a day. She'd continue the story, her way, on the following evening.

"I'm assuming you work," she said.

"I don't know. I haven't been for two days. I thought I'd quit. I have some money saved—"

"Nothing doing. You don't live in Tourisme, my dear."

"But what do I tell them? I've been out for two days. I never even called in sick. They've probably been trying to reach me at home."

"Tell them you had a nervous breakdown, a little ugly spell."

"Is that a pun on my name?"

After all this time, she didn't even know my name.

"Jennifer Spell," I announced.

"Go to work, Ms. Spell. Here are some rules. During the period of this story, you are not to see that boy."

"What is this," I objected, "football training?"

"Two. This is quite important. At midnight, when I finish, try not to talk to me. I like to stay alone in my story when I talk about it. Don't interrupt to tell me about your boyfriends or your career plans."

"Well, we'd better arrange where we'll meet."

"Not necessary. I'll find you."

"How?"

"Don't worry. There's the cardinal rule for gracious living. Just go home, take a shower and feed your cats—you ought to invest in a lint brush to get the cat hairs off your clothes. Then get up in the morning and take the cattle car to work, read the paper standing up. Then go home again, take a shower again and feed your cats again—what are your cats' names, incidentally?"

"Freud and Skinner."

Mildred sighed. "Do whatever crosses your mind. If I decide to tell you the rest of the story, I'll find you."

"Where do you live?"

"Don't worry. Preen your records. Note how lovely the yellow daisies look near your legal pad. Do laundry if you have to do laundry; bring a book. But don't see that boy. You're wasting your time."

"I counted on him."

"All you can count on, sweet child, is death. Here's Rule Number Three." Mildred was pouring salt into her glass idly. "No philosophizing. I don't want to hear your ideas on anything, if you have ideas. You don't know anything I need to hear."

"How would you know?"

"I don't want to discuss your ideas on ideas. Promise me."

"I won't have ideas," I said, "if you don't have ideas."

We were not drinking in my neighborhood, and I didn't feel entirely safe at the bar, with my back to tables where men in loosened ties argued sports and the economy. Speaking of the economy, while I was not cheap exactly, I was aware that Mildred and I between us had consumed eight drinks. Five were hers; she would undoubtedly move onto her sixth. In my head I was trying to multiply eight by all of the possible prices of Scotch and Manhattans, nine by all of the possible prices of Scotch and Manhattans, then add that amount to the total amount I already owed on my Master Charge; but because I was drunk, this process seemed exceedingly difficult. I needed to know how much I'd spent. My math superimposed itself over Mildred's speech and seemed to lend her a clarity as she continued to speak of a place that existed outside of the socioeconomic grid that maps Manhattan.

"Passado!" she said.

"Passado?" I said, but she put her finger to her lips, closed her eyes, cleared her throat, asked the bartender for another drink, belted it down, skipped a few years, and began her story again in 1914.

# 4

Casey and Katey O'Brien heard about World War I from some Americans staying at the Sanity Inn. They told Kitsa Maginski, who told her mother, the president of Tourisme. Pia was airily swinging herself in the garden hammock.

"Momma," Kitsa purred. "There's a war."

"I know, darling. Isn't that dreadful?"

"Stinks. Casey shot a squirrel once."

"Darling, don't you have any other friends? The O'Briens are getting on in years—"

"Please don't say 'getting on in years.'"

"—and they need the twins' help around the inn."

"Does the sky light up? Casey says you can stay up all night chatting in a trench and not giving anything but your serial number—"

"War, young lady, is no fun at all. You should thank your lucky stars—"

"Please!"

"—that you're not in that war, and pray God you won't be."

"Momma, can we have a treehouse?"

"What on earth for?"

"Casey says we could see the bomber planes from here if we had a treehouse."

"There are no bomber planes, Kitsa."

"I love the helmets! Like turtles' backs."

"Kitsa, have you been attending to your history? There are no bombers. Casey and Katey must have heard that from their parents. Your grandfather Parnell predicted bombers for the next war."

"There's going to be another war?"

"Several."

"Then we can get the treehouse finished in time for the next war if we miss this one. Can we borrow some paintings to hang?"

"Perish the thought!"

"Do you have any idea how fussy you sound, Momma? I detest 'Perish the thought.' I want a treehouse, Momma. Please dear Momma, may I have a treehouse?"

Although Kitsa's life remained a musical comedy, the war did affect Tourisme. It was very difficult to import chocolate mints, which Kitsa liked to eat chilled before bedtime. The tourist trade was understandably slow, and Tourisme was in no position to get arms bids. It was almost impossible to get musicians together for a serenade in Kitsa's bath or the lifeguard for her midnight swim.

The treehouse, however, was built. During World War I, Casey, Katey, and Kitsa—that indomitable clan, those fast-to-hyperactive friends—were moving into their treehouse, singing the latest hits from America.

They were a Siamese trio. Tourists viewing Pia's house could see the twins sprawled on a divan whilst the president's daughter did her morning exercises or brushed her astounding hair. Their friendship was legend among the townspeople. Kitsa's affection for the unregal twins spoke well for the democracy of the human spirit—the development of which was, after all, the point of Tourisme.

The children did not look alike. The twins were dark and angular; Kitsa was fair-to-pallid with dimpled cheeks and elbows. Her most notable feature was her eyes. One was brown, like Maginski's; the other reproduced the emerald green that had crowned Pia's beauty before her horn-rims.

For years the children wore matching outfits. Even their educations were identical. What one wanted to know, the others learned at once. An instructive example is their mutual discovery of Jesus Christ. Both the O'Briens and Pia had neglected to mention him. When a shipment of medieval art arrived at the president's, the then ten- and eleven-year-old threesome asked for a briefing. Pia, delighted with the opportunity, had the reverend summoned from the tavern, where he liked to hold sermons informally. The children's main interest was in why Christ was always bleeding, and why did he have those moles on his hands? The reverend told them about the crucifixion.

"You're a liar," Kitsa shivered. "I'm going to tell Momma you're trying to scare us."

"You may not believe in God," the reverend said, "but you must believe in the crucifixion. That is not open to interpretation."

When Pia couldn't convince them either, Casey agreed to monitor a search through the extensive Parnell/Maginski library, where he discovered evidence that crucified people weren't nailed at all—they were simply hung. Death was due to the caving-in of the innards and ensured by the stab, which was, however, mostly decorative.

The clan's fascination with Christ was brief and enthusiastic. They mailed away to the Louvre for every available postcard of this incredibly wrong-headed man; they shredded each view of the crucifixion and threw the pieces over the cliff at the beach. They even went so far as to consider whiting out the bloodied palms of Christ in Pia's collection of paintings, but decided it was not worth incurring her wrath for the sake of verisimilitude.

Pia had discovered early in her career as a widow that there was pleasure to be had in a good scream, especially when tantrums had no consequences but hoarseness, readily cured by honeyed tea. Her fits were rivaled only by Kitsa's.

One frequently broken bone of contention was Kitsa's friendship with the O'Brien twins.

Pia liked the twins. She even worried that a tinge of favoritism might be said to exist in her dealings with them. By their tenth birthday, they'd been granted employment at Pia's house during off-seasons at the inn—Katey as companion to Kitsa and Casey as museum guard. This arrangement soon became troublesome because the twins neglected their duties at the inn and because, predictably, all three children could be found howling and running in the museum, playing jacks on the parquet floors and cutting up the tapestries for doll clothes. Also, while the twins were bright, articulate, and witty, they had a peasant disrespect for education, and doggedly worked to distract Kitsa—who lacked their natural gifts—from her studies.

Kitsa's tutors found their charge "politically opposed" to history and science. She'd ask if Shanghai was part of New York; she simply refused to accept the most rudimentary principles of biology. For instance, she did not believe in photosynthesis, on the grounds that "if plants could figure out how to do that, people could too, and women would be freed from their kitchens." She proposed several all-night camping trips for herself and her companions to demonstrate that plants are cannibals that eat other plants at night, while no one is looking. The only thing that impressed her in all her years of science lessons was the Venus flytrap. She lined her ledges with them and tried to wean them on fruit. The relish with which she would "scarify" a stalk of broccoli by doing a headstand and saying the words JESUS CHRIST WAS OUT OF HIS MIND (a pagan phrase remaindered from her atheist days) was distracting during dinner, where Casey and Katey were frequent guests—in fact, Kitsa would refuse to eat unless they were there, insisting that the charm against vegetable-death was invalid without three voices. She also refused to practice anything on the piano that wasn't in waltz time, although her piano teacher was dismayed to discover that after six years of lessons, she couldn't really tell the difference anyway.

All three children had a unique ability to fall. Frequent excruciating scrapes and sprains of ankle, knee, and toe meant the twins had to spend the night at Kitsa's—which meant the staff kept up all night by giggles and crashes from the youngster's bedroom. The morning would find the children gone, not to return until the hours for lessons and duties were past.

Pia could have accepted these exploits tolerably well. They were children, after all. The real problem began when they reached puberty. Casey's stays in Kitsa's canopied bed, behind locked doors, seemed less innocent then. More of their time was spent in the unchaperoned treehouse, which was halfway between Pia's house and the inn and not visible from anywhere except Kitsa's bedroom, to which Kitsa kept the key.

"In America," Pia scolded, "the children must leave their doors open. If they get out of line at parties, their parents can suggest some activity that might be fun. How about a spur-of-the-moment scavenger hunt? Or maybe you'd like to make trifles?"

Having forgotten her connection to the twins, Pia thought the children were defying decorum, not nature. Her advice to her daughter was entirely conventional: "If anyone tries to get fresh with you, you don't have to slap his face and run. Take both of his hands in yours, grin into his eyes and say, 'Ambrose, you're quite a guy.'"

"If I ever meet anyone named Ambrose," Kitsa assured her mother, "I'll kick his teeth out first thing. Now Momma, why don't you go to your office and play?"

By fifteen, Casey O'Brien was six feet tall and shaving, with a throaty hum, each morning. He promised to grow more—his hands, feet, and ears were large as a puppy's. Casey's ease was as disturbing as his height. At dinner he'd clench a cigar in his teeth ("One musn't smoke," Pia reprimanded), light it with a match struck in one carefree motion on the heel of a boot (crossed on his sturdy thigh), and turn his face (gentle, quick, almost girlish, were it not for the big bony nose) toward his sister, who would want the salt or Casey's opinion on Kitsa's opinion that Aristotle was "scabby" and had "unforgivable blind spots."

In a red shirt, Casey was magnetic as a Christmas tree against the bright grass. Everything he did made Pia catch her breath, and he did plenty—he was always moving. That was the key to his charm; he was never quite still.

His sister, on the other hand, was remarkably composed. His sister! In fatal flashes, Pia shuddered at the thought of the two children in the womb, drowning in natal cheese—a splotchy, psychedelic yin-yang. As a child, Katey had been serene, and a healthy influence on Kitsa, who was wild and loud. But as a teen-ager, Katey was a tomboy. The more frilly Kitsa grew, the rougher Katey grew—and Katey was too fleshy to be climbing trees. Her leisurely blush, even her gums were fleshy. There was too much flesh and yet, at unpredictable moments, Katey attained a look of sexy innocence bordering on majesty. Even tying a shoe, Katey was settled into her body in a way no fifteen-year-old should manage. The very way she flexed her feet in her tan kid pumps spoke to it. She had a dulcimer's repose and clarity. Beside her, Casey was hard and smooth as wood, expansive as pipe tobacco in the woods. Yet with all this impending sexuality, the dinner conversations still centered on Kitsa's bad manners and fussy eating habits.

"Your Sunniness," Casey would say—picking up, always picking up—"how cometh your asparagus to be uneaten?" Kitsa would explode the wine in her mouth all over the tablecloth and gag in laughter as Pia admonished her to be a lady.

Other parents of teen-agers have these problems. But Pia

didn't talk with other parents, so when problems came up—like the night in 1919 when she couldn't find her hookah—she had no choice but to deal with them herself.

She found the door to her husband's study ajar. Someone had picked the lock. Inside, Katey was asleep, naked, on the divan, her fist pressed to her mouth. Bare-chested Casey was relaxing with his feet on Edward Maginski's desk, reading a book; Kitsa was asleep in his lap, in pink silk pajamas, grinding her teeth. The hookah was on the desk, atop an open book, its snaky arms crammed with yellow wallflowers.

The study was Pia's only room. It was her sanctuary, her mausoleum, and she'd told the children more than once to stay out. But how should she fight back? She knew the effects of absence on the heart. Seventeen winters before, when she'd stared at the obstinate hill facing the inn where her newborn twins were hostaged, she'd felt as if she'd melted the blue snow herself, with the laser of her desire. The oxalis and tuberose studding the hill in March were musicians come to sing the sweet song of her grief. As late as the summer, she'd wanted to count every hair on the babies' blue heads, every lash protecting their blue irises. She was as fascinated with the twins' development as she would have been with the scab forming on a harmless cut. When Pia made her isolationist declaration in 1919, the twins were getting under her skin, where she'd long ago ceased expecting to find anything but her bones and her vital organs.

"I want nothing to do with any of you," she announced. "Fight me like crusaders if you wish, but I shall give you no more advice. Do not use my study or my house for your shenanigans. Eat at the inn. Sleep in your treehouse. I don't care. May you dig your own graves. May you go straight to Hell in a— in a—"

"Handbasket?" Casey prompted.

"Clever boy," Pia said, loudly enough to wake Kitsa and Katey. "You think you're a clever boy, don't you?"

"I don't think about it much," Casey said.

"May you all stew in your own juices," Pia said, as she left the room. And stewing in their own juices was exactly, in a manner of speaking, what they planned to do.

# 5

By the hookah was the leather-bound, gold-embossed volume of Oriental erotic art that Casey had just found behind the stout Russian dictionary.

The book must have been Parnell or Maginski's personal favorite, for someone had traced the women's breasts, kneaded their nipples and cartoon caves so often that the oil of fingerprint had worn the paper thin, smudged the ink into a numinous possibility of breast, of vagina. From this glow protruded the stark, steely outlines of male genitals like scimitars and cannonballs, and the lovers' toothy, triumphant grins.

For a moment Casey was disarmed. An adolescent like Tourisme itself, he could barely conceive of people having had ideas before him. He was also a virgin. His only consolation was that the imaginative lovers pictured there were foreign, almost savages—he still had time to be the first man in Tourisme to stand a woman on her head.

When Pia found them, Casey had been alternately examining one particularly nice picture in the book (girl on her knees, her pink ass rotating in air like Bambi's) and his sister's exposed breasts. Katey's arm was thrown behind her head; Casey was grateful for this detail, not present in the book, and grateful too for Kitsa's breasts against his side, the pressure of her rump modifying itself periodically to orchestrate his perusal of book and twin.

"What did she want?" Kitsa yawned, as her mother left. She offered her mouth to Casey, soft and smooth inside as a raw oyster.

"She washes her hands of us," Casey announced, but it was garbled by the kiss.

"Keets, Case, stop, will you? I want to hear."

"I can't help it," Kitsa said, and she was right. Tongues were a new development. The clan was still adamantly virginal. They'd made a blood pact many years before that none of them should do anything that they all couldn't do. Since propriety and good taste prevented Casey from making love to Katey, he renounced the right to enter Kitsa until such time as Katey should find suitable similar company. Everything but intercourse seemed innocent enough to them, Casey with Kitsa and Kitsa with Casey and Katey. Katey and Kitsa had kissed, and kissed still, though more with affection than passion. They began to kiss with tongues several days after Kitsa had quite accidentally discovered the joys of that organ. Kitsa was puzzled by the fact that although Casey and Katey's mouths were quite similar anatomically, Katey's "wasn't as much fun." She also reported that Katey wasn't as much fun to cuddle with or press up against.

Katey was, however, an ace at O.S. (Oral Sex), which they'd read about but not tried until a cat wandered into the treehouse and casually demonstrated the technique on languishing Kitsa, who found it sensational. The cat, she said, did it best, although the cat was unreliable in its attentions; next Katey (who also rated the new thing, as practiced by Kitsa, on the top of her list of amusements, "like," she said, "being burned at the stake but having someone hose you down with cool water the whole time"); then, last and decidedly least, Casey. He was indignant at being third fiddle, slightly placated when Kitsa modified the technique for his organ (which, when erect, still made both girls giggle), and determined to make up for his reduction in rank by making the girls promise to adhere to a new set of sexual guidelines, which limited the sphere of activity between Kitsa and Katey to hugging, kissing, holding hands, and stroking, with Kitsa allowed to perform O.S. on Katey but not Katey on Kitsa. Kitsa agreed to this plan with the provision that Casey would brush up on his O.S., which he did with dispatch.

Things went reasonably well for almost a year. Katey and Kitsa didn't habitually stroke, except for hands on knees or around shoulders and Casey thought they looked pretty doing that. But trouble arose, most notably the curious development that the okay areas—e.g., hugging, holding hands, and kissing—became less popular and clustered around O.S.; which, combined with Casey's monopolization of Kitsa, led to Katey being left out more than she liked; which precipitated overtaxing of Kitsa's albeit enormous energy (a situation not improved by attempts to harness the cat or other cats into consistent or sustained efforts in O.S. toward either Katey or Kitsa) and mounting pressure toward intercourse.

"The bat!" Kitsa said. "Her toes are webbed, you know, and long as pinkies. I'm glad I didn't get her toes."

"What do you mean, 'washes her hands?' " Katey asked.

Casey shrugged. "No more dinners, I guess."

"I've always known Momma killed Poppa Chopin and Parnell," Kitsa said. "Can you imagine her and Poppa Chopin having O.S.?"

"Stop calling him Poppa Chopin," Katey sighed. "You never even met him. What's that book?"

Kitsa had moved behind her half-brother, so she could read over his shoulder as she rubbed his neck. The sensuality of her pose—shoulders thrust back, hair languid over the green eye—made Katey nervous.

"We've got to find someone for Katey," Casey said.

"Let's not start this," Katey begged.

"What about Chappy?" Kitsa said.

Katey gagged. "John Chapman? Who never closes his mouth right because his tongue's too big? With all those freckles he looks like a pond with scum on top, and he smells."

"That's not his fault," Casey scolded.

"My exasperation mounts, Casey. You wish on me a stable-boy?"

"Think how well his tongue will do for O.S."

"He can put his tongue flat against you," Kitsa agreed, "the way you like."

"I'd rather sleep with Uncle Nose," Katey said.

Kitsa scoffed, "You can't make love to an old man who climbs into trees to urinate on folks."

"He only does that to people who deserve it," Katey said.

"There must be someone you can tolerate," Casey said.

"You're erect," Kitsa announced.

"I don't want to hear about it," Katey said.

"Then you'd better think of a plan," Kitsa warned, "because any minute now"—she began to calligraph Casey's back with her nails—"we're going to quit waiting around for you."

"Knock it off," Katey hissed, as her friends began to cuddle and as Pia entered without knocking.

All dissent between the friends was dissolved in the solidarity with which they confronted their oppressor. Pia didn't need to tap her gold-slippered foot on the door jamb to get their attention. They were already defiantly taking in her hair flattened on the side where she'd tried to sleep, the scrawny breasts beneath an elaborate monogram, the eyes small and sharp as pebbles in their shoes.

"I may seem ancient to you," Pia said, with an edge to her voice which her children knew she thought was self-control. "But I am only thirty-six. I know very well what boils in the cauldrons of your bodies and I cannot condone it. I have already taken on the responsibility of running Tourisme; I haven't time to be a bodyguard as well. Take advantage of the O'Briens if you must, but I don't want you in my house."

"I'm not welcome at all," Kitsa taunted, "even to take my vitamins?"

"Take your vitamins with you—walk. The carriage is no longer at your disposal. The staff will be instructed to ignore any orders from you."

"Go drown," Kitsa suggested.

"You may hate me," Pia rejoined, with a tranquility which even her daughter had to acknowledge, "but you have my blood. You will drag me after you, me and Tourisme, wherever you go. You will never be at home anywhere else. Only here can you think yourself witty. In Paris your demonstrations will be taken as provincial and pedestrian; you will miss how we doted on you, how much of a 'character' we thought you were, no matter how dreary you find us. A taxi won't stop for you in Paris."

"How would you know?" Kitsa snapped. "You've never been to Paris. You're so lazy it's a wonder you ever get out of bed. And just because you're Parnell's daughter doesn't make you a prophet. I know, I know. 'Which way I fly is Hell; myself am Hell.' Say anything, but don't give me Milton!"

"You have kept me up too many nights," Pia said. "I expect to find you gone in the morning."

If Katey and Casey hadn't been there to reinforce archness, Kitsa might have found herself hurt by her mother's genuine indifference. Perhaps if it hadn't been summer, if the treehouse hadn't been so open to the cozy night, if the blueberries hadn't been so plump and plentiful, if the air hadn't been chilled to exactly the right temperature, Kitsa would have missed in advance the rosy kitchen staff, aproned in crisp gingham, carrying endless plates of steaming venison. As it was, however, Kitsa rejoiced. Pia was pathetic. Kitsa and her friends spent the rest of the night on the floor, doing dry runs of positions in the book. At dawn they headed back to the inn under a sky the precious blue of the Virgin Mary's robes, a sky goosebumped with birds that never sang the same song twice and never stopped singing, except to listen to the children sing.

Mr. O'Brien was at the back of the inn, plucking a chicken for lunch; his wife was making breakfast for her guests. The coffee, already perked, was strong enough to help the children forget they hadn't slept.

The children were fond of the O'Briens, whose eccentricities seemed harmless enough. At over ninety, the O'Briens lived in Parnell's future as most old folks live in the past. The fact that Tourisme had, in such a short time, turned into a bargain basement of anachronisms didn't seem to disturb them at all. Their lives wouldn't be significantly changed by the Sputnik or the television, and since they were fully confident that men would land on the moon eventually, it didn't much matter who planted whose flag first; in fact, it didn't make much difference whether men really planted a flag on the moon, or had Buck Rogers do it in a talking film. The film would be miraculous enough.

"A new one came about three last night," Mrs. O'Brien told them. "Taller than a telephone pole and every bit as heavy, his pockets full of American gold. We'll get telephones here soon enough. It took Pia five years to come around to the light-bulb. Ah, but they haven't gotten around to television yet, and they've known how to do that for years. There's just a backlog of miracles! With our luck the Russians will think of the talking movie first and we won't get to see one until after the Cold War. The Russians wouldn't have shared the shoelace if they'd thought of it before the Babylonians. But all in good time. We'll leave it to America. We're descendants of the father of invention; we don't have to prove ourselves to anyone. You can help with breakfast, though. That means you too, Miss Maginski."

"You're crazy, Mother," Katey said affectionately.

"Crazy," Mrs O'Brien snorted. "Your mother gets the papers,

Kitsa; they run about a week behind, but old news is better than no news. Now run along and tell Mr. O'Brien that we need beans for the stew. Don't torture him, mind."

Accustomed to being served, Kitsa found the chores at the inn amusing. Her favorite job was writing guests' names in the register in peacock blue ink. She didn't go home at all for nearly three weeks. There was always room for her at the inn when it was too chilly to sleep in the treehouse, and Katey's clothes fit well enough. When Kitsa finally relented and went home to pack her things, Pia looked up from her paperwork to greet her daughter with a curt nod. Both were content with their stalemate.

Astonishing things happened all the time. The very morning after Pia banned them from her house, for instance, there at the inn was Rory Kirn, the red-headed entrepreneur. Oh he was tall! His feet hung over the end of the bed by at least a foot. He had a thyroid problem and he was very rich. Katey served him breakfast in bed. He immediately fell in love with her.

Rory was a key figure in the construction of the boardwalk in Atlantic City, New Jersey. His visit to Tourisme was a business trip; he was collecting ideas for his own holiday resort. He told Katey about roller coasters and cotton candy; he told her about shooting galleries and about how you could buy a plastic comb from a machine for a penny. For another penny, another machine would tell you how much you weighed and how many children you'd have. Rory told Katey that he wanted to show her a strip of the Chesapeake Bay in Maryland near his home town where, he claimed, there were dinosaur prints embedded in the cliffs, sharks' teeth in each handful of sand—millions of sharks' teeth, polished and honed by the centuries. Katey found the attention flattering. The compliments of businessmen and barons who frequented the inn improved Katey's self-esteem, and took some of the pressure off Casey and Kitsa to entertain her. Although Katey refused Rory Kirn's marriage proposal, she did spoon with him nightly on the beach, and after a week she'd inspired him enough to assure that he'd send her gifts.

Within weeks, she received a large carton from Paris. Inside was a live monkey, dressed in the latest Parisian fashions. Katey crocheted a tiny Tourisme sweater and a tasseled hat, and taught him to pour cream and pick daisies. Unfortunately, the monkey didn't take too well to the climate and died peacefully in its sleep after less than a month, just in time for the arrival from London of the *Encyclopaedia Britannica*. When Rory returned to the States, he sent Katey a certificate which announced her a shareholder in General Electric. "Stock's cheap now, dearest," he wrote, "but wait. I promise you'll never have to marry for money." Katey liked the idea of Rory making his affection for her known to American corporations and kept the stock certificate in her keepsake box, along with the one for Bell Telephone which arrived the following month.

Tourisme itself was full of news. In early fall, the town blacksmith invented the laundromat. The fact that his machines were still crude—hand-cranked and not at all kind to satin or silk—didn't dampen local enthusiasm. And in late fall, Uncle Nose came down from the mountains as he did annually to stock up on sugar and flour. Though Uncle Nose was nobody's uncle officially, his avuncular joviality, as well as his taboo status with the elders, endeared him to children. Nose was the only defector from the original Tourisme settlers. He'd argued violently with Parnell about the beach, and some still thought that Nose was the ax murderer. But even if he was, he didn't have the adrenalin in him for further harm, except to subject villagers to loud, sloppy kisses.

Katey learned to come by having a man take her face in his hands. While Kitsa's mechanism remained more demanding, she was tractable enough to respond to Casey's devoted attention. They may not have known how a radio works, or what to do with decimals, but their bodies were finely tuned. They had pet names for each other's moles; they read each other's skin as

Uncle Nose read his footing in the Alps. Such sexual ease—especially without intercourse—is no mean accomplishment in teen-agers. They were nothing less than sexual geniuses. They also had a natural bent for the avant-garde, because they laughed at anything new, and they loved anything that made them laugh. The flying hats and winged pigs of the Surrealists were better than nitrous oxide; *The Rite of Spring* made vaudeville look funereal. Duchamp's urinal brought tears to their eyes. They were, in short, practiced idiot savants, competent dilettantes. They'd developed an effortless air that would serve them their whole lives, wherever they went.

To their credit, they were only bored once.

They didn't invent boredom. They discovered it. Boredom was there all along, massive and immobile as America.

It was a mild day in April, a day on which you could hear the daffodils pulsing right under the ground.

They were the only people on the beach. It was too early to "swim," too early in the season for many tourists, and they had made O.S. on the beach that morning, partially clothed; they'd taken their time, but in their mock-privacy there was some wish to be caught in the act: they made love as people get in the shower when they want a phone call, or light cigarettes when they want a bus. Now they were trying to decide what they'd do with the rest of their afternoon. The town was upset because the doctor had just announced his decision to move to New York, where he had a niece and nephew. Pia was less concerned about the loss of the doctor than about the loss of her nursemaid, who had married the doctor, and would leave with him. Pia and the nursemaid were the best of friends. When the nursemaid left, Pia lost, in essence, all traces of her past—that glorious past when nannies were loyal depositories for one's secrets. That left the town doctorless and nannieless, and several people had been dispatched to Paris to recruit replacements for both positions; but there had been some concern about whether a doctor could be found who would live in a one-room cottage with no plumbing and work for his room and board. The loss of the doctor had provoked another in a long series of town meetings about whether or not Tourisme should modernize. While Katey, Casey, and Kitsa hadn't attended that morning's meeting, they knew this discussion like the back of each other's hands: knew that Pia had sighed about tradition, or bemoaned the town's increasingly sad finances. The advantage of being in the Alps was that they were unlikely to be invaded by German troops; the disadvantage was that they were unlikely to get subsidized for telephone wiring. It was on the subject of the telephone that people disagreed most fiercely.

The town had had to sell almost a quarter of its holdings in art to fund electricity. Having telephone service installed would cost them the rest of their art and more, and they didn't have the expertise to provide their own labor. The telephone would also, some argued, cost them their independence, for if Tourisme allied itself with France or Switzerland for funding, the children of Tourisme might have to pay taxes. On the other hand, if they didn't get telephones, Tourisme's feasibility as a tourist mecca would be limited. Pia couldn't justify the financial risk of committing the town to a technology that could soon be rendered obsolete. Tourisme had survived without telephones until now, and would undoubtedly continue to survive. Furthermore, Tourisme's identity rested on being slightly out of sync with the rest of the world—no, *adamantly* out of sync. Her opponents pointed out the paradox of her position: true, Tourisme had a tradition of independence; but to adhere to that tradition, they must adhere to *modernism,* for Tourisme's tradition was to be one big step ahead of the rest of the world, not one giant step behind. Tourisme thus needed not only the telephone, but a more sophisticated telephone—perhaps one that allowed people in three different places to talk all at once. Such a phone, however, was simply not economically possible—so the argument raged on, always in the abstract. The conservatives, led by Pia, argued that Tourisme should not take any chances with the world. The radicals, led by the blacksmith, argued that they fight back—fight fire with fire or, in this case, fight telephones with better telephones. The moderates, led by the O'Briens, argued that telephones would certainly be nice, but if they couldn't have telephones, they should simply try to make the best of what they had.

The telephone debate was so heated that it had even caused some friction among Katey, Casey, and Kitsa. Casey was an advocate of the telephone; his sister and girlfriend were indifferent to it. When Casey tried to discuss the question again that afternoon, Kitsa cut him off:

"I'm tired of the telephone. I wish my mother had never started talking about that. Maybe there's a secret room at her house we can discover. Maybe the ax murderer lives there, or maybe Parnell and Maginski aren't dead after all, and Pia keeps them bound and gagged there, without any light, and makes them eat raw meat out of dirty bowls, or maybe there's a torture chamber—"

"You're just like your mother," Casey said. "You'd think Tourisme was the only place in the world. You were so excited about the laundry machines—well, that's just dirty clothes! The least you could do is get excited about the telephone."

"Well, I'm not excited."

"We could ride the horses," Katey said. "We haven't done that in a while."

"If you had a phone," Casey said, "we could find a man for Katey."

"Maybe Rory'll send something," Katey said.

"He hasn't sent anything but stock in months," Kitsa said crossly. "Couldn't you write him to send more fun things like the monkey or those French ticklers we read about?"

"If you had a phone," Casey said, "you could call him and

the new things would get here much sooner. But French ticklers wouldn't do us any good, since Katey refuses to find a man."

"Here we go again," Katey said. "You know this isn't a man's town."

"Quite true," Casey said. "We could discuss how, in a society run by women, there aren't any wars or sports—"

"No discussions," Kitsa said.

"How about a revolution of some kind?" Katey said. "We could see how many people we could turn into Bolsheviks in a predetermined period of time, or Buddhists?"

"Or Jews," Kitsa said.

"There's an idea," Casey said. "There's the whole bit in Parnell's will about how he foresees a time when Tourisme's ideals and independence will be threatened—not physically, as we share with Switzerland the inhospitable Alps, but spiritually. He therefore suggested that sometime around 1920, as a vote of confidence in world freedom, the entire population of Tourisme convert *en masse* to Judaism."

"Why would he suggest that?" Kitsa asked.

"Probably because Jews are a small group, like our own. The point is, it'd be solemn and serious. Your mother would love it. 'Good lord!' she'd exclaim"—here Casey commenced his Pia imitation, which made the girls laugh—" 'what a charming idea! I'll have my seamstress make up some of those blue tasseled cloaks and adorable caps.' We can hang a Star of David beside the Tourisme flag—"

"We don't have a flag," Kitsa said.

"All the better. We should. We'll design it today. Your mother will love it; we can get on her good side again, and maybe influence her about the telephone. Now we can incorporate our Judaism right into the basic design. A Star of David on wings? Too diagrammatic. A Star of David carried in the beak of a dove with PEACE OF MIND written on its torso in Hebrew and Gaelic?"

"Who'll be the Rabbi?" Kitsa asked.

"Uncle Nose?" Katey suggested.

"Uncle Nose would be a nice touch," Casey agreed, "if Pia would approve. First he'd rule out flags, printed napkins, and matchbooks on the grounds that we can have no heathen images; then he'd rule out a dancing band and attack the menu. No wild boar, he'd say. No escargot or other crawler. Roast chicken would be acceptable, but if we have meat at all we can't have cheese or cream."

"How dreary," Kitsa said.

"That's the point. I've been reading about it in the *Britannica*. I guess that's why Parnell liked it. If you want fun, be a Christian. Then at least you get the Resurrection. Or go to China and then you can have New Year's floats and Peking duck. As it stands, all you get is heartache."

"And the Song of Songs," Katey said. "What time is it?"

"Afternoon," Kitsa said.

"What do you think?" Casey asked.

"The fact that I've changed the subject," Katey said, "should suffice as an answer."

"What do *you* think, Kitsa?"

"I went along with the change of subject."

"What is the new subject?"

Katey put her arm around Kitsa and said, "How about a little O.S., just on the spur-of-the-moment?"

"Fine with me," Kitsa said. "Any objections, Casey?"

"I guess not," Casey said, as Kitsa started in on Katey. "But I still like the Judaism idea. I'm sure we could pull it off and it would keep us busy for at least a week. Parnell recommended it anyway."

"Oh," Katey said.

Luckily, she came quickly, so Casey didn't have to talk to himself for very long.

"A lovely day," Katey said, pushing wet hair from her eyes and removing some grass from her toes.

"I wish someone would die," Casey said, as he started in on Kitsa.

"Oh," Kitsa said.

"Maybe someone new will show up," he added.

"Shut up," Kitsa said. "That's better. Oh."

"Someone interesting," he added.

"Casey, please!"

"Someone for Katey."

"Now," Kitsa said. "The circle part!"

As it turned out, someone would die very soon—two people, in fact. And someone new and interesting would show up for Katey. Luckily, Casey wouldn't remember his lazy wish, or he might have felt guilty, had he the time to feel anything at all in the confusion that followed.

# 6

I met Mildred in Washington
Square after work, as I'd done the night before. I hadn't yet
quit my job. I worked for a recording studio, playing piano
and doing back-up vocals and some mixing. That Thursday,
we'd taped a commercial for a long, slick gas guzzler called a
Panther. I had to sing a song about cars ("I'm gonna make you
a Panther lover") and play the simple-minded beat of panther
paws on the piano. Leland, my boss, had put his arm around me
and told me I needed some rest. I hadn't talked to Argyle in two
days. Everyone I'd ever known had left me. I was therefore quite
grateful to Mildred, who was waiting for me on a park bench,
as we'd planned. I wore a white linen suit with a bright red
scarf. Mildred wore the same clothes she'd worn the day before,
and the day before that, minus the pearl choker.

"I was thinking about Tourisme at work," I said. "I had a
thing for Christ too when I was a kid. I always used to scurry
past crucifixions in museums. The height of my revulsion to
the icon came when my father took me to see the Pietà at the
New York World's Fair. Jeremy Spell is hardly religious, but
he's positively fanatical about culture. He made me wait in line
for hours when I, of course, was much more interested in 'It's a

Small World' and the Belgian waffles. Finally I was there, shoved right up against the statue. When you think about how hard it must have been for Michelangelo to puncture those little limp marble hands and feet, the gruesomeness of the crucifixion is driven home. I bolted right out of there and got lost. My father found me in about half an hour—I hadn't gotten far—but he was furious. I never understood why parents get angry at lost children; the separation is its own punishment. The only other time I saw Jeremy that angry was once on the boardwalk in Ocean City, when he handed me a ten-dollar bill for a caramel apple and I gave the change to a blind beggar. Jeremy actually shook me that time. I didn't know if I was crying because he shook me in front of so many people, or because I was over-whelmed by my own magnanimity."

"Did your father's anger always invoke your epiphanies?"

"Pretty much. He couldn't keep up with me."

"A typical complaint about any parent."

"No, he was too old for a child. He was a riot at PTA meetings—all the sexy young mothers thought he was my grandfather."

Mildred didn't say anything.

"So what happened to your characters?" I asked. "Let me guess. They intermarried, gave birth to a monster, interpreted this tragedy as an acid test of their incompatibility, separated, and died of cobwebbed souls. Thus what we have is a parable of the high cost of great expectations, with Tourisme disintegrating into something like a suburb."

"You slip," Mildred remarked sadly. "Your feet are caught in the quicksand of sarcasm. You can't be kind to other people, because you can't be kind to yourself."

"You learn that in California?"

"Casey was like that too. Even as an old man, he some-times inflicted his past with facileness—a youngster's sacrilegious prank. He believed he could have a snappy dialogue with fate, tip his top hat, and saunter off, swirling a jeweled walking stick.

But fate followed him and took the lead, burned his bridges before he even reached them, cutting off his future—for what is the future but the past, how it rules us? Fortunately, there's comfort in such fatalism."

"Fortunately."

" 'The best way to guard yourself against the superior qualities of another person is to love him.' "

"Meaning?"

"It's Goethe."

"But meaning?"

Mildred shrugged. "It just came to mind."

"That's the problem with this story," I said. "You talk all right, but sometimes I'm not sure how it's supposed to pay off. What I can't figure out is why you're bothering to make all this up. Obviously the mention of public figures from the past is meant to lend your narrative the sheen of historical accuracy, but why tell the story to begin with?"

"Casey," Mildred said, bending over so that her head fell jerkily between her knees.

"What about him? If he was your lover, maybe you ought to start there. I mean, why do I have to hear about his adolescent sex life? What's your emotional investment in all of this?"

"Casey. Casey and the basic vulgarity of the magic world," Mildred said, her voice muffled by her plaid skirt. "Casey understood that it couldn't go on. Tourisme was a children's place. Its founders were children, suffused in the present as adults never are. Casey was the only one who ever grew up without losing all the magic. Most of the time, when people try to set up their own little world, they lose all connection and become puerile. Look at Venice, California, if you need evidence."

"I wish you'd pick up your head. You're hard to hear that way. Why are you all hunched over like that?"

"I don't feel well."

"What's wrong?"

"I don't feel well, Jennifer."

I helped her up and put the back of my hand to her fore-head. She was hot. I offered my place for aspirin, tea, and a cool place to sleep. She refused. She said she had to go to sleep immediately and asked if I'd help her to move her bags to a bench on the opposite side of the park.

"You're not going to sleep here," I said.

"I might."

"I'll take you home."

"No, sometimes I like to sleep in the park and think of Casey."

"And you call *me* boy-crazy. You'll be robbed."

"No I won't. Besides, I'm too tired to go home. But I have to go to those benches. Otherwise the sun will start in on my face too early in the morning."

"You're nuts."

"Be that as it may."

I left her there, curled up on a bench, her handbag punched into a pillow. She told me to be there right after work because, she said, she was dying.

"You just have a cold," I said.

"You never know. You have to take care of yourself and count on the worst."

When I arrived at five-fifteen on the following day, a Friday, Mildred felt much better. "There you are," she said cheerfully. She was sitting on the exact bench where I'd left her, filing her nails. She hid the file guiltily when I approached.

"Now we're going to move onto Frog and Gato!" Mildred said. "You'll like Frog and Gato, I wager."

"Don't you want to hear what happened to me?" I objected.

"No."

"I broke up with Argyle."

"About time."

"He didn't call me so I called him. A mistake."

"I could have told you that."

"He wouldn't talk. I told him he was scared of me. I said

that people can be very generous if you're generous enough to allow them to be. He said, 'I know. I've known generous people in my life and I'm about ready to know another one.' I thought about that. I realized that he was saying I wasn't generous, so I hung up. Mildred, you don't think I'm ungenerous, do you?"

"You don't seem terribly interested in Frog and Gato."

"I called him back ten minutes later to say, 'I don't like loose ends. What an odd phone call.' He said, 'Let's forget the whole thing.' I said, 'Do you think that can be done?' I had to repeat myself because the connection was bad. He said, 'Quite easily.' I realized that, as usual with Argyle, the 'it' was ambiguous. 'Do you mean the phone call,' I asked, 'or the whole thing?' He said the whole thing. I told him curtly to have a good time wherever he was going, although I know perfectly well where he's going, and then I hung up."

"Where's he going?"

"After a week of celibacy, probably to Seattle on borrowed money to visit Girlfriend Number Two. But after that, he's going to New Zealand."

"Why?"

"To make distance the excuse not to make a commitment to her, as she was an excuse not to make a commitment to me; and to teach art."

"How did he manage that?"

"He has relatives in New Zealand. I hated hearing him tell people he was going to New Zealand. He'd say it casually and half-smile, because he knew he was going to be able to answer the questions you've just asked. He'd never just tell anyone, 'I'm going to New Zealand, where I have relatives, to teach art.' His parents were lawyers and even before they got divorced, they'd tell Argyle never to write or say anything that might incriminate him. Argyle is stingy. Given that, it's surprising how good his work is. But the trouble is that so much of his life is small. His apartment is small, which isn't his fault, but his paintings are much smaller than they should be. He parcels out all usable space, nitpicks at all the boundaries. If his leg is resting on your leg then you have your share of him and you'd better not expect him to touch your face or talk to you. Sometimes he opens up a bit during lovemaking. In the beginning he'd get so sheepish as we moved into the bedroom; he was tickled to please me. But the rest of the time he's so anal; and finally, anality is not terribly interesting in the world of problems."

"Then why are you talking about it?"

"It's like the first time I saw how recordings are made. I always imagined that the orchestra would get together and play until they got it right. Instead each instrument, including the voice, does its part solo, perfecting it, until they all get combined in the 'mix.'"

"He who travels alone travels fastest."

"It's easier to be nice. I know that I shouldn't be upset about Argyle, and then I'm upset with myself for being upset with myself, because obviously A. Argyle Lovett whom I've known a year has little to do with the price of coffee or success, with my disappointments or—Mildred? Mildred, you're not listening. I'm upset!"

"I realize that."

"Don't you care about me?"

"There are people I've known most of my life I don't care about."

I was still standing. I sat. Mildred patted my hand. "Argyle didn't matter anyway," she said.

"That's the problem in a nutshell."

"Don't give it another thought."

"Easier said."

We sat in silence for a moment. "Mildred," I whimpered, "what's wrong with me?"

"Don't worry. You're not alone in the world anymore, Jennifer. I'm like your twin, sitting here being sick with you."

"So you think I'm sick."

"You're fond of your complaints."

"Can't you be serious?"

"I'm always serious."

"And you? Are you neurotic?"

"My body is going fast."

She told me that she was anxious to get on with her story, because she was dying and hadn't much time, and I let her—it seemed as good a way as any not to think about Argyle.

When I went to the park the next night after a miserable Saturday of overtime, Mildred wasn't there. I took a circuitous route around the park back to my apartment on Bleecker Street. No Mildred. I unlocked the front door and walked up the flight of steps. No Mildred. I unlocked my door and went to turn on the air conditioner in the kitchen. There were several M. Howells in the phonebook. I called information to see if they had a Mildred listed, but they didn't. The doorbell rang. It was Mildred, of course.

"Why do you live on this street?" she greeted me. "It's so noisy. In the summer, on the weekend, so many tourists."

"I've always lived here. Used to live a block down. Why can't I have your phone number? What am I supposed to do if I can't find you?"

"I don't have a phone."

"Do you have an address?"

"What's your problem? I'm here." She appraised my apartment with a squint and the twitch of a smile for each object she'd predicted—the posters, the butcher block table, the violin.

"You're just like Argyle," I said. "For the first two months I was seeing him I never saw his apartment. If he was here, he could leave when he wanted. Why the secrecy?"

"Let's go," she said.

"To your place?"

"To dinner. Your treat."

"I only have eight dollars," I said, checking my wallet. "How about your treat?"

"All right. My treat."

I suggested a place that had cheap moussaka. That seemed to agree with her. We strolled. It was too hot to walk fast, and I walk slowly when I'm thinking anyway—I was thinking about a way to reintroduce my complaint about her secrecy. At one point, we stopped to listen to some street musicians who were doing a Bach trio-sonata. I looked at the boy playing the violin and felt a pang of nostalgia for my father—nostalgia and fear, because I'd said my father was sick to explain my absence from work the week before, and with my luck, he would be.

Thus lost in music and thought, I hardly felt the tug on my shoulder. I turned to find two hands in my purse: the hand of a huge, unscrupulous-looking man and, grabbing his wrist, the dainty hand of Mildred Howell.

"He was going to take your wallet," Mildred told me. "You should be more careful, Jennifer. What would you like me to do with him?"

They were playing an allegro movement. "I don't know," I said—then, indignantly, to the man, "You're not nice!"

Mildred still had him firmly by the wrist. When he tried to move his other hand, she caught that one too. They stood— Mildred at about the level of his armpit—linking hands tensely, like children at their first dance class. Her purse was swung diagonally across her chest, like a beauty contestant's sash.

"Check his back pockets," Mildred commanded.

I reached into his sweaty pants. I found two good watches, twenty credit cards, and over three hundred dollars in cash. From his stunned expression, I half-expected to pull out, as if from Harpo Marx's shoe, a swordfish, a telephone, and a can of sardines.

"Good enough," Mildred said. She looked into the man's impassive face. I think he was shocked to be accosted by her; he couldn't have been held by her geriatric grip. "What's your name?" she asked. "Where are your friends? Working alone isn't a good idea. Now I'm going to let you keep a hundred of the dollars you've stolen. You can live on that for a week, can't you? That'll give you time to look for a job. I'd like you to tell my friend how much money went along with each of those credit cards. Do you think you can remember? Jennifer, do you have any paper? No? Here, reach into my bag. That's it. There should be a scratch pad under the matches."

Our scene had by now attracted a small crowd. As I scrounged for the pad I noticed her wallet. It was crammed with bills and I mean bills. Fifties. Hundreds. This was a different wallet from the one she'd showed me before, the one with the driver's license. I thought I must be wrong, but I opened the wallet a bit, all under the pretense of looking for paper. Mildred was carrying a lot of cash.

"Hurry," Mildred said. She looked more nervous about the police coming than the pickpocket did. Mildred held his wrists and listened to the music, which had started up again, while the man dictated his sources of income. Then Mildred told me to give him a hundred dollars and to put the rest of the money in her purse. "Go ahead," she prodded.

I handed the man a hundred dollars.

"You won't do it again," Mildred told him. "Got that?"

He nodded.

She released his wrists. Then we watched him run off and we walked in silence toward the restaurant, with the Bach behind us like the noise of pinball machines from the basement bars.

"Thank you," I said.

"Sure."

"Do you think he'll stop?"

"Of course not."

"Then why didn't we turn him in? What are we going to do with the credit cards and all that money?"

"Return it to its owners. What did you think?"

"Why don't we give it to the police?"

"The police keep it."

"Mildred?" I said cautiously.

"Yes, Jennifer."

"When I was looking for the pad I couldn't help but notice another wallet in there. I don't mean to pry, but where did you get all that money?"

"What money?"

"The money in the green wallet."

"Why do you ask?"

I noticed we were walking in step. I said, "You know perfectly well why I ask. If you have all that money, why are you living like this?"

"How do you know how I'm living?"

"You sure don't spend much on clothes."

She laughed and put her arm around me. After a while she took her arm off my shoulder and linked it through my arm. She began to talk softly but very quickly.

"I'm rich. I don't want you to think I'm ungenerous because I made you buy the drinks and asked you to pay for my dinner. Whatever you need, just ask. I just don't like to hold money in my hands. I hate the smell and texture of money. I don't care about spending it, I don't need it, we could go to the Plaza now and get a hundred-dollar bottle of wine, drop five C's on veal, that's fine—six hundred is nothing, I could wipe my ass with that. But if we're going to do it, I'd like to give you the money before we go in. I'd rather you hadn't found out, because now you may not trust your interest in me, but there you have it. All I care about is the story I've begun to tell you. That story tugs on my sleeve. I'd rather not think about it, I'd rather move on with the business of living, but it's like when you've gotten three hours' sleep and try to wake up in the morning for work: you know how dark and heavy sleep is then, like the barnacled underbelly of a ship, but how sweet at the same time? I go back to my story because one can't help returning to a dream. Besides, if you stick with me, you'll love Casey too. I know it's hard for you to grasp. You're so young. Your pull is forward, onward, toward the future; for you life is water-skiing—"

"That's not so," I interrupted. "My mother committed suicide when I was six. I'm often depressed."

Mildred shook her head vigorously. "Did I say I was depressed? Did I say I was unhappy? I don't want to sound like a Taoist, but I've danced on graves. I'm probably the happiest person you'll ever meet because those categories don't apply to me. Do you ask an eggplant if it's happy? Do you ask a highway or a teabag or a chunk of moonshine?"

"You're saying you're inanimate?"

"No, no, no, no, of course not!" Mildred tapped out each *no* on her thigh with her purse. "It's just not a question of happiness with me anymore. Happy people wake up and wonder, Am I happy today? They're afraid their freckles will fade. They're afraid to go outside if it's raining, or they sing in the rain just to prove how happy they are, and then they're afraid it'll be sunny and everyone else'll be happy too—and all it does is escalate, until even their chauffeurs and psychiatrists are complaining—who needs happy?"

"I'm happy," I said. "Here. With you."

"But you'll listen, won't you? To the rest? As long as it takes?"

There was a hint of panic in her voice. "Naturally," I said.

I *was* happy. I felt an iridescent peace with my arm linked through Mildred's. My back and shoulders were cool, dry. I had color in my face. For at least twenty minutes, I didn't think about Argyle, even to think that I wasn't thinking about him. I didn't think about money. Only later would I be troubled by Mildred's wealth—how, for instance, she guarded her purse for all those years; why, when so much of her money was in a locker in Grand Central Station, she bothered to have a will; why, if she never spent any money, she bothered to carry it at all.

"We missed the restaurant," I said. "We walked by it blocks ago."

"I have a friend a couple of blocks from here who sells hot dogs."

The friend, a gnarled old man, spotted Mildred from a good distance and began to wave. She reclaimed her arm to wave back. I waved too. For a second I could smell the Mildred Howell I first met, the Mildred of Grand Central Station and stale cigarettes. But only for a second. After I waved, I turned to Mildred and smiled. Seen in profile, she was blonde and radiant as a sixteen-year-old posing for her high-school graduation picture.

There was a gentility in the old hot dog vendor's face that made me trust he was one of us.

*One of us!* That's what I thought.

# 7

$\mathsf{F}$rog and Gato Haggerty arrived in Tourisme with their mother the morning that Mr. O'Brien died.

Katey, Casey, and Kitsa were at the Sanity Inn, in a bedroom they'd set up to resemble a stage. Boredom had driven them to art. They'd spent the last week rehearsing scenes from great plays. Kitsa did a competent Cleopatra. Katey, though usually stuck with the role of maidservant or wicked competitor, played her roles with infectious dignity. Casey had true acting talent, and might have pursued a career in the theater had not the following circumstances compelled him to spend the rest of his life in Tourisme, pandering first to a woman he hadn't chosen, and then to a woman he'd disliked his whole life.

It was Friday, and Kitsa, as Hedda Gabler, had just executed a superbly funny, hyperkinetic suicide; Casey scooped her in his manly arms to kiss her neck.

"No tongues," Katey said. "You're dead, Keets. You don't have control of your tongue muscles."

But art, as usual, led to sex; and art and sex made fierce competitors for daily life, so when the bell at the reception desk began to ring downstairs, the threesome ignored it. The tinkle persisted, however, and since they couldn't agree who should be forced to leave a scene that was building so rapidly to O.S., they all went downstairs together.

From the top of the landing they saw a tapping, gray-slippered foot below, which was soon revealed to be attached to a gray-haired woman dressed entirely in silver. She was an aging flapper, a type they'd seen before. All the glitter in her clothes did not disguise the lusterlessness of her skin. The woman said she had a reservation for three. The head of an attractive young man appeared at the door.

"Better come out here," he said. "One of these is stone cold."

The O'Briens had lined up their chairs along the wall of the inn as usual. The boy pointed to Mr. O'Brien. The old man's eyes were closed. A contented smile played along his mouth.

Another youth, a girl, was leaning over Mrs. O'Brien, listening to her heart.

She looked exactly the same as the boy, except for her figure and her mouth, which was enormous. Casey, Katey, and Kitsa had never seen another set of twins before.

"How old are these, anyhow?" the girl asked. "This one's pulse is slow as a riverboat down the Nile."

She cocked her head at Casey. "Know them?"

"They're my parents."

"Not anymore," Mrs. O'Brien said, almost jovially. "We are not your parents and never were. There. Now you know."

"Delirious," the boy pronounced, as the silver lady appeared in the doorway. The twins flanked her sides, their arms identically folded. "I'm Gato," the boy told them, "and that there's Frog."

"Do you have to use those vulgar nicknames here?" their mother pleaded. "Your names are Lucinda and Percival Haggerty."

Katey had knelt in tears at her father's feet. Kitsa was staring at Gato.

"We'll help you ditch the corpses," Gato whispered to Casey, "if you help us ditch our mother."

"How'd you do it?" Frog asked jauntily. "Arsenic?"

"You understand," Mrs. O'Brien told Mrs. Haggerty. "We had over half a century, Mr. O'Brien and I. More! I'm sure I know you. Who are you?"

"Helen Haggerty."

"I'm going to close my eyes, Helen Haggerty, and when I wake up, I'll be dead."

Mrs. O'Brien kept her promise. She would not open her eyes again until the instant of death, which came two days later. Casey and Gato carried the bodies—one dead, one playing dead—upstairs to the O'Briens' old four-poster. Katey followed, sobbing. Kitsa, Frog, and Mrs. Haggerty remained downstairs.

"Get rid of her," Frog hissed to Kitsa. "Send her off. Is there a tour?"

"If you'd like," Kitsa gulped, "you can walk to the museum, ma'am. It's an easy stroll. We'll carry up your luggage."

"Is there no taxi?"

"Not at the moment."

"Very well, then. I know where it is."

Frog turned to watch her mother amble off, then grabbed Kitsa's elbow.

"We're getting out of here. Gato's the brains. You better cooperate."

Upstairs, Gato and Casey were conferring outside the O'Briens' door. Gato smoked a filterless cigarette, flicking the ashes on the carpet. Katey had crumpled on the floor and stayed there, weeping quietly. The pentagon of teen-agers was speechless for a moment, taking in the possible permutations of five and listening to Katey cry.

Gato put an authoritative hand on Katey's shoulder.

"Don't cry," he said.

All eyes, all light in the hall focused on his hand, which was darker than the skin on her shoulder. In that $f$/stop, every-

one knew precisely what was going to happen. The only unknown variables were the depth of Katey's grief, and the extent
of a friendship between Mrs. Haggerty and Pia.

Pia and Helen met on Pia's grounds. They found they had
much in common, as wealthy widows with responsibilities and
unmanageable children. The late Mr. Haggerty had been an
automobile magnate in Detroit, and Helen had taken on much
of his business. She'd visited Tourisme years ago before her
twins were born and had vowed to return. Helen found Tourisme
quaint, whereas Pia loved to think about dailies rolling off
assembly lines in Detroit. We don't know if the women, drinking cognac in the drawing room, discovered that they both had
illegitimate twins, or that they'd both been in love on an artificial beach in 1901, with a sexy "sailor" whom neither would
ever hear from again.

Helen Haggerty's husband had been alive at the time of her
infidelity, so she'd simply raised her twins as her own. She
never entirely suppressed her wish to find her sailor. But there
was enough to occupy the women without comparing their
pasts. Helen showed Pia the latest dance steps, and Pia charmed
Helen by showing her heirlooms that would be worth a fortune
in America. Even news of the O'Briens' deaths didn't daunt Pia,
who hadn't had such good company in years. She was so happy
that she sent a note to the inn suggesting a reconciliation with
Kitsa.

Kitsa didn't answer the note. She was preoccupied with
Gato.

As the golden-haired only child of a president, Kitsa was
used to being something wispy and aglimmer in the night, like a
firefly, that caught everyone's attention without even trying.
But Gato didn't even comment on her mismatched eyes. *His*
eyes were riveted on Katey.

Katey presided over Mrs. O'Brien's living wake. Mother
and daughter mourned together. Katey mopped her mother's
forehead, rearranged her sheets, and tried not to look at Mr.

O'Brien's corpse on the other side of the bed. All Katey's crying had made her luminous. With Mr. O'Brien dead and Mrs. O'Brien trying to die, there was no one to run the inn. Katey cooked and turned down sheets that night with a mournful propriety, and she seemed, to Gato, like European royalty he'd read about.

Frog and Gato were most American in their hatred of America. They'd spent most of their lives wrangling their ways out of homes for delinquents. This was the first time they'd been out of the country, and they didn't intend to return.

"You've been arrested?" Kitsa asked.

They were in the lobby very late at night. All of the guests were asleep, except for Mrs. Haggerty, who was still at Pia's. Pia had sent a man to say that Mrs. Haggerty would spend the night. Gato wore gabardine and wine-colored riding boots that he'd found in a trunk in the attic of the inn. He reminded Kitsa of Vronsky, Anna Karenina's smooth customer.

"For what?"

"Little things," Frog said. "Just robbing liquor stores and such. We never killed anyone or set a live dog on fire."

"You don't look like the types."

"What do the types look like?"

"I'm not sure."

"Clam up then."

Vicious looks between Frog and Kitsa. Kitsa thought Frog was coarse; and Frog thought Kitsa was flouncy as the debs she'd spent her life avoiding. Frog was also possessive of her brother, and since she had no excuse for snapping at Katey, who sat silently, she picked on Kitsa.

The main discussion was about how Frog and Gato would get to Paris without their mother.

"She won't leave here without us," Gato said. "We tried in the States. She always has us tracked down. The only solution is for her to go away from here alone, convinced that we're dead."

"Easily done," Kitsa said. "Over the cliff at the beach."

Kitsa suggested that they hide the twins and say they'd strolled off and accidentally fallen; the bodies, of course, would never be found. In fact, if the accident happened during the O'Briens' funeral—scheduled for the next day—they could "fall" amidst the commotion, since the cemetery was just off the beach. That would make it more convincing and easier for them to get away.

At the mention of the O'Briens, Katey began to cry again. Gato stopped pacing, knelt before her, and cradled her face.

"Come with me to Paris," he said.

"That's all we need is extra baggage," Frog said.

Kitsa stood up to exclaim, "Katey can't leave."

"Katherine, Katherine," Gato said. "You can be a model, you can be a countess. You'll be mine forever."

"Until he finds the next one," Frog added.

"She wouldn't leave Tourisme," Kitsa said.

"Why?" Frog said. "It's a dive."

"Is not."

"Is too."

"How would you know?"

Kitsa and Frog proceeded to argue about Tourisme. Frog proclaimed the genius of America in everything, from the Grand Canyon to the invention of strip poker; she laughed off Tourisme's beach as minor-league inventiveness, lower in rank than miniature golf or George Washington Slept Here. It was a stupid argument, considering that Frog had defected, and that Kitsa had mocked Tourisme her whole life. But the argument served to distract them from watching Katey and Gato.

Casey watched.

Gato ran his thumbs over Katey's cheekbones, over the bridge of her nose, repeating her name; Katey looked at him numbly and murmured, "I don't know. I don't know." Casey knew that if Gato moved his thigh a little to the left to press on Katey's thigh, Katey would come. Her face would flush from the cheekbones out; her eyes would get clearer; her hands would swirl thank-you's through Gato's hair and she'd make the sweetest sound, so that Gato—who was probably not used to such responsive women (for there aren't many)—would be determined to keep her; and Casey was pretty sure Gato's determination would not be easily broken.

Kitsa was pacing now as she argued with Frog, but she still glanced at Gato occasionally. Casey watched her watching Gato, saw Gato for a moment as Kitsa must have seen him. He imagined Gato robbing a bank, and placing the money—crisp green bills, lined up neatly like shoes in a shoe store—beside him on the seat of the getaway car, a forest-green Lozier that shone in the sunlight. Casey imagined Gato's self-confident smile, and knew that he'd lost Kitsa—lost Kitsa, Katey, and his parents.

What Casey didn't know was why he wasn't more upset.

He'd expected loss to make more of an impact. His father had died with less pomp than an old dog deciding to nap, on a day that, with almost mocking deference, had been clear, mild, and utterly unexceptional. As for Mrs. O'Brien, she'd decided to die; but there was little heroic about her decision. Everything was dispensable. Even Kitsa, with her even teeth and bitten hands tiny as a doll's, might be dispensable. Casey's coldness surprised him, but in it he imagined he might find a new strength.

"Frog," he said.

Frog turned from her argument.

"Frog, do you want to make love?"

"Funny," Kitsa said. "Your parents just died. Show some respect."

Frog laughed. Her laugh was just the right notch higher than her speaking voice. "Don't worry," she said. "I don't feel left out." She gestured to Katey and Gato in each other's arms. "He does this all the time. He's a sucker for that innocent look. Once we were in the middle of a holdup and he got a sweet tooth for the check-out girl. He stood with a gun in his hand telling her how her hair was the pig's wings and her body the ant's eyebrows, with the sirens getting closer and closer. We got four months on probation for that. I'm used to it. But it's not going to happen again," Frog added ominously, "at least until we get to Paris."

"Let's go upstairs, Frog," Casey said. "What do you say?"

"Why not? But we've got to get some word down about how we're going to do the escape tomorrow. Hear that, Gato?"

Gato nodded.

Kitsa began to scream. She clenched and unclenched her fists. Gato and Katey turned to her dreamily, as if they were looking at a tacky plaster statue on a neighbor's lawn.

"I don't know," Katey told Gato. "I just don't know."

Casey and Frog found an unoccupied room upstairs. They didn't turn on the lights, so Casey didn't know what Frog looked like undressed—he didn't want to know. But her mouth, so horrible to look at, fit his entire penis into it down to the root as Kitsa's never had, and Frog seemed never to run out of breath. She later confessed that she'd wanted to be an opera singer—she had a strong voice. She worked on Casey as if she were holding a climactic note. She trilled on him. He came once in her mouth and again inside of her; she was worked up from his O.S., and their lovemaking went so well that he didn't even have to confess he was a virgin.

Kitsa had long ago stormed out of the inn. She spent the rest of the night masturbating in the treehouse, lubricating herself with tears from her two-colored eyes. It was the first time she'd been alone in the treehouse. They hadn't used it in a good while, and as she came, Kitsa had a spidery feeling along the length of her body.

She went home in the morning, entirely composed, to change and to make perfunctory amends with her mother. She drove to the beach at ten o'clock with Pia and Helen for the funeral. Though she hadn't slept, she knew she looked good in her lacy black dress. Her friends hadn't yet arrived at the cemetery.

There was a scream from the beach, loud at first, then trailing off. Moments later, Casey appeared. He walked briskly to where Kitsa stood with Pia and Helen Haggerty.

"There's been an accident, Mrs. Haggerty. I tried to warn them, but—"

"The twins," Pia said.

"I drove Frog and Gato over to see the beach on the way here, and I'm afraid that before I could warn them, they—"

"Dead?" Pia asked.

Mrs. Haggerty fainted. All of Tourisme surrounded her then—almost sixty people, for there were still other people in Tourisme, however little they mattered to Casey, Katey, and Kitsa. They soothed her, recalled other unfortunate deaths, provided handkerchiefs and smelling salts. Casey and Kitsa slipped to the periphery of the group where they could talk freely, near the O'Briens' identical coffins.

"Where's Katey?" Kitsa asked.

"She went with them."

"They're off?"

"They took a carriage. They'll be gone well before we get done with this. They're going to drive to Chamonix and leave the carriage for us to pick up. Kitsa, I'm sorry about last night. I was jealous. Let's get married. Katey promised to write. Kitsa, please don't cry. Kitsa!"

Kitsa ran fast. Since everyone wore black, she was only recognizable by her white-blonde hair as she fought her way through the crowd of mourners toward the village. Casey would have run after her, but Pia caught him and begged him to help with Mrs. Haggerty.

He didn't get back to the inn for an hour. He smelled fierce from an afternoon of lifting coffins and fainted women.

He found Frog sitting in the lobby of the inn with Uncle Nose. Nose was eating the marrow from a leg of lamb with great gusto; he was nude except for a tattered loincloth.

"What are you doing here?" Casey asked Frog.

"The bastards left without me."

"Where's Kitsa?"

"She went after them. I told her they didn't want her but she went anyway. Said she was going to make a million as a Parisian whore. What a tacky little twat. Who *is* this man? He's cutting up paper dolls."

"Down for the festivities," Uncle Nose told Casey.

"I fixed him something to eat," Frog said. "Who *runs* this place, anyhow? Is this supposed to be a hotel?"

"Aren't you going after your brother?"

"I'll tell you. Gato isn't dependable. That's where the name comes from, in case you haven't figured. Wave some yarn in his face and he's off. I'm not crazy about your sister, and I can't stand that Kitsa character."

"But what if your mother sees you? You're supposed to be dead."

"She won't. Or you can make a big show of rescuing me from the Alps. Listen, I enjoyed last night."

"Me too."

"Care for a repeat?"

"I've got to watch the hotel."

"All the guests are at the funeral. Get that lunatic to man the desk for you. Lunatic, will you man the desk?"

"He doesn't know what you're talking about."

"Sure he does."

"Look, Frog, the guy's completely shell-shocked. He can't man anything."

"Sure he does," Nose said proudly. "Shell-shocked."

"You see?" Frog said. "He can handle an idiot's job."

Uncle Nose placed one hand on Frog's breast and offered

her a decimated leg of lamb with the other hand. She brushed him away. Casey was impressed with her equanimity.

"Casey," Frog said, "I want to make you shiny as a choir-boy praising the Lord."

Which she did, for several hours. Despite all her gruffness, Frog was an angel in bed. Perhaps Casey's vision was blurry from his second and third bouts of lovemaking, but she seemed almost pretty to him.

When they came downstairs around five in the evening to make dinner, they found Uncle Nose at the reception desk in a clean pair of the late Mr. O'Brien's overalls, looking almost official, if a little glazed.

"I'm going to stay," Frog announced to them both. "I just turned eighteen but I've lived quite enough. My mother'll go home, I'll drag myself up from the Alps and we can have a great time, all by ourselves in this ghost town."

She made her pronouncement with such certainty that Casey wasn't sure he could talk her out of it, although he wasn't sure he wanted to.


Mrs. Haggerty, however, had no intention of going home.

She told Pia that with Lucinda and Percival dead, no one needed her in Detroit. Her eldest daughter, she confessed—Pia was the first to know—had been put up for adoption.

"Why!" Pia said.

"I just didn't want children. I didn't want the twins either, but I didn't think I could get away with the same trick twice."

"But what did your husband think?"

"I told him the baby was stillborn. Then I gave it up for adoption."

"How dreadful," Pia said.

"I know," Mrs. Haggerty said. "Dreadful."

Helen Haggerty telephoned her lawyer and told him to sell everything she owned and send her the money, so she could invest it in the beautification of Tourisme. Her money was in a Swiss bank long before the stock market crashed.

"Are they lovers?" Frog asked Casey.

Casey had just brought the news of Mrs. Haggerty's decision to stay. He'd been at Pia's, consoling the president about Kitsa's disappearance with, it had just been discovered, several valuable pieces from the museum. Actually, Pia didn't need much consoling. She'd never much cared for Kitsa anyway, and told Mrs. Haggerty so.

"What do you mean?" Casey asked Frog.

"Lesbians. They do exist, you know."

"Not Pia and your mother," Casey said, although the idea delighted him.

Frog was "rescued" from the Alps a week later by Uncle Nose, who was now a regular visitor at the inn—Frog and Casey took care of him as they would have tended a pet. Frog and Helen were tearfully reunited (the tears were mostly Helen's, and mostly show), and Frog and Casey were married.

It wasn't a bad marriage. In some ways, it was even a good one. They got along fine in bed, and had enough beds for variety. (With World War I and then the Depression, the tourist trade dwindled away almost entirely; Helen's money basically kept the town alive.) Frog entertained Casey by reading from American magazines and realistic French novels. Casey took Frog for outings in the Alps; after Detroit, she found the landscape mouthwatering. Only when Kitsa's letters from Paris arrived did Casey miss his golden girl, remember her pout of a mouth, her walnut-flavored labia. But as the letters became more cursory and less frequent, Casey settled into a life much like his father's—his adopted father's. *Peace of Mind* was Tourisme's motto, in gold leaf on its postage stamps, and Casey had some love of peace in his blood. He was content with his life even after Frog left him, even after a German bomber blew away all of the remaining buildings in 1944 and left Tourisme a true ghost town. Casey's survival—like his birth, like his marriage—

was a fluke. He must have loved Tourisme, though, for he stayed even after the bombing, living as Uncle Nose had lived, not talking to anyone but himself and an occasional salesgirl in Chamonix until 1964, when a sixty-three-year-old woman had trouble with her car, and he got to tell his story.

# 8

had to work overtime on Monday. I had earphones on and I was in the mixing booth, so I couldn't hear anything but music—if you can call the theme song for cream soda music. Indeed, cream soda was music to *my* ears, so sick was I of Panthers and of cars in general. The music stopped. My boss was gesturing to me impatiently with his ringed forefinger. Leland was an enterprising young man who'd hitchhiked light-years from Harlem. He was nothing if not hip. If I were to excuse myself to copulate in the supplies closet with a delivery boy, Leland would nod wryly; but a phone call made him angry. Never mind that I'd skipped lunch; never mind that all the secretaries in New York spend eight hours a day on the phone, examining their split ends. Leland returned to the mixing booth to smoke. The call was from my Aunt Mara in Boston. "I just called to chat," she said.

"To chat? Mara, I haven't spoken to you in months."

"This is one thing I thought we might chat about."

"How are you?"

"Better than your father, who, you may recall, has recently recovered from a mild stroke."

Leland, his arms folded, was narrowing his eyes at me through the mixing booth, blowing menacing smoke rings.

"If this is going to be a guilt session, Mara, don't you think we should talk after the rates go down?"

"No guilt. Your father is going to sell the house. I just thought you should know. I've been trying to convince him either to move to Boston, or to get into a nursing home."

"A nursing home? You're mad."

"I don't see you offering to take care of him."

"He's doing fine."

"Absolutely. He's ready to disco-dance."

"All right, Mara. I'll call him. I'll worry. Okay?"

Leland knocked on the glass of the mixing booth.

"You know we love you," Mara said. "In fact, *we* worry about *you*. Are you dating? Do you have any friends? You want to wind up all alone like your father and your poor Aunt Mara?"

Leland approached to suggest that I haul my ass back to my job.

"I heard that," Mara said. "Go. We'll talk later."

"Love you," I said.

I apologized to Leland. It was three more takes and almost seven o'clock before we got the cream soda right, and I had an awful headache. I closed my eyes and rubbed my temples. When I looked up, I saw Mildred fighting off Leland and a large armed security guard, her nose pressed up against the glass of the mixing booth.

"It's okay," I mouthed.

"You *know* her?" Leland asked, as I came out of the booth.

"Yes, I do."

"You're so popular," Leland smirked.

"See you in the morning."

I took Mildred's arm as we got off the elevator and began to head toward the subway, but she told me we were eating dinner nearby, and commanded me to follow her.

"What are you doing," I asked, "testing me?"

"You were late. I waited in the park as planned."

"I know. If I hadn't been so busy, I was going to spend the last hour hunting down those credit-card holders. Mildred, I'm terribly bored with my job."

"Boredom is the opiate of the masses."

"Yes indeedy. One yawn and before you know it, you're onto the hard stuff. We're eating here? This is awfully fancy."

"My treat."

The headwaiter tried to share a knowing grin with me. From my distressed look—my headache, really—he thought I was embarrassed to be out in public with such a poorly dressed grandmother or aunt. I ignored him. I think Mildred was nervous because I hadn't been able to spend much time with her over the weekend—the Panther soundtrack had gone on and on and I needed the overtime. Before we went in, Mildred had bade me to take three hundred dollars from her purse. The headwaiter put us in a back room, of course, so Mildred wouldn't distress the other customers. At the only other occupied table in the room, two impeccably dressed Chinese women were trying to keep five boisterous children in check. One child kept knocking its chair over backwards to fire an imaginary machine gun at Mildred and me. The mothers were discussing wallpaper in careful English. I had beef Wellington; Mildred, after a long argument with the headwaiter, had bacon and scrambled eggs. Toward the end of our meal, one of the Chinese women got up to go to the bathroom. As she stood, she ran her hand lightly over her ass as women do to smooth their skirts, or to assure themselves that their bodies are still there—the privacy of the gesture almost undid me. Mildred saw it too. We'd hardly spoken.

"Let's get out of here," she said.

The bill was outrageous. I tipped ten dollars of Mildred's money. We strolled out and realized we were close to the Waldorf, so we walked there and wandered around in the lobby a bit, until we found ourselves in the empty ballroom.

"A piano!" I squealed.

"Do you play?"

I closed the ballroom's heavy door and walked to the piano slowly, stretching my arms like a tennis player in between sets, looking back at her over my shoulder.

"What'll it be, M'lady?"

She sat on the dusty parquet floor.

"Chopin," she said. "Nothing else will do."

When I touched the keys of the grand old Steinway, I felt as if I'd just recovered from a long amnesia. The keys seemed far away as the handwriting and names in an old diary. But the Chopin: the Ballade was in my blood. I was in my element.

"I didn't know you could play," Mildred said.

"There's lots you don't know about me. I was a prodigy, you know."

"What happened?"

"I grew up. Here it comes. This is my favorite part. I hope my fingers will accommodate me here."

"Lovely," Mildred murmured.

"We're floating off to sea."

"Yes. Yes. I hope we never land."

And I thought, but had the good sense not to say, Mildred, let's never come back.

# 9

My father took me to Paris for three days in 1967. I was old enough to have heard of Twiggy and the Six-Day War. Although it was a business trip for him, he thought it essential that I see Montmartre, Napoleon's Tomb, and the Louvre. The Louvre gave me a headache. What excited me most about Paris was a pen I bought in a souvenir shop. The pen wrote in three different colors and depicted a tree-lined view of the Seine; as you wrote, a barge flipped back and forth on four inches of river. I left the pen in a restaurant on our last night in Paris, and moped the whole flight back to the States. The pen loomed so large in my view of Paris that I didn't pay any attention to the Eiffel Tower.

I suppose I got stalled out in some infantile stage of grief, but knowing that doesn't change anything, just as saying I know nothing about Paris—especially Paris in the 1920s—doesn't change the fact that the city was there for Katey, Kitsa, and Gato. The city and decade had to make a difference to them somehow, no matter how sheltered they were—and they *were* sheltered, living as they did in the Louvre.

They could never have lived in the Louvre if they hadn't met Marcel; they would never have met Marcel if Kitsa hadn't become a whore; and Kitsa would never have become a whore if Gato and Katey had paid more attention to her.

The first thing Katey and Gato did when they got to Paris was to lose Kitsa in a crowd.

There appeared to be a political gathering of some sort. Kitsa wasn't sure what side she was on, but she was determined not to care. She was in Paris! People everywhere were speaking French. The rich people wore shiny fabrics and feathered hats; the poor people had a spirited look. Kitsa wanted to get to know everyone's soul over *escargots* on the top floors of buildings made of plush white stone.

A man with a too-long mustache asked Kitsa in French what she charged.

Kitsa was trying to remember the French for *whore*, so she could tell the man she wasn't one, when she heard her name and spotted Gato gesturing to her with Katey's hat.

"Charge him twenty francs," Gato called. "Katey and I are going to get married. Meet us at 58, rue Rembrandt in a couple of hours."

The mustachioed man, Rodolphe, was a poet who told Kitsa about *Surréalisme* in the heat of a tiny restaurant. Kitsa's broth had globules of chicken gristle in it and the walls were an unfriendly yellow, except where the paint had flaked away to reveal hospital green wallpaper. There was a potted geranium on the ledge of each shuttered window. Most of the geraniums were sick or dead. Men with cigars spoke too loudly. They made maps in the air with their smoke. Kitsa watched the corner of the poet's mouth as he spoke and she thought about Gato.

Rodolphe took her to a room with angry cats and a mattress that was too soft. His kiss had a fuzzy texture, as if he had hair growing inside his mouth. His mustache was so long that it tickled her chin. This was the first time Kitsa had kissed anyone but Casey or Katey, and she wasn't sure if she liked it. Nevertheless, she got involved enough in the kiss to imagine the dark of Rodolphe's mouth as a relief map of Europe. Her tongue was a finger that pointed to London and Rome, to Tourisme over his upper left molar where she perhaps should have stayed—but Rodolphe was taking off his pants, and Kitsa had to remind him that she was not, was decidedly not a whore.

Rodolphe thought her shyness was part of her repertoire. High-class whore-virgins were popular at the time, modeling themselves after Garbo and other proud actresses. Rodolphe was patient. They might not make love that night, or even the next, Rodolphe thought; but when they did, it would be sublime. He was paying on the installment plan.

Kitsa didn't get to 58, rue Rembrandt until the following morning. Katey and Gato were cross-legged on the bed, in a small room on the fourth floor, eating croissants off each other's laps.

"Look who's here," Katey said.

"About time," Gato said. "How much did you get?"

"Dinner."

"You've got to pay your way. We used the last of the money on breakfast; we'll have to sell the things we took from our mothers."

"We're married," Katey added.

"And I'm going to get a job," Gato said, "as a maître d' at a place with roses on every table and lace napkins. I'll lie about my citizenship."

"You're not married," Kitsa said.

"Of course we are," Katey said. "Get used to it."

Gato saw Kitsa's astonished look, grinned, said "Love and war, love and war," and tossed her the last croissant as someone knocked on the door.

Gato's gruffness was show. He was a pussycat. The moment Kitsa saw that, she lost interest in him, and knew she'd be a whore. Her favorite customers would have a gloomy, impatient look, as if they were waiting for something that would never come—the expression of refugees in foreign countries, of people in love with ideas they haven't arrived at yet. Gato had seemed that way when he first arrived in Tourisme, but Katey had already domesticated him. Now he had the contented gleam of a housewife reflected in a polished plate.

At the door was a skinny young man in a bright beret. He was pale; his teeth were almost the same green as the wallpaper in the restaurant. "Rodolphe sent me," he said.

"You see?" Gato told Kitsa. "Business is already booming."

But the pale man looked at Katey. "Please, Mademoiselle."

"Madame," Katey corrected.

"Madame, hold your hair up with your arm. Look over your shoulder at the other girl."

"I'm Kitsa," Kitsa said.

"Smile. There! Ah, there's my odalisque."

Katey did odalisque poses in her blue nightgown.

"Take off the robe," the man said, "and drape it over you."

"Look here," Gato said. "That's my wife."

"Not to misunderstand. I am Étienne, I am a painter. I want her to pose."

Gato said he didn't think so, but Katey brightened.

"Why not? It'll give me something to do while you're at work, if you ever get work; in the meantime, it'll keep us in croissants."

"No," Gato said.

"It's all right," Kitsa said. "She isn't used to so much attention. Remember, she was the odd-woman-out in Tourisme."

"Keep out of this, will you?" Gato said.

"I can't pay much," Étienne said.

Kitsa tugged on Étienne's shirttail. "They're having a lover's spat," she said. "Take me to lunch."

First he circled Katey several times, touching her right armpit, her left earlobe, putting his thumbs under her eyes, as if to erase the dark circles there, checking the perimeter of her waist, while Gato looked on uneasily, shifting on one foot, holding in his hand the remains of a croissant.

"Men," Kitsa sneered.

But she got her lunch, and the next day she'd get a bath, in the marble tub of a Latvian count. The water came in an arc from the miniature penis of a bronze curly-haired boy, a replica of the statue in Brussels.

He was an exiled count. His money was being systematically pissed away on women like Kitsa. Most of her clients were poor or near-to-poor; she was their only luxury. All of her clients were artists or philosophers. Kitsa wondered who flew the planes, who built the fountains, with all of the men out enthusing about nature, writing or painting or singing songs. She wondered how so many men in Paris heard of her and why they paid, with so many love-starved widows about. She especially wondered why they paid when she refused to make love. She'd only let them run their fingers through her hair, kiss them if the mood moved her, let them praise her beauty, and give them a sense of community. Who would break her will? They talked about her to each other, and about each other to her, and she listened.

After four months, Kitsa still wasn't quite sure if the Great War was over or not, but she could discuss phenomenology in its relationship to Dada. She knew about *Ulysses* and Cubism. When she saw a tanned man on a ladder, painting a wall whiter, his back turned to the street where cars fell down the hill slow as leaves, her mind would hold the scene in high relief. She understood. She knew the man on the ladder without ever talking to him, knew his ambitions, knew how his ambitions fell away from him—she would always know him, no matter what happened to the stock market. She watched the cars as if they weren't real, as if she had to close her eyes and flesh them out on the back of her eyelids.

She liked it in the streets better than in the room on the rue Rembrandt. There wasn't enough space for her there. She had to sleep on the floor, and before dinner she was often shooed away so Katey and Gato could have a pre-meal bout of love as fresh trout swam in a basin at the foot of the bed. They wouldn't let her watch. Kitsa had a change of clothes in twenty different places, and was fairly used to her rootlessness. But when Marcel—one of her customers, a sculptor and night guard at the Louvre—proposed that they live in the museum, Kitsa liked the idea, as did Katey and Gato. Katey said she could use the extra space; Gato said he could use the adventure.

They moved into the basement of the Louvre on New Year's Eve, 1920. Kitsa had just turned twenty. All of the guards were drunk or off at parties. They spent Marcel's salary for that week on a fine bottle of champagne, which they drank to celebrate; they kept the empty bottle for the remainder of their stay at the Louvre, on the stump of an armless statue, to commemorate the fateful day.

The furniture only needed to be polished, dusted, and rearranged into proper groupings. While the rooms were badly lit, they could burn as many oil lamps as they wanted at night without anyone noticing, and they weren't there much during the day.

They were excited, of course. They'd tasted enough poverty to savor their spacious new home. The Louvre, at that time, was so much like Tourisme that it *felt* like home. They were not, after all, the only squatters in the museum—it was huge, a town all on its own, and ever-expanding. Construction workers gabbed over lunch or entertained their mistresses in kings' beds; *grandes dames* rented rooms for parties and dinners; blind men and poets begged outside; and the basement itself was labyrinthian, so even when someone went downstairs, they were unlikely to stumble into the apartment.

Marcel drilled a hole in a corner on the first floor of the museum, through which he lowered rolled-up notes on a string and tapped overhead if there was any danger, but there was rarely danger. Once or twice they had to sit in the dark for a minute, watching the tip of Gato's cigarette, until Marcel tapped again. But most of the time the Louvre was home, and they were a family (with Marcel something of a boarder or a trusted servant). Katey snapped at Gato to get a job and at Kitsa to stop staying out so late; Kitsa told Katey to stop telling her what to do; and Marcel told all of them to shut up and do some work.

Within half a year, Marcel, a wiring genius, had provided them with electrical outlets. His biggest accomplishment was the bathroom. Let other Parisians shit in Turkish holes and eat by candlelight; he was going to have proper facilities. The project was as risky as the beach at Tourisme, but Marcel planned to do justice to a salon where their ashtray was a Wingless Victory, dating about 200 B.C.; where their hatrack was a screen depicting Diana the Huntress, behind which Kitsa sometimes entertained her guests on a Louis XIV four-poster; where the headboard was an undersized first draft of Courbet's *The Painter's Studio*; where the men's smoking jackets had belonged to Napoleon and the women's robes to Marie Antoinette. When the bathroom was finished, they lived in high style for four years.

Later in their lives, they might have bragged about their ingenuity. But at the time, the Louvre was home. Their pride was the pride of homeowners, not thieves, and the home might have been anywhere—a split-level in Scarsdale, a treehouse in Tourisme. They complained about the heat in summer and the cold in winter (a log-burning fireplace was Marcel's next project); they complained about bugs and rats all year round.

Kitsa was still a virgin. Katey and Gato had decided to have children and were working on that vigorously, happy as newlyweds.

Sometimes, to pass the time, Katey and Kitsa would dress up to visit the Louvre. They particularly liked the hallway where Étienne's portrait of Katey hung. The Louvre wouldn't buy it, so they'd bought it themselves. Katey was nude in the portrait, with a scarlet cloth draped over part of her pelvis; she wore a bird-of-paradise in her hair, and held a half-opened book. From her mournful expression, you'd think her lover had left her. Katey would lean against the wall beside the painting, miming her own expression, waiting for someone to remark on the resemblance, but no one ever did. That hallway was not often visited, but Katey wanted the painting to have some visibility, despite the fact that Étienne's portrait was too dark and not piquant enough; it was not Old Master and not Impressionist, and as such, already dated. Kitsa and Katey didn't mind. They loved the painting as unselfconsciously as mothers love their children's baby pictures. Surprisingly, living in the Louvre did not make them art connoisseurs. They'd inherited Pia's spotty taste. They liked Corot and Rembrandt well enough, but they were equally fond of sixteenth-century portrait painting—especially the funny portraits, like *The Beautiful Gabrielle and the Maréchale de Bolagny*, circa 1596, which had for a while hung in the room where the secret passage to their apartment was. The portrait depicts Henry IV's fiancée in the bath with her sister. Their gazes are prim, their poses are pompous—and one woman is reaching out formally to tweak the other's nipple. Katey and Kitsa would often stand before the picture and reminisce about Tourisme, about the old days before Gato when they still touched; but Katey would get defensive and remind Kitsa that in Paris she could certainly find a lover. They'd sometimes mime the gestures of the bathing women, stiff as marionettes, for the amusement of guards and tourists; and it was this innocent play, one lazy afternoon in the year 1925, that attracted the attention of Klaus Frankovich.

He waited until they stopped the routine. Kitsa sighed and walked off to examine another painting. The middle-aged man approached Katey, bowed quickly, and asked, "Who's your friend?"

"That's Kitsa, and you can't afford her."

"A Polish name," the man observed in English, as Kitsa turned around.

"She's half Irish," Katey said. The man grinned.

By the time Kitsa reached them, the man was gone.

"Who was that?" Kitsa asked. "He was cute."

"Cute?" Katey scoffed. "He was old enough to be your father."

"He looked a bit like Casey, don't you think?"

"No, I don't; Kitsa, he's awfully skittish, and he's in the next room, still staring at you."

"Do you mind if I leave you here?"

"Of course not, but be careful."

Kitsa passed the guard and walked toward the stranger who was pretending to be absorbed with Théodore Chassériau's *The Two Sisters*.

"Are they twins?" Kitsa asked, in her best French; but he answered in English.

"I don't know."

"You look familiar," Kitsa said.

The man leaned toward her. He smelled like Dutch tobacco. "I want to make love," he said. "Please. Now."

"Not so fast. Do you have a place?"

"Your place."

Kitsa shifted until she could see Katey swinging her purse in the other room, cocking her head at the fat Ingres nudes.

"Let's go," Kitsa told the man.

"Your friend?"

"She'll be fine."

By then Kitsa knew the museum. She knew where the guards were sparse. There were whole rooms that were closed off, where no one ever went, beyond rooms where the guards took three-hour lunches or snuck off to play cards. Kitsa took the middle-aged man's hand (the fingers were callused) and walked with him for ten minutes, going up one flight of stairs and down another yards later, past one sleeping guard and another half-asleep, until they were stepping over the velvet cord that blocked off a passageway leading to an immense room quiet as a monastery and empty of furniture except for a Persian rug too natty to hang for display. On the wall was a life-sized tapestry of St. Sebastian being deposed from the cross. The positions of the men deposing him were extremely awkward. Their backs faced the viewer, but their heads were turned almost all the way around on their necks, so they were gaping at the viewer as if they'd been caught at something. The perspective was all wrong.

"My mother would love this tapestry," Kitsa said.

"Not here."

"Choosy, aren't you? There's a bed downstairs, but we can't get to it now. It's in the other building, which is heavily guarded."

"Take me to the bed, please."

"I can't."

"Then tell me how to meet you there later."

"You go to the green Corot room in the East wing and—no, it's too complicated. You'd have to go there with me. We live there, you see, but in the day we have to be very careful—"

"You live in the museum?"

"Yes, and we—"

The man took Kitsa by her waist. His kiss was harsh and tasted somewhat like chutney. Kitsa broke away to protest that she didn't know his name.

"Klaus," he said. "Frankovich."

"Are you German?"

"Half Polish."

Klaus didn't want to chat. He had lowered her to the floor before she could say Klaus and was inside her before she could try to say Frankovich, and he came before she could explain that the screams he was muffling indicated pain, not pleasure.

"Next time," he smiled, "I promise more, and slower."

He put her hand in his mouth and bit it, not quite tenderly. "You were a virgin," he said, as he began to dress.

"Yes."

"I can find my way back."

He waved at her, smiled, and backed out of the room.

Kitsa didn't dress right away. She leaned on her elbows and watched a drop of blood and fluid languish down her thigh onto the carpet, where it blended with a large scarlet diamond.

She tried to figure out if she felt different as a non-virgin, but it was impossible—like trying to figure out where a year has gone on your birthday. She tried to decide whether Klaus Frankovich was mean or just shy. She had a feeling that she wouldn't see Klaus Frankovich again. She probably had this feeling because she wanted to see him again and was protecting herself against disappointment. In either case, she was wrong. Paris was a small town then—much smaller than New York, where, that evening, Mildred Howell had been granted an audience with J. Pierpont Morgan to sell him a piece Klaus Frankovich had recently smuggled out of the Uffizi.

# 10

The next week, art began to disappear from the Louvre.

Kitsa, Katey, Gato, and Marcel didn't notice at first. Paintings and statues were everywhere in the basement apartment—stacked against walls, piled under tables; lamps sat on end tables made of crates full of Greek statues that had never been unpacked. When Katey noticed, she just assumed that someone had moved the things, and scolded her friends and husband to be more careful. But soon they missed a Ming vase they'd been using as an umbrella stand. The umbrellas were on the floor. No one among the four of them had moved the vase.

Soon afterward, their Wingless Victory was gone.

What could they do? They could hardly go to the police. The only way to catch the thief would be to have someone on guard all the time. That would be almost impossible during the day, however; they were far more likely to get caught themselves.

Kitsa said she'd take the day shift, if they helped her set up a net over the bed, so if she caught the thief, she could lure him into bed and hold him there until the rest of them got back.

Kitsa wasn't exactly sure why she was expecting Klaus, but

the next day, her first on guard, she was waiting for him. He showed up around noon. He was sloppily dressed and carried a knapsack; he began shuffling through a pile of small jewelry and china they'd set up as bait.

"Hello, Klaus," Kitsa said, from the floor in the corner.

He pointed a gun and a flashlight at her.

"You," he said. "I was looking for you."

"Lame. This isn't nice, Klaus. Do you expect to walk out of here with that stuff in the knapsack? Let me see your gun."

"No."

"Don't worry. I just want to hold one. I never have."

Klaus gave her the gun reluctantly. She had planned this routine, and performed it well: she pulled up her skirt, put the gun slowly back through her underpants, and began to masturbate with the barrel, her bare toe pointed like the Persian women's in Maginski's books of porn.

Klaus put down his knapsack.

She slipped the gun under a chair cushion as they moved to the bed. But she didn't put down the net, not then. She *wanted* to make love. She thought it might be the last time she ever did, and she was right.

By five in the evening, Kitsa was quite embalmed.

She'd left a bottle of cognac on the nightstand as part of the plot. They drank cognac like mineral water. The drunker she got, the more Kitsa told herself that sex would have been divine with anyone. It didn't have to be Klaus. But Klaus liked her too, apparently, or he was exceedingly drunk as well, for he began to tell her details from his life of crime that, he claimed, he'd never told anyone, not even his girl in America.

"Do you like her better than me?"

"Do you want to hear my story or not?"

"I'm a great listener."

"My best years were at the turn of the century."

"Well, I'm *usually* a great listener. It would help if you moved your hand from between my legs."

"You're sweet. I was a schemer! My friend Jack found this small town in the French Alps called Tourisme, believe it or not. Have you heard of it?"

Kitsa stopped herself from saying yes.

"You're too young to have read about the trouble there. Jack and I had this plan: We were going to take over the government of the place and never have to work again. No one had heard of the town; no one would ever have known. There was money there. I was too young for serious crime, though. First thing I see in Tourisme is a sunbather with red in her hair. Sixteen I think she was, and laying her would be like climbing to the bell tower of an old church to ring out high noon. I point her out to Jack; Jack does the legwork and finds out she's the president's daughter; her name was Pia. Since I was sexier than Jack, and since Jack was the more cold-blooded, the plan was that he'd bump off the president and I'd marry the president's daughter. This was 1899. As usual, Jack went overboard. He used an ax on the president. The murder got bad press and I'd have been balling the jack to come on to Pia right away, so we waited; but before I could get to her, she married her father's lawyer."

"Is this true?" Kitsa asked weakly.

"Sure. The husband was a pompous little gigolo with a pedigree from Warsaw. We discovered he'd gotten her pregnant. There was no point in trying to seduce a pregnant woman, so we were forced to wait even longer before we could act, but it was worth the wait. Pia grabbed me so hard on the beach—they had this fake beach there, sand but no water, craziest thing I ever saw—that you'd think I was saving her life, which it turns out I was. I took a quick shine to the girl. Death and kinky sex had made her a bit bilious, but that somehow only made her real innocence stand out. She never asked for much. I wasn't sure if I wanted Jack to do in the Pole. I could have stayed for years and lived off her with plenty left over for Jack, until the husband died more natural-like. Jack didn't see it that way. We fought about it, and to get even with me Jack axed the husband and skipped town without even telling me. Luckily, I found out before I saw Pia. I couldn't have stayed. Pia would have suspected me; no way to keep a low profile."

"Then you personally didn't commit the ax murders?"

"I'm no murderer. Mainly I do forgery, middleman work in art theft. You know the bronze horse the Met made such a stink about finding? That was my deal. They think it's from 800 B.C. It's fourteenth century. But it's a nice horse and they'll never know the difference. I love my job. I get to travel. One picture covers the same hole in the wall as the next picture. This love of originals is a lot of balloon juice if you ask me. I never hurt anyone, even with the Tourisme bit, although I suppose the girls missed me some."

"Girls?"

"I didn't mention Helen? She was an American tourist, freckled, sweet if we were banging but if we weren't, whiny as a one-legged beggar. She kept me busy while I was waiting for Pia to drop the Pole's kid. Jack wanted her and I was perfectly willing to hand her over, but she wouldn't cooperate. I got both of them pregnant."

"How do you know, if you left?"

"While I was in Tourisme I used Jim O'Brien as an alias, but it is my mother's maiden name, O'Brien. I still had cousins in Dublin who were O'Briens, and who happened to be friends of the O'Briens that Pia dumped her children on. They were twins Pia had. The O'Briens sent the story back to Dublin—it was a big secret so of course it got around. Fraternal twins, a boy and a girl. Funny thing, the Haggerty girl had twins too."

"Are you sure?"

Klaus laughed. "She might have been baiting me, I suppose. She looked for me, Helen did. She took an ad in every paper in Europe. She's probably still looking for me. JIM OF

TOURISME COME GET ME AND YOUR TWINS HH. I saw the ad quite by coincidence in Munich."

"Lot of coincidence here."

"True. I shouldn't have known Jack in the first place. I've never liked Germans."

"Where is he now?"

"Back in Munich. Jack wasn't his real name, his real name was Heinrich something. He's working on getting some Vermeers for the Krauts last time I heard, but as I said, we don't keep in touch."

"Did you ever think of telling the police about the ax murders?"

"With my record, you don't call the police for anything. You know that. You didn't call the police about me, did you?"

Kitsa got up from the bed casually to stretch and pulled the string to the net. Before Klaus could protest, she'd gotten the gun from her chair cushion.

"Careful!" he said. "That's loaded."

Kitsa cocked the pistol. "You're not shy," she said.

"Come now, honey, don't be jealous. I'm with you now, aren't I? I'm holding up a lot of work to spend this time with you."

"It's not that. Where do you think I'm from?"

"Ireland and Poland. Your friend told me. It's a combination close to my heart. I suppose you're attracted to your own. Now take off this net."

"I'm Irish and Polish all right, but I'm from Tourisme. And guess who my mother is."

Klaus made a lunge for the gun, but he was netted fairly well. Kitsa stepped back. She was naked, and felt funny being naked, a gun in her hand.

"Pia Maginski," she said. "Small world. Edward Maginski was my father. Casey O'Brien, your son, was my lover for eighteen years. You know that girl you saw me with in the museum? That was Katey O'Brien, your daughter. And guess who Katey is married to."

Klaus tried for the gun again. Kitsa got the handcuffs Gato had given her and, after a struggle, put them on Klaus.

"Gato Haggerty," he said. "Helen Haggerty's son."

"I don't believe you."

"You don't? Casey O'Brien, your son, is married to Frog Haggerty, your daughter."

"I don't believe that."

"It doesn't matter whether you do or not. You're going to stay put until we decide what to do with you."

"I was just kidding about Tourisme," Klaus said. "Just to show off. I made the whole thing up."

"We'll get you for the Louvre thefts first. Then we'll backtrack to Tourisme. You can tell your story to Gato and Katey when they get here, which I hope will be very soon indeed."

"You wouldn't let anyone hurt me."

"Don't be so sure."

"You're in love with me."

"How can I be in love with my father?"

"I'm not *your* father," he reminded her. "You're pure Parnell and Maginski. We're not related at all. Besides, I didn't kill anyone. I only started forging because no one would buy my work. If people liked to buy imitations of other people's work, it was fine with me, but I still think my work is better than some of the junk that sells."

"Always a bridesmaid, never a bride," Kitsa soothed.


The morning after Frog O'Brien's miscarriage, there was a telegram.

Casey picked it up at the post office but didn't open it. He was too upset about the loss of his child. He'd worked hard to get Frog pregnant; he wanted the child badly, perhaps more than Frog. Frog was on her feet within several days, and she discovered the telegram slipped under the blotter at the reception desk of the inn.

FROG CASEY, it said. URGENT COME TO THE LOUVRE AT ONCE ASK FOR MARCEL HE'LL TAKE YOU TO US FOUND AX MURDERER AND MORE LOVE.

Casey said he didn't care about the ax murderer.

"Let's take a trip, Case. Maybe it'll help you relax. We haven't seen them in so long."

But Casey wouldn't go, so Frog went to Paris alone.

She didn't have to find Marcel. Kitsa was pacing in front of the reception desk at the Louvre. Frog embraced her warmly.

"Where's Casey?" Kitsa asked her ex-nemesis.

"He couldn't come. Where are Katey and Gato?"

"Katey's gone."

"Gone? Where to?"

"She called Rory the moment she heard. She's on her way to Atlantic City. How she got a passport so fast I'll never know, although I can guess."

"Heard *what*? Where's Gato?"

"He's with Klaus and in terrible shape."

"Who's Klaus?"

"Your father."

Frog spent the night in the basement of the Louvre. She was only in Paris that day. She didn't see the Arc de Triomphe or the Mona Lisa. The next morning, in panic, she got on a ship to the States, leaving Kitsa with Gato (who was rendered almost catatonic by the loss of his wife) and the prisoner, whose fate still hadn't been decided.

Kitsa was the only one who didn't fall apart. Her two bouts of sexual intercourse had given her the strong serenity most often found in pregnant women. Nothing surprised her; she resented nothing, not even the stupidity of the plot in which she was presently implicated. The thought of her mother as a sexual creature didn't shock Kitsa; in fact, now that they'd shared a lover, she felt she understood her mother better. She hoped that Klaus had impregnated her, and she vowed not to raise her child as Pia had raised her. Kitsa's child would know how to live alone.

"You're a lousy sister," Gato told Frog, as Frog left.


"I can only stay with one of you," Kitsa announced. "Who wants me?"

Father and son looked at her numbly.

"I suppose you have a claim on me, Klaus, on account of deflowering me. But you've lived with me for almost five years, Gato. I came to Paris to be with you. Don't everyone speak at once."

Klaus said he'd be more enthusiastic if she took off the handcuffs.

It was the end of the summer, Kitsa said. She suggested a picnic.

"The end of my life," Gato added.

"I doubt it," Kitsa said, as she poked around for a pen. Casey never answered Kitsa's letter asking him to come to Paris, decide Klaus's fate, and take Kitsa back to Tourisme. Kitsa didn't expect him to answer it. She mailed the letter on her way to the picnic. Gato and Klaus, handcuffed to each other, watched the sky as she ran across the street to the mailbox. It looked like rain, as it had on the day Kitsa arrived in Paris; they'd passed the corner where, once more, a political gathering was under way, filling the street with argument, familiar as rain on cobblestone. Kitsa wore a bright green dress that a client had given her years ago; at any moment a man much like Rodolphe might mistake her for a whore. Her life would go on mass-producing its symmetries. But as the letter dropped, she got a final feeling. The letter, though not that long, sank like a two-hundred-pound tumor into the belly of the box. Kitsa thought she'd never see anything stranger than Klaus and Gato handcuffed to each other, docile and dumb, scanning the sky for rain. She knew people were staring at them as they walked (Kitsa alongside with parasol, straw basket, and bagged bottle of champagne).

Except for the handcuffs, the slight rain, and the fact that no one spoke but Kitsa, the picnic on the Seine was utterly conventional.

"Cheer up," Kitsa said. "The sun's still here. The day after Lear's storm, the sky was clear and mild, a perfect day for kites in the park. His was no tragedy or mightn't have been, if he'd stuck around for the ending. The past was bad, the future might be worse, but the present's best. Amen."

As she spoke, she imagined herself in a book, torn between two equally wonderful men, both of whose desire for her was pure and true. Her voice would be softer then. She might not know what to do but she'd seem lovely in her indecision. In her sympathetic state, everything she saw—the child in his tree in the park, the chicken strung up in the shop window—would speak to her.

"Done in by a woman," Klaus said. "Once more done in by a woman."

"A toast," Kitsa said. "To family. To us. To us in love in the rain by the Seine on a Saturday in August 1925."

She poured the champagne. Klaus spilled his on his shirt, quite intentionally.

"At least let me go to the water and wash myself off."

"Fat chance."

"Let him go," Gato said.

It was the first thing he'd said since Frog left.

"What do you mean?" Kitsa asked.

"I mean let him go. Get rid of him. Let him leave."

"Good idea," Klaus said.

"You'd leave your own children?" Kitsa asked.

"Yes."

"You'll return to your girl in America?"

"Perhaps."

"You don't care about us?"

"I didn't say that."

"Let him go," Gato repeated.

Kitsa unlocked the handcuffs. Klaus stretched. His face was sad, leathery. He shook hands with Gato. He put one hand lightly on Kitsa's wrist.

Kitsa took an apple from the picnic basket and bit into it as Klaus walked away. "We shouldn't have let him go," she said, and passed the apple to Gato, who kept it, chewing thoughtfully. It was a long apple or a long thought. They were still there by nightfall in the damp grass, and they still hadn't exchanged a word. When Kitsa broke the silence, her voice was moist, like something that had been alive for a long time alone, under a rock.

"Sometimes I try to remember what Casey looks like, and I can't. I can muster a general sense of him—how he liked his eggs, how I felt with him, how I sometimes knew what he was going to say before he said it. I remember a way he'd squeeze my legs after I came. Sometimes when I'm almost asleep I hear him call my name. I'm not expecting his voice at all, but there it is. Does that happen to you?"

Gato didn't answer right away. When he talked, he said only, "Frog's mouth."

"What about it?"

"The way it trembled when she was scared."

"That's it?"

"She pretended never to be scared but she almost always was. Once we almost got caught stealing Valentine's Day cards. When we saw the police coming we ran home and dumped the cards in the dumbwaiter. The police followed us to the door and when they saw where we lived they only snarled and went away. We were six. I remember Frog's face when we walked into the den, with Dad looking at us like he knew. Or whoever it was we thought was Dad. Dad could well have been watching from the window. Just something about the frightened look she had then."

"But you can't forget Frog's face. It's your face."

"Almost."

"That's a point. What will you remember about me?"

"Your eyes, I guess."

"Do you like the green one best, or the brown one?"

"No preference. I like the lashes."

"Thanks."

"It's dark."

Kitsa squinted. She could just make out the trees on the other bank of the Seine, black against black. Gato's thoughts were like that.

"Gato, did you like Klaus?"

"No."

"Not at all?"

"Not at all."

"I liked him. I felt sorry for him. He didn't know what he was doing. Do you like me?"

"Yes."

"Did you like me right from the beginning?"

"No."

"I grew on you. I'm glad, because we've known each other a fairly long time. Five years is fairly long, isn't it?"

"Fairly long."

"You'll miss Katey?"

"Very much."

"I'll take care of you."

"Thanks."

"What will you remember about Katey? No. What will you remember about Paris, if we leave?"

"Katey."

"Do you realize that we've never made love in the five years we've known each other? I wanted you so much, you know, in Tourisme. I've never even kissed you. We've never held hands!"

Gato felt for Kitsa's hand. His fingers were like his thoughts, like the trees across the bank. They weren't cold; they just weren't hers.

"We don't know each other," Kitsa said. "I don't think I've been alone with you for this long in my whole life. We might have just met. Is this true?"

"This is true."

"I don't mind," Kitsa said. "In a way, I even like it. I think it's nice. It's nice, isn't it, Gato?"

"It's nice," Gato said. "It's very nice. "

# 11

Too much fluorescent light was making me sterile. Too much shuffling back and forth on industrial carpeting was making me dim-witted. I hated the skyline, I hated the philodendron in its big bold pot, I hated the receptionist's cheerful voice. I was going to strangle my boss. Why couldn't I have lived in Paris between the wars? Why did I have to work and, if I had to work, why couldn't I do something I loved?

I didn't know whether to curse or bless Mildred, for reminding me of the more colorful possibilities. All I knew was that when I got home from work on Wednesday, I was happy to see her.

As a change from the park, she'd consented to meet me at home. I found her sitting on the hood of a truck parked in front of my building. She was drinking a Dr. Pepper through a straw. For a moment I jumped because I thought the truck was Argyle's, but it wasn't. Argyle hadn't called all week. Of course I hadn't been there much to answer the phone, but I'm sure he didn't know that. If I'd jumped into the Hudson, Argyle wouldn't have known. Even my father wouldn't have known. The only person who would have noticed was Mildred Howell.

"Hard day at the office?" she said gayly.

"Don't make fun. It's miserable."

"I know. Are you hungry?"

"Sort of. There's food upstairs. Your eyes look awfully green in this light."

"Contact lenses. They're tinted—my only touching vanity. I used to have nice eyes. Actually, they've been bothering me lately."

She almost bounded up the stairs.

"What are you in such a good mood about?" I asked.

"Nothing," she said brightly. "Just making sure I can still bound."

She couldn't. She was breathless.

I unlocked the door to my apartment, opened the door, and closed it again. "Damn them," I said.

"What's wrong?"

"This isn't my floor. I must be really tired. Do you know that one key fits all of these locks?"

"Look again," Mildred said.

"Do you know something I don't?"

"Many things."

I opened the door. There was Skinner on my orange chair. There were my curtains with their print of watermelons, my brick-and-board bookshelf with my Riverside Shakespeare and the small-print *Oxford English Dictionary* I'd gotten cheap when I joined the Book-of-the-Month Club. But there, taking up more than half of the available space in one of my three small rooms, was a Steinway baby grand.

"Surprise," Mildred said.

Freud appeared from the other room, jumped on the piano, and sat on the keyboard around middle C, flicking his tail.

"It's brand-new," Mildred said. "You're not exactly bubbling over with joy and gratitude."

"I don't know what to say. How'd you get it up here?"

"It wasn't easy. But it wasn't as hard as finding one in stock, as getting it delivered immediately, or as breaking into your apartment. Your security isn't bad."

I leaned over the piano and played the first bars of the right hand of a sonata by Scarlatti, one octave too high, just to the right of Freud's tail.

"It's a good piano," Mildred said proudly, deposing Skinner from the orange chair. "Rich tone. Play something for me."

"Thank you. Bartók? Beethoven?"

"How about *Rhapsody in Blue*?"

"I don't know that."

"Then play what you know."

The only things that came to me offhand were the commercial we'd been doing that day (for a blow-dryer that didn't give you cancer), the Chopin Ballade I'd played for her at the Waldorf-Astoria, and a Bach two-part invention I'd known as a child. I opted for the Bach. But I'd forgotten the fingering and missed a flat. "I haven't played for a while," I apologized.

"You'll need to practice. Do you have the makings of a BLT?"

"Yup."

"With toast and mayonnaise?"

"Thank you, Mildred. I've never gotten a present like this. 'I appreciate it' is not the phrase. I'm overwhelmed. Maybe I'll start playing again."

"You most certainly better."

"This piano might change my life."

"Let's hope so."

From the kitchen, where I was brewing coffee and making sandwiches, I could see she was still in the orange chair—the only chair (the other had been moved into my bedroom, to make space for the piano)—reading the paper with her feet up.

"Maybe this Scarsdale strangler will get you," she said, "and you'll have an excuse not to go to work."

"No thanks."

I felt awkward over dinner. Perhaps it was merely her being

there in my tidy apartment. I wasn't sure how she wanted to be entertained. More likely, though, I was trying to figure out what change in our relationship the piano was supposed to certify. A piano is not a casual gift, not a house-warming present; a piano means business, but I didn't know what to do to return her kindness. She wouldn't want a car even if I could afford one. The only thing I could think to do was to listen to her story better, to be more enthusiastic about her story.

"Where did Frog go?" I asked.

Mildred shrugged with her mouth full. "We lost track of her. We still don't know, and probably never will. We know she stayed with Katey and Rory for a while in Atlantic City, but then we lost track of her. Do you have any friends?"

"Sure I do."

"I mean nice ordinary women-folk you can go out with on a Thursday evening for a beer and a movie."

"A couple. We're all usually pretty busy, though. We get together occasionally to complain about men."

"You ought to have a couple of good friends. You'd feel much better, I think."

"You sound like my Aunt Mara."

"There are probably worse fates."

"Thanks for the piano."

"Maybe it'll help you patch up your self-image. You're likable enough, Jennifer. You're fairly sharp and you're not painful to look at, although it wouldn't kill you to smile a bit. If you'd stop trying to come on strong like a Russian woman, you might find that people were kinder to you."

"Do you know I'm Russian, or are you just guessing?"

"What was it, Spellovsky?"

"Something like that. How did you know?"

"When you've lived in New York as long as I have, you know from a Russian Jew."

"I'm only Jewish on my father's side. My mother was raised Episcopalian. It killed my grandparents, but not, as you'd imagine, because she wasn't Jewish. They just thought my father was too old and confirmed in bachelorhood to marry, and he was. I come from a long line of late bloomers. Furthermore, my grandparents lived in Wellesley and would have liked everyone to think they'd been Americans since Plymouth Rock. I don't remember them too well. My father wasn't close to them. The Spells suspected that my mother had been around too much. She'd lived a while in Europe, held blue-collar jobs. From what Mara tells me, Lucy refused to play family tree with the in-laws. They liked her all right after a while, but they were angry at first—she didn't even invite any of her relatives to the wedding."

"So you have no mother and you have no ethnicity. Your mother died very young."

"She died when I was young, but she had me very late in her life. She was fifty-one when I was born, believe it or not. She was fifty-seven when she died. I think the reason I got pushed so hard was to prove that my mind was fully functional."

"That's most unusual," Mildred said. "Fifty-one. Perhaps you were adopted."

"Don't think it hasn't crossed my mind. But why would a fifty-one-year-old woman adopt a child?"

"I can't imagine," Mildred agreed.

I felt like I might cry. I avoided talking about my mother because, after seventeen years, I still cried when I talked about her.

"So did Kitsa and Gato stay together in Paris?" I asked.

Mildred shrugged. "I think I'd like to leave Kitsa and Gato alone for the night, quiet and thoughtful on a bank of the Seine. The fact is, my throat hurts. I think I'd rather you talked."

"Do you want a spoon of Robitussin or a Lifesaver or something?"

"I want to hear about your family."

"Couldn't I play you the *Moonlight* instead?"

"No drumrolls, please. I'm not going to beg."

"I'd rather not."

"A dying lady asks for an evening's entertainment and you clam up."

"It's hard for me to think of my mother's suicide as 'entertainment.'"

"There, there. Sorry. You don't have to talk if you don't want to."

"I'm sorry," I said. "I might as well."

"You don't have to say a word."

I closed my eyes, opened them to my new piano, and tried to remember what the weather was like in the spring of 1959 in the suburbs of Baltimore, Maryland.

# 12

Mozart spiced up a house that always smelled like cedar. I needed to sit on two dictionaries to reach the piano, which was respectable, black, and dimly European. On Thursdays, Lucy washed it with lemon to soak up the sun that coasted, at three o'clock, from my school to the high old window.

I was pigeon-toed and skinny, with flakes of dry skin at my elbows, wrists, and knees. I thought that *eczema* was a pet name for my special relationship with the sun. The sun, I thought, could be owned, like goldfish, and I owned it. Wherever I went, the sun was directly overhead, more stubborn than a shadow.

My father, who could fit his hand around my elbow, didn't challenge this misconception. He thought it was endearing in the Santa Claus sense. Like most fathers, Jeremy Spell was a huge man. He was far too big to call Jerry, so I forfeited the nickname Jenny at an early age, to be fair.

My father and I had the same initials—J.S., as in Bach. We also looked alike. Jeremy Spell had, the reviewers liked to say, a "spacious heart." The reviews of his violin-playing were taped to the side of the refrigerator. I learned to read from them.

Sometimes I was allowed to draw faces on the reviews in crayon, adding mustaches and long gaudy tongues.

Lucy Werner Spell was my mother. She was something brought back, at great cost, in a suitcase. She always had a suntan; she wore colorful high-heeled shoes and an ankle-bracelet. When she put on bright lipstick, there was nothing else in the world but her mouth. For all my talents, I hadn't mastered pronouncing L's and W's. As these stubborn sounds were my mother's nimbus—a written recrimination on some of her handkerchiefs and on her pocketbook—I was often made to recite, with my father:

> Let's lay a week in Lucy's lap,
> That bicycle built for two,
> And as a celebrational nightcap
> Let's sing the Honolulu Blues.

*Blues* came out *booze*, which made my mother laugh, then cry, because laughing hurt. While Lucy didn't play an instrument, her laugh was as foreign as a mandora or a carillon, rare instruments I'd marked with red ink in my World Book. She never looked right in pictures. In the one my father still has on his dresser, she's on a horse in Massachusetts, her face lit from underneath—majestic, diabolical.

I do remember the zoo. I went on my father's shoulders, the week before the family fell apart.

"Say a sentence," I said, looking down on my mother's careful hair.

"Mind over matter," Jeremy said.

"That's not a sentence. Say a sentence, Lucy."

"The blue moon ate a rarity," Lucy said.

"That's stupid. Say a paradox."

"Nothing's either good or bad; 'tis thinking makes it so," Jeremy said.

"Is that a paradox?"

"I don't know. Ask your mother."

"Is that a paradox, Lucy?"

"It depends," Lucy said.

Lucy was a master of equivocation.

Walking to the car wasn't pleasant. The pavement was strange after the pink, disfigured shine of an orangutan's ass. Lucy cried in the car. During the drive, the sun hid behind a tree nastily. When I sat down to practice, my mother cried more.

This was not unusual. There was something wrong with my mother's brain. It wasn't going to kill her, but it would always hurt. One time, as an eloquent demonstration of chronic pain, she'd brushed my hair so hard that it came out in dramatic clumps. But then she'd scooped up my face in her hands and told me about nerve endings. Hers were disintegrating. I looked the word up in my dictionary.

"If the nerves are being destroyed," I asked, "then who is destroying them?"

"I wish I knew," Lucy said. "When you find out, will you let me know?"

I promised I would. Her hands, thanking me, were cold. The fingers were long, bluish, and knotty. All the pictures are like that too—blue and cold, like ice about to melt.

The night of the zoo, I'd insisted on kissing my fish good-night, despite the time. It was late, and my goldfish ritual was protracted as the balcony scene in *Romeo and Juliet*, which we'd been reading out loud, curled up on a couch.

"Absolutely not," Lucy said. "You're too attached."

I was not used to argument. I was a lucky person who owned the sun, five goldfish, and a happy childhood. All were gifts, I sensed, from my parents. Each dinner was Christmas. Each book was an intricate wind-up toy that my parents set in motion. So I cried. This was odd in a child who could use the word *incalcitrant* wrong, but with great aplomb, in a sentence, so my mother relented.

Five fish were dead.

They floated on the top of the bowl, on their backs, innocuous as seaweed.

Lucy took the fish out and rested them in her palm. She held them out to me.

She tickled one fish with a long fingernail. With Lucy's arm bent at the elbow, she brought the fish right under my nose. They didn't smell.

"You see?" she said. "Death isn't so bad."

I felt green. I wanted to run from the bathroom, but Jeremy framed the doorway, impassive.

"Careful," he said, over my head.

"You see the big fish?" Lucy said. "She's pregnant. That's why her belly is so translucent. Do you know why mother fish eat baby fish? Because there are lots of fish, and it's no great loss."

Jeremy said, "Your mother means to say that nothing's indispensable."

I didn't know what *indispensable* meant. The word filled the room, medicinal as air freshener. My parents, too, seemed clean, clean and big.

Lucy was cross. "I meant to tell you just what I said, Jennifer. Put it this way: never eat a whole box of chocolates looking for the one with the cherry center when all you have to do is poke the bottoms."

She still had the fish in her hand.

"Easy," Jeremy warned.

I clung to his leg. Lucy glared at both of us and briskly flushed the fish down the toilet. I threw myself on the bathroom floor and started banging my fists on my mother's toes.

"These are fish," Lucy said. "Even people aren't worth this."

There were new fish the next day. Lucy brought them in the cardboard boxes used for take-out Chinese food. She had a bright scarf on and she was humming, but her eyes were red, and I could tell that she'd cried most of the night. We cleaned the bowl and inaugurated the new fish.

"You see, you can't tell the difference," Lucy said, without much conviction.

I could tell that she thought I thought she killed my fish, and she was right, but there was something worse. The night before, I'd known my fish would be dead. I felt it in the lining of my stomach—a kind of low-grade dread. But if a kiss had no curative powers, what good did it do to know things ahead of time? I watched my new fish tour their plastic shipwreck and worried.

I didn't worry for long, though, because I had to practice. My first recital was on Bach's birthday, the first day of spring. I woke up that morning with the stomach-feeling.

"Nerves," Lucy said. "You'll always have that before you play, even when you're famous. Your father still does."

I was in the doorway of my parents' bedroom. Lucy was cross-legged on the floor, sorting through a heap of clothes. She still hadn't dressed.

"Are you going somewhere?" I asked.

"No, dear. Just spring-cleaning."

Lucy was a bad liar. I knew she wouldn't be at my recital, and she wasn't.

I spent the morning in the library, as I did every Saturday, and then walked directly to my piano teacher's house. Neither of my parents was there, but Jeremy turned up, breathless, right before the recital started.

The seat next to his was empty. He looked small, gray, and hung over. I don't remember what I played. My hands just reached an octave; I had a Band-Aid on one knee.

Jeremy told me Lucy was gone when we got in the car.

"To Aunt Mara's?" I asked.

"No. She's dead."

"When?"

"This morning."

"Her head hurt."

"Yes."

We were driving badly. We passed the church with the huge mosaic of Jesus Christ which I hated. The Spells did not believe in God. We didn't like melodrama. We were, from what I could gather, more Behaviorists than anything else.

"You were at work," I said.

"Yes."

"Well, if you were at work, and I was at the library, then neither of us killed her."

"Jennifer!"

"Then she must have killed herself."

He admitted I was right. His eyes were big and hollow as a cartoon's. He even told me how she did it. She lined her stomach with toothpaste, so it couldn't be pumped, then took some drugs.

"You are six years old," Jeremy said, as if that were news.

"Yes," I said, "but that won't last long."

I didn't want to remember my mother in a Roadrunner cartoon, going off a cliff or slitting her wrists. Still, it didn't mean much. It wasn't dead goldfish; it wasn't a frantic bee trapped between the window and the screen. *Suicide* was like *eczema*. It could have meant hot chocolate spilled, or someone dented the car at the shopping center. *Your mother is dead* was a sentence like any other sentence. It could have meant *Wear the green dress* or *She's in the shower*.

By the time we got home, it was raining a bit. I excused myself to practice. Jeremy sat on the porch while I played. After I finished, I came out with two bowls of bananas and cream. Neither of us was very hungry. We ate slowly, listening to moths knock into the streetlamps and the spoons click against our teeth, until it got entirely dark.

Jeremy put his arm around me. I think he was crying. I know *I* was.

"You'll miss your mother," he said.

"Yes."

"Me too."

Jeremy sat on the edge of my bed that night for longer than he had to. I could tell that he wanted to talk.

"Your mother wasn't crazy," he said.

"I know," I said. I smiled a bit and feigned sleep.

I could tell that Jeremy didn't want to go into their bedroom. He didn't want to hang up his clothes in the closet with her rows and rows of delicate dresses; he didn't want to shave next to the windowsill with her bottles of perfume and her one azalea blossom, hot pink, floating in a long-stemmed glass. From my bed I leaned over and watched him open his bedroom door. He opened it wide enough so I could see their bed. It was made. The pillows were against the wall, and the spread slightly rumpled—before she died, Lucy had sat there doing crossword puzzles.

Jeremy closed the door and began to do push-ups in the hall, right outside my door.

I couldn't tell whether he wanted me awake or asleep.

Both of us, I think, were angry with Lucy. I've learned a lot about Lucy over the years from my father's sister Mara, who was around fairly often to keep my father from becoming an alcoholic. Mara is about the only person who would talk to me about my mother. She is the only person who totally forgives Lucy. She says that none of us could even have begun to deal with pain as gracefully as Lucy did. It seems to me, though, that my mother's suicide was inept and desperate, like any suicide.

What we know about the suicide is that Lucy took pills and left a note taped to the bedroom door: *Don't open the door. I'm dead in here. Don't be angry, and by all means think of a decent way to tell Jennifer!* I've seen the note. Jeremy still has it in his bottom desk drawer. Mara thinks it's vulgar of him to have kept it, and so do I.

The door was locked from the inside. My father called Mara, who promised to get on a plane from Boston; then he called the police. He'd never seen a dead body, even in the war, and he wouldn't see one now. They brought Lucy out covered by a sheet. Jeremy waited for the ambulance to leave and then got sick.

I can barely imagine how he went through all that and then managed to sit through my recital, his hands folded in his lap. He probably worried the whole time about the trace of vomit on his breath. The whole time he stared slightly to the left of me, where my piano teacher sat. She had a finger missing, the middle finger on her right hand. Jeremy had never noticed it before and I'd never had the heart to tell him how repulsive it was, watching her play with the stump. Throughout the recital, Jeremy muzzled a look of radical disgust.

Lucy had a last fit of bad taste, which we didn't notice until later. First she left a vase of fresh roses on the piano, like it was Mother's Day. Worse than that, the next day we found a casserole in the refrigerator with a note tucked into the tinfoil: *350° for 50 min. P.S. I love you.* It was her handwriting, large and childish. Jeremy carried the dish outside to the trash and threw it away, Corningware and all.

My father is the kind of person who actually remembers to have the newspaper delivery stopped when he goes on vacation. I don't think he had a response for a suicide. I suppose Lucy left the notes to make us feel better, but it didn't work. We wished she'd gone on a vacation, mailed us an ordinary loving postcard, and made the suicide look like an accident. She could have fallen off the roof at a dark party. She could have floated, blissfully, too far off at sea. Her note was an affront. It was too light, almost incidental. This was hard on me, but it was even harder, I imagine, for my father, who had loved Lucy right from the start, from across the lobby of a Cape Cod hotel.

Mara says my father rubbed lotion in Lucy's back as she sunbathed in a slatted chair; he watched her hold a hat on with one downy arm, her pelvis knocking the pier. If you listen to Mara, Lucy was clear and pink as a Forties scriptgirl. I find this hard to believe—my mother was over forty at that time, and already had her disease. She told him about her brain then, but it hadn't seemed credible, with Lucy so appealing, a book in her lap as he practiced the violin. He proposed quickly because he figured he'd waited long enough; and Lucy thought she didn't have long to wait.

My grandparents were still alive then. Lucy and Jeremy were married at my grandparents' house in Wellesley. My grandparents never took to Lucy, who was to move to Baltimore, where my father would continue to play in the orchestra, and where Johns Hopkins might be able to say something about Lucy's disease.

The way Mara tells it, there was a generalized happiness that didn't last long. I got born in five minutes during a luscious remission, but then my mother's condition got worse and worse, and Mara would approach the suicide—at which point my father would come home, or Mara would get nervous and tell me to go do my homework.

I don't think about my mother when I think about the day of the suicide now. I think about my father in the hall, doing push-ups. I think about how gingerly and slowly he opened the bedroom door the second time and how, after a moment, I heard him say *"Shit"* and start flinging open drawers. Soon he was running violently all over the house, throwing open cabinets and cursing. He was in the linen closet right outside my door, shoving sheets and towels onto the carpet. Then he was in the guest room, where my mother kept her wedding gown in a plastic bag and her hooded sewing machine. He was screaming, *"I'm going to kill her."*

I heard the front door slam. From my bedroom window I could see Jeremy walk down the steps separating our lawn from the median strip. It was still drizzling. He stood against our neighbor's car parked in front of the house. The car was new, shiny as a paper cut-out of a car. Then he started banging his head rhythmically against the glass of the car window, gripping the car with both hands. I didn't know what to do.

A taxi threaded down the street. I was relieved for a moment when I saw Aunt Mara get out of the car, but I couldn't hear anything and what I saw was awful. Mara put her suitcase down and tried to hug my father. He pushed her down. As she was getting up, he just fell over backwards, until he was flat against the pavement.

I crawled under my bed, dragging my blanket after me.

They came in the front door. I could hear them hanging up their coats. "She wouldn't do that," Mara was saying. She spoke slow and loud, like a nurse. "You can't see anything in the dark anyway, and you're going to wake Jennifer. Wait until the morning."

They moved into the kitchen, which was directly below my bedroom. I couldn't make out their talk over the ice hitting the sides of their glasses and the drone of the refrigerator.

I couldn't seem to get the room dark enough.

Then I heard my mother's voice, tiny at first as a key in a lock but soon wide and lucid in the dark room.

We were going somewhere in the old mint-green Rambler. There was honeysuckle out and the smell of freshly cut grass. We pulled up in front of a house. It became clear that I was going to a birthday party, and that the present in my lap—a box cleverly tied with licorice rather than string—was for a friend. It also became clear that neither of us was in any great hurry. We just sat there with the windows rolled down, taking the air.

Lucy had sunglasses on and was drumming the steering wheel with her nails, her head resting on the palm of the other hand. Her scalp seemed soft; her hair was blue-black, the bruised color of hair in comic books. In fact, her whole face looked puffy, the way it sometimes did when she came back from the hospital. She didn't seem in a good mood. I heard a lawnmower and the bell on an ice cream truck. I began to sing, and what I sang, clear as day, was this:

> Miss Spell
> Won't go to Hell
> And stay there ever after.
> Her mother is dead;
> She was sick in the head.
> This is no laughing matter.

Then I flinched, because I thought Lucy was going to hit me, but she didn't. In fact, she smiled.

"Look at yourself in the mirror," she commanded.

I craned my neck to center myself in the rear-view mirror. In the mirror *I* was *her.*

This is hard to explain. It wasn't as if I, six years old, was suddenly 57, married, unmusical, and dying of a brain disease. It seemed something very simple, like something in Latin written on a coin—something to notice and not to do anything about.

*I* was *her.*

No wonder I've been feeling so strange, I thought. I'm *her.*

"I suppose I should go in now," I said, in *her* voice.

Lucy bunched her knees up under her chin and asked me winsomely, in *my* voice, if there was anything she could do for me.

"Nobody can do anything for anyone else," I said. I said it to be flip, but somehow I felt as if it were the truest thing I'd ever said. The present felt minuscule and false in my lap.

Lucy reached into her purse and handed me a pen and a piece of paper. Then she gave me a large key, maybe a skate key. I tried to look in the mirror to see if I was still her, but she held me down.

"I want you to remember what you just said," she told me. "I want you to write it down, sign it, and date it."

"I don't know how to write yet," I reminded her.

"Don't be ridiculous. If you can read music you can write a declarative sentence."

She was right. Not only could I spell all the words correctly, but I wrote them in cursive—*her* cursive. I expected her to praise me for this, but she took the paper from my hand, folded it, and pressed the fist in which I still held the key.

"Put this piece of paper in the storage cabinet behind the linen closet," she said. "I want you to have this so you remember, so you don't blame me. But don't *ever* tell anyone you said that when you were six, because they're not going to believe you. They're going to think you make it up. Promise you'll never tell a soul what you said."

"I promise," I said.

"You promised," she said. "Now go inside."

The next thing I knew, Jeremy was lifting me back into my bed. Mara was standing behind him.

"I was cold," I said. "I fell asleep."

"Turn the air-conditioner down, Mara," Jeremy said.

Both of them seemed fairly satisfied with my explanation. Jeremy tucked me in and Mara gave me a kiss on my forehead.

"Do you think you can sleep now?" Jeremy asked.

"Yes," I said cautiously, "but there's one thing. Are you looking for Lucy's things? Because I saw her pack some stuff this morning. Did you check the storage cabinet behind the linen closet?"

Jeremy almost knocked us both over to get to it. In the cabinet were neatly wrapped boxes. Lucy had even labeled them.

"Of course," Jeremy said. "I just wasn't thinking straight."

Mara was staring at me, arms crossed, trying to read my mind.

"How much do you know," she asked, "about what happened this morning?"

"Here's everything," Jeremy said. "I just wasn't thinking. I should have thought of it myself."

One of the boxes, smaller than the rest, said: *For Jennifer.*

"How much do you know?" Mara repeated.

"I know that my mother killed herself," I said, "because her head hurt."

"You're awful cold-blooded about it."

Jeremy said, "Leave her alone." He jogged into his bedroom and came back with a pair of nail clippers. He turned one of the boxes onto its side and started to undo it.

There it was: a little room with everything belonging to my mother, behind the linen closet, right against my bed.

"What on earth are you doing that for?" Mara asked.

"I just want to make sure everything's here."

I was in what is called a double bind. If the note my mother had asked me to write was in the box addressed to me, then Mara and Jeremy would see it and I would have betrayed my mother. If the note weren't in the box, then I'd have to disbelieve my mother, or think I was crazy.

"Please," I said. "I don't want to open my box."

"It's probably jewelry," Jeremy said. "There's no point in leaving it here."

I began to cry.

"Please," I said, "please let me open my box myself when I'm old enough. I'm not ready now, I'm sleepy. Please, Daddy, please please don't open it now."

I'd called him Daddy. Even he had to listen to that.

It seemed like a long time before Jeremy finally repacked the boxes and closed the cabinet. We stood there even longer while Jeremy leaned against the wall, looking tired, with Mara still staring at me like I was a cripple on a bus.

"I think you should go to bed," she said.

Jeremy snapped out of it. "You sure should. I'll tuck you in again."

"Jeremy?" I said. "You don't think Lucy could be back, do you?"

They assured me she couldn't. As they tucked me in, even Mara's face was gentle and solicitous.

"Maybe she'll be back," I said. "If she's not back, then I'll get to see her in Heaven, right?"

I didn't believe in Heaven, of course. But they seemed to like me best as a child, and I didn't want to displease them.

Two

# 13

Lucy's body, in a yellow skirt and loose maroon T-shirt, was donated, in accordance with her will, to the brain research doctors. Her soul was left to its own devices. I often imagined it soaking in the rain gutter along the upstairs windows, like a paper hat, although it didn't rain much that summer; it was very hot. A week after we threw out the flowers and condolence notes, a chipmunk wrangled into the crawlspace through the gutter and built a nest over my mother's boxes. Every night the chipmunk tap-danced over our heads. We paid two hundred dollars to get an exterminator up there, but as the chipmunk was out for the day, the man just jangled his keys against his legs, fumigated halfheartedly, and told us we were probably imagining things. Maybe we were: the chipmunk never came back. I learned the *Appassionata* and netted tadpoles in the stream behind our house.

What stands out in my memory from the years that followed are the hamsters in the back of the class, a boy with bangs obstructing his face whom I chased around during recess, a ferris wheel in Ocean City, a chemistry set in the basement, Chinese food on Sundays, Kennedy's funeral, and the dinosaur bones in the Smithsonian. Life with Jeremy had the seriousness of purpose, the earnestness, of a Girl Scout camping trip. I loved going to the jewelry store with him to choose a cat's eye for Mara's birthday, or to hardware stores to compare prices on fertilizers. I loved reading with him in the library on Thursday evenings. By the time I was ten we had read *The Brothers Karamazov* together; we discussed the concept of redemption over a pot roast I'd cooked myself, with a recording of Liszt's Hungarian Rhapsodies in the background. We also discussed the economy, black holes, Khrushchev banging his shoe on the table, and my homework (when I did it), especially the math; we discussed my friends, with whom I went ice skating, played baseball, and talked about boys.

Saturday afternoons were holy. I had my own seat at the symphony. The same woman sat beside me at each matinee. I loved to feel the hush of mink that separated her arm from mine on the armrest. She knew that my father was the first violinist and she treated me like a first lady. After the performances, I'd go drinking with Jeremy and his symphony friends. They'd drink liquor and I'd drink ginger ale. I'd watch my father's eyes turn clear and spacious as his bourbon went down. When we walked from the new car to our house, my father would rest his arm on my shoulder and I'd feel tall then, tall and sure of my love for the world. Sometimes his friends would bring their instruments over and we'd all play, until the room was richer and brighter than a toy store.

There was, in short, nothing to be unhappy about, no cacophony between the notes in my head and the notes the world played for me. My only worry—even then—was that by opting for comfort, I was allowing bad luck to amass, that it would hit me later—an unlucky streak like a killer heat, heat like the summer after Lucy died, when some chemicals dumped into the Chesapeake washed dead fish and stingrays onto the shore.

It was, in fact, very hot when I finished telling all this to Mildred. Even my air-conditioner seemed to be whining.

"No wonder you're so snide," Mildred said. "Poor dear,

you've never exorcized your anger. When my mother died (I'm talking about my adopted mother now, of course), I went straight into the living room and smashed a glass coffee table with my fist. I needed to have twenty stitches in my hand, but I felt much better."

She showed me her palm. A jagged white scar crossed her life line. "So what was in the box?" she asked.

"I don't know. I never opened it."

"I don't believe that."

I shrugged and went into the kitchen to pour Pepsis. My wandering Jew was ominous in the window, silhouetted against the fire escape. My eyes, reflected in the window, were dark and puffy from crying. When I handed Mildred her Pepsi she said, "Why didn't you open your Pandora's Box?"

"It isn't a Pandora's Box. I can tell you by process of elimination what's in there—some jewelry, some snapshots, maybe a note to me on one of her monogrammed blue cards, saying how much she loved me."

"Or saying she killed herself because you were such an obnoxious child."

"I helped around the house. I was even-tempered. I was a genius."

"Genius," Mildred sneered.

"Was too, and I can prove it."

I opened the closet, pulled out the stepladder, and got the box where I keep old papers from the top shelf. I resisted reading anything else and went straight for the black-bound composition book I'd written in the fall of 1963.

"This was written in green ink on September 16, 1963," I told her. I began to read one passage aloud:

"My first year accounted for 100% of my experience. My second year accounted for only 50% of my experience. That same day—my second birthday, August 24, 1956—accounted for only $1/18,032$ of my father's experience. Each day gets

less and less important. The older you get, the more accouterments you need—calendars, watches—to remind you you're
living inside a particular day. Adults only notice the day if
their cars won't start or if they have a doctor's appointment.
You have to be very fast to catch time. It's quicker than a
hare on a neighbor's lawn, and more ruthlessly graceful."

Mildred yawned showily. "You didn't write that in 1963."

"I was nine."

"Nine-year-olds don't say 'accouterments'; nine-year-olds
don't say 'ruthlessly graceful.' "

"Okay, I admit I had some help from my father on the big
words."

"Anyway, that's not genius. That's precisely the kind of
defensive precociousness that hinders you today."

I replaced the box and went to stand by the window. Across
the street, a man in a suit and a woman who looked like a
dancer, in a lavender leotard outfit, were arguing animatedly,
gesturing with drinks in paper cups. Their movements cut the
mugginess.

Mildred said, "Naturally you realize I wouldn't spend my
last evenings with you and give you a piano if I didn't think
you were basically a decent person, so stop being so touchy and
tell me what happened to your piano playing. Did you get your
wires crossed the day of the first recital and turn morbid about
music forever?"

"I had some talent for music; that, combined with great
ambition on my part and on my father's part for me, put me in
the peculiar position of graduating from Juilliard at sixteen."

"So why don't you play anymore?"

"I started school when I was five, like most other kids, but
then I skipped a year and took English in the summer so I could
start my conservatory training early. For the first two years at
Juilliard, I commuted from Baltimore, but then I insisted on
getting a place of my own in New York. I rented a tiny apart-

happen to discover the secret of everything. My fingers were as elastic as they'd ever be. According to my orthodontist, who took an X-ray of the bones in my hand when I got braces put on my teeth, I wouldn't grow much, either. I was five foot five. I'd sprouted breasts and read Nietzsche. At that moment I could play everything that Rubinstein could play. What inscrutable light shone on Artur Rubinstein that did not shine on Jennifer Spell?

"By process of elimination, I decided that I suffered from a poverty of spirit. I didn't want to be competent; I wanted to be *charmed*. But the moonlight in my sonata would never be as lush as the moonlight in Rubinstein's sonata because I could not see, touch, smell, or embrace moonlight deeply enough.

"I took a day off from practicing to wander about the city. Golden, barelegged women in lilac and vermilion were eating lunch together everywhere. They sat over plates of glistening pasta, over baconburgers and carafes of wine. All of them gave the impression of having explored the world enough to be as comfortable in every corner of it as they were in their own kitchens. Everything they said sounded either relevant or buoyant.

"I didn't want to be any of them. Still, I didn't see how it could hurt to prove that I *could* be one of them, if I wanted.

"I got my hair cut. The edges just brushed my shoulders, soft with the aura of other edges. This sensation was so pleasant that I almost believed it could replace being great, at least for a while.

"Of course, I didn't really believe that a painfully thin, gray sky could spread itself over me. I envisioned instead— rather superstitiously—a furious black clock buzzing in the back of my own head, obscuring the sun of the old Jennifer-centric days. So all I had to do was ignore the cloud by not acknowledging it, and the cloud would doubtless disperse into a harmless shower. If I did have real spirit in me, it'd make itself known; if not, I wouldn't have wasted any time waiting around for it.

ment down the block from the school with money my grandfather left me, and I was so happy there that I didn't move until
a year ago. I loved having my own checking account and my
own plants to water, but I got tired of people at parties asking
me if I knew how to cook and if I liked boys. I got especially
tired of boys saying, 'I keep wanting to treat you like you're
thirty.' I knew that they treated me like a Raggedy Ann or a
nymphette because they found me threatening, but the effort of
making them comfortable eventually seemed more trouble than
it was worth. I didn't find most of my classmates very refreshing
anyhow. Their breathy metaphysics like seawater, heavy with
an undertow of nonchalance. I was playing Scriabin at the time,
and was given to grandiosity like all adolescents. But in publi[c]
I was demure, sometimes sullen. I began to spend most of m[y]
time alone, and my father, who had never liked the idea of [my]
living alone, began to worry about me."

"Just answer my question, Jennifer."

"I am answering. He wasn't as worried as I was m[y]
I'd expected to be snatched up for a Town Hall recital[]
after graduation. Instead, my teachers patted me on the he[ad]
recommended private tutors. It wasn't that they didn't [?]
was good; on the contrary, they assured me that I w[as]
nomenal *for my age*. So far as I was concerned, that wa[s]
enough. It'd only be four years before I was old enou[gh]
everything adults do in every state in the union, and b[?]
be almost too old. Child wonders, I knew, always bur[?]
take a look at the statistics—stockbrokers now, insu[?]
men, all of the stars on 'It's Academic'; name in l[?]
ten, and by twenty you have to light a match [?]
names on a check. My father and everyone else I [?]
was nonsense, but how would they know? My [?]
competent violinist. If my teachers were that goo[d]
have been stuck at Juilliard. I knew that nothi[ng]
for me. Musicians aren't scientists, after all. [?]
looking through the right instrument at the r[?]

"I looked for a job the following morning and had no trouble finding one, with my sightreading ability and better-than-average singing voice. While the recording studio was paying me much less than they'd have paid a unionized adult in my position, eight thousand wasn't a bad start for a sixteen-year-old. I went home that first weekend to have my braces removed. Jeremy was proud but, as usual, a little uneasy. He'd been thinking that it wasn't too late for me to go to medical school.

"What mainly kept me going was boys. The first one I loved was an eleventh-grader and part-time Boy Friday at the studio named Tommy, who had auburn hair, no ass, and hands as big as his feet. He liked to sway with his hands in his pockets and his high-topped sneakers pointing outwards, to compensate for his knock-knees. Sex gave our relationship the safe, warm feeling of rain on a study window. His penis made immediate sense to me. Even after the fact, walking hand in hand to a gangster movie, sex felt like a responsible memory, as if we'd toasted marshmallows together over a campfire. The only trouble with Tommy was that he liked horrible rock music and didn't have much to say. I moved on to 'older men.' The only kind I could get, though, were the kind who are interested in screwing cute, ambitious sixteen-year-olds. Meanwhile, I worked. Eight years now. Eight years! Eventually I'll get a gold pin."

Mildred had a coughing fit.

When she stopped coughing, she clutched her neck, rotated her head, and sighed, "Sorry I asked."

"Sorry I answered."

"You didn't. The simple answer to my simple question 'Why don't you still play the piano?' is that you were scared of failure."

"That's what I said."

"It's a common reaction in women, especially women pandered to by their fathers. You probably made the right decision, though. You might have been a competent pianist if you'd worked at it, but you would never have been a great one. You're not mathematical enough."

"How do *you* know?"

"I saw you trying to figure out the tip at the restaurant—you were too slow. Also, I've heard you play. You rush certain parts and slow down others; your pacing's all wrong. You don't have a pianist's patience. You don't at all have a pianist's mind. A pianist needs a thorough coat of peace, a primer of quiet energy."

"What does a painter need?" I was thinking of Argyle. I wanted her to say that a painter needs a good heart.

"A good eye."

"But a pianist doesn't need a good ear?"

I leaned forward in my chair until I could see my foot in the mirror on the back of my closet door. I pointed the foot and sat back. Mildred wiped some condensation off her glass.

"Now that I think of it," she said, "peace and patience are the personality traits required for accomplishment in any field, from cancer research to opera-singing. The only thing you could do in your present state of mind is to write poetry. You wouldn't be a good poet, of course, but then most of them aren't."

"I thought you were going to be quiet tonight. I thought this was Jennifer Night."

"Point. Let's open your mother's box."

"I don't have it here."

"Yes you do. If you have your old diaries, you have that box."

"It's at my father's house in Baltimore."

"No it isn't."

"We're not going to open it."

"Yes we are."

"There's no reason to open it. I knew from the moment I saw it that there was no reason to open it—that there was nothing left to know about my mother's death, or about death in general, that I didn't know when I decided never to open the box; that asking for more would be tacky and sentimental. Perhaps if I have a daughter, I'll give the box to her."

"Passing the buck," Mildred laughed, but then her face turned grave. She hadn't moved from the orange chair since she'd arrived, except to eat, and from her drained look I thought she was going to be sick again. But her voice was clear and tender.

"Jennifer, it's not healthy for you to nourish these fantasies of a deep, secret past. You're not old enough. You've had a nice suburban life and you're reasonably successful. You've got to confront your own limitations. If there's nothing left to learn, then admit it already." She paused. "I'll tell you what. If whatever's in the box upsets you, I'll let you call in sick tomorrow."

"I'm shocked that you take such a rabid interest in my mother's ashes."

"I'm not interested in your mother. I'm interested in you. You've got to worry about a child that calls her parents by their first names at age six."

"We were progressive."

"You progressed right into imbecility, then."

"Don't insult my family."

"Then don't play poor little orphan-child."

I relented. I got the box. It was behind a pile of empty boxes in my closet; before that, it had been in the back of my last closet. I put the box on the floor by Mildred's feet.

"Go ahead," I said.

"You."

After almost two decades, the masking tape on the box was mottled and cakey. The lettering on the box, however—*For Jennifer* in my mother's cursive—was fresh enough. I'd looked at that writing hundreds of times, amazed at the casual flow. My hands should have been trembling but they weren't. I felt safe, I suppose, with Mildred there. Actually, I was almost glad. When the lid came off, no blast of foul air greeted us. There was no smell at all.

"And the winner is," I said.

On the top of the box was something white and lacy—my mother's bridal veil. The headband was made of small white pearls. I put on the veil and looked at Mildred through the yellowing mesh.

"I wonder what she did with the gown," I said.

Mildred said, "Next."

Next was a purple velvet sack that obviously contained jewelry. As I lifted the sack from the box, I could see the blue envelope underneath, and I got the sinking feeling I used to get before a recital.

In the sack were a pair of gold earrings with garnets in them, an emerald pendant, my mother's wedding band, and an exquisite bracelet—delicate rubies sinewing down a white-gold curve to a large, flat diamond. I handed the bracelet to Mildred. She examined it under the overhead.

"Quite old—eighteenth century. Russian, maybe. I'd have to ask Weldon. That's very pretty indeed. I wonder where on earth your parents got this. Did your parents collect antiques?"

"You can have it."

"Wear it yourself." She bent forward from her chair to clasp the bracelet on my wrist. "Now, read that letter."

"There's a picture!"

"Open the letter."

I pulled out the picture from underneath the letter. It was a black-and-white snapshot of me, at about age five, playing the piano. I wore a flouncy dress; my saddle shoes dangled a good foot above the floor. I'd turned partly around to look toward the camera, making my face a blur—dark areas for the eyes and the smile. My hands, too, were out of focus.

Mildred looked at the picture without emotion and repeated, "The letter."

"You read it to me."

Mildred opened the letter. " 'What can I say to you, sweet one?' "

"What do you mean?"

"That's what it says."

"No 'Dear Jennifer'?"

"The salutation is 'What can I say to you, sweet one?'

"I can tell you to live simply. I did and it would have worked. Hopefully you won't understand pain for a long time. Your father is a good man. Stay with him, don't flee to Mara. Your father will teach you how it feels to have a family, to have built a family that can stand on its own, like a strong old house. Don't ask for too much and you'll get more than you asked for. I've got to go now. Please remember me fondly if you can."

"That's it?"

"That's it."

"No 'Love always, Mother'?"

Mildred shook her head.

I turned toward the window, where my porcelain teapot on the ledge, blue, was decomposing quietly.

"You're disappointed?" Mildred said. "What did you expect? It's a fine note, affectionate and to the point."

"I shouldn't have opened it."

"Why not? Your mother was right about you. Is that all?"

I rustled through the tissue paper and nodded.

"That's not much for a box that size. Your mother must have had a real sense of humor."

"Wait."

I'd found a picture flat on the bottom of the box. As I lifted it out, one corner snapped off. The picture was very old and brittle. Lucy was young in it, dressed in a crisp dark suit. She wasn't smiling. She leaned against a car in such a way that you could tell the suit was new, that she didn't want to get it dirty. The street in the background was one I didn't recognize.

Mildred looked from the picture to me several times, then

asked unsteadily, "Is this the only picture you have of your mother?"

"My father has some at home."

She got up from the chair and moved it to the other side of the room, where she examined the picture for a long time under the lamp on the end table.

"I'm almost positive this is Detroit," she said. "Are you sure this is your mother?"

"What kind of question is that?"

Mildred went to the window. She steadied herself on the ledge, then turned to me, trying to smile. "Jesus Christ," she said.

"What?"

"Holy mother-fucking mother of God."

"Mildred!"

"How old did you say your mother was when she had you?"

"Fifty-one. What is this? Tell me."

"Had she ever been married before?"

"I told you, she married late."

Mildred looked at the picture once more, then crouched on the floor and began to laugh and moan.

"Mildred, this isn't fair."

She was pounding her fist on the floor, laughing so hard that no sound was coming from her mouth. I began to cry. Soon I was crying so hard that no sound was coming from my mouth either. Mildred, still laughing, shuffled around in her bag for a while until she drew out a photograph from the red billfold where she kept her driver's license.

It was a poor, out-of-focus photograph of someone, taken from a good distance.

"So?" I said.

The face in the picture was half-turned and hard to see.

"Look carefully," Mildred said. "There's your mother."

"Don't be silly."

"Look again."

The face was dark and thin, like my mother's, although it was hard to tell—the photograph was bad, and I hadn't seen my mother in seventeen years.

"That's Frog Haggerty," Mildred said. "Your mother is Frog Haggerty. She left Atlantic City, went to Cape Cod, and married a stranger. We've found Frog."

"That's amusing, Mildred, but my mother's maiden name was Werner."

"Your mother's maiden name could have been Magdalen with a short trip to County Records or a decent forger. How lovely. She had no living relatives; she invited no one to her wedding, and called herself Werner."

"My mother wasn't from Detroit."

"Your mother just didn't happen to *mention* that she was from Detroit."

"Don't be absurd."

Mildred patted my shoulder, then hugged me hard. "You should be happy," she said. "Such is the fortuitous event that makes New York the best city in the world. You should be overjoyed! You pick up an old lady over breakfast; lo and behold, she's your rich half-aunt. You should sing with bliss."

"First of all, I'm not convinced that these pictures are of the same woman. Second of all, even if my mother were Frog, which I find highly unlikely since her maiden name was Lucy Werner—"

"Lucinda, Lucinda, of course—Lucinda Haggerty."

"There are millions of Lucys. Anyway, even if my mother were Frog, which she wasn't, then how does that make us related?"

"Because I'm Frog's half-sister. We haven't gotten to that yet. I'm Helen Haggerty's secret daughter; I'm the illegitimate thing delivered to the doorstep of an infertile factory worker in Detroit, raised in poverty, while my mother trotted about in

Europe. I can't believe you look disappointed. Jennifer, this is beyond beautiful. How history repeats itself should be a comfort to you, a true comfort."

How history repeats itself was, apparently, a comfort to *her*. She looked very peaceful. She wore the contented half-smile of a woman enjoying an elegant meal with a dashing lover, confident that he'll propose over dessert. She'd decided that I was her half-niece, and that was that. She'd refuse to entertain any doubts about our blood relationship, and I had plenty of doubts. I didn't *want* to be her half-niece. Blood relationship seemed to me a cheap climax; it undercut all the special beauty of our attraction to one another. Only later could I accept why Mildred needed to cling so fiercely to her artificial closure. She was a spinster who didn't want to die alone. She wanted to leave her story in good hands and, despite all evidence to the contrary, she was old-fashioned enough to believe that family has the best hands. It wouldn't serve me to believe in family. I wanted to believe in friends. As Mildred's friend, I played half-niece, but I never fully believed the part, and told Mildred as much right from the beginning.

"Suspicion within bounds is perfectly healthy," she said. "This has been a most productive session. Tomorrow in the park we'll continue the story, and I'll bring you more photographs of your mother. I think I have one of her taken on that same street, in that same suit, leaning against that same car."

Mildred began to cough, but this time, she coughed for about five minutes, until her face was scarlet and she was fighting for breath.

"Can I get you anything?" I asked.

"It's been too much excitement."

She got up with difficulty and began to gather her things. I was aware of the box, still on the floor, with my mother's legacies to me strewn about like discarded Christmas decorations. I couldn't wait for Mildred to leave so I could pack up the things and get them back in the closet, but I said, "You're welcome to stay. The couch folds out."

"Not anymore, because the piano doesn't fold in. Do you have any Valium?"

"Who, *me?*"

"Take two aspirin, then, and get some sleep."

She put her palm against my face and shook her head, smiling. Her palm was cold. "Also," she said, "take off that silly veil."

I'd entirely forgotten I had it on.

As she walked down the steps I called after her, "Thanks for the piano. Thanks for everything."

"Sure. Good-night."

"Mildred?"

I walked to the landing so I could see her several flights below. She was looking up at me. She was so tiny.

"Mildred, what do you like least about me?"

"Can't we discuss it tomorrow?"

"No. What do you like least about me?"

"Your stubborn insistence on asking that question. Good-night."

"Thanks. Mildred?"

"For God's sake, Jennifer."

"What do you like best about me?"

"Your stubborn insistence on asking that question," she said, and left before I could ask her anything else.

# 14

If the sun got hot enough you didn't have to think. If you thought at all, it was about how close Europe was when you squinted, how much closer than the end of the boardwalk where men in white were nailing down planks. If you tried, you could just make out the nails being driven—a sound like the last wan notes from a wound-down music box. If the tourists got obstreperous, all you had to do was concentrate on the hammers, and the crowds became silent-movie crowds, their movements choppy and comical.

Katey O'Brien Haggerty got very dark. Her hands were brown on top, white on the palms, like her servant woman's. The lines of her bathing suit were indelibly etched. Her teeth and the whites of her eyes were very bright against her face. Except for the tan, she looked as she'd looked when Rory Kirn first courted her in Tourisme, just as she'd looked in the photographs she'd mailed him from Paris.

Rory didn't find the tan so becoming at first. Paleness was still considered aristocratic, and most women carried parasols, letting their cheeks get flushed from the heat. But Katey had never been most women, and Rory liked to watch her sunning herself—one arm thrown behind her head, one knee raised, her eyes closed.

He'd waited a long time for her. She came unannounced, ragged and thin after a month on a boat, and begged him to take her in, which he promptly did, although she said she wouldn't marry him. She'd live with him, cook for him, make love to him; but she saw no reason why they should rush into marriage. *"Rush?"* Rory said. But he was a patient man, a peaceful man, and he settled for what he got.

What he had, in most respects, was plenty. Denizens can still point to his large house, which he more than once had to defend against highways and condominiums. Some can still remember what an honor it was to lean against his mahogany staircase, holding a cocktail. But Katey's ambiguous status in his household caused a scandal. The couple was easily recognized: Rory stood almost six foot five, and the dark lady on his arm almost never smiled, never wore the furs and jewels that Rory most certainly could have offered her.

The scandalous couple grew private. Rory had thought Katey's gloom was homesickness that would fade, but it didn't, and soon Rory too had a misty look as he listened to the radio or ate on the sunporch. Farsighted enough to invest in the resort, Rory was farsighted enough to predict his country's disaster, and started to save regular sums of money in the mattress of the least attractive guest room. By 1927, his investments had fallen off sharply. People thought it was un-American of him to retire so young. He sent away for books that would teach him how to read Japanese, and spent most of his time on his grounds, constructing a Japanese garden with pagodas and waterfalls.

Katey found his new hobby endearing. She wasn't indignant, as the townspeople were, that Rory was more interested in his dwarf shrubs than in plans for the new convention hall. She perfectly understood why Rory would want to cultivate six square yards of grass on a knoll near the Atlantic Ocean. She herself had cultivated several basement rooms in the Louvre, as Pia Maginski had cultivated a tiny museum in the Alps. A child of Tourisme, Katey understood escape, by which she didn't mean the escapism of the movies—she found the largeness of the faces on the screen disconcerting. Katey thought that smallness, attention to detail, was what growing up was all about. After dinner, she and Rory would retreat to the den, put the radio on low, and stretch out; as the announcer talked, Rory would repeat the words under his breath in Japanese, and Katey would smile, focusing on the shock of pale skin between his shoe and his pants leg. She felt tenderness toward Rory and tenderness, she thought, was enough. Her mistake with Gato had been asking for more. When she imagined Gato, he took the steps to the Sacré-Cœur two by two, extending an arm which held a loaf of bread to the sun, and proposed a toast to his odalisque. Sometimes, when she listened to the radio, Katey imagined that Gato had come to the States, that he had gotten a job as the technician for a radio station, that he was about to grab the mike from the speaker's hand and cry out her name. But she'd look up to see Rory practicing his Japanese and every time she'd feel a tenderness for him and a gratitude, and she started—slowly—to forget Gato, at least until Frog showed up.

The first thing Katey said when she saw Frog at the door of the house in November 1926 was, "Rory doesn't know about Gato."

Frog said, "I'll tell you now and get it over with."

"He isn't dead!"

"You know the bonds Rory gave you, that you kept in your jewelry box at the inn? I took them. I brought them to Paris because the inn needed the money; I'd hoped to sell them there. But I left fast and I needed the money to survive. I never got any of it to Casey. The money's gone now, so I come to you. I'm sorry."

"That's all right."

The women embraced. They were half-sisters and sisters-in-law, but they'd spent a total of two days together in their lives. In each other they saw their brothers' eyes, their brothers' hair, their brothers' complexions; this might have made them happy, but instead it made them melancholy.

Katey introduced Frog to Rory as her sister, and asked if Frog could stay. Rory said certainly.

It was a harsh winter. They closed off most of the rooms. Rory didn't mind Frog. Frog was even more melancholy than Katey, and talked even less, but Frog was stronger. She chopped the firewood and carried it in; since Katey, Frog, and Rory between them could take care of all the chores, they fired the last servant. Sometimes while she chopped wood, Frog would belt out angry workers' songs she'd learned at the car factory in Detroit, for that's where she'd gone when she left Paris—back to Detroit to work for the company her father had been instrumental in establishing. At first she'd found her anonymity in her home town comforting, even adventurous; but Tourisme had accustomed her to something better than the factory worker's lifestyle. She enjoyed Rory's quiet house on the beach, which was as big and old as the Sanity Inn. Like Katey, Frog didn't often want to disturb the peace by discussing Tourisme or Paris. It was enough to have people about. She also liked Rory and his Japanese. She'd had a chance to see New York when she got off the boat, and although the city frightened her, she'd been drawn to Chinatown, where the colors were bright and happy as those in a five-and-dime store. In the summer, Atlantic City too was colorful. From the hill, Frog saw the candy-colored umbrellas on the beach, the women in their pastel hats strolling the boardwalk slow as sun. When the crowds were thick enough, Rory would accompany the two tanned women down the boardwalk. He'd now been totally ostracized by the natives, not that he cared. The trio would fish cigarettes out of a glass box with a stiff crane, although none of them smoked; they'd eat candy apples and watch the lovers file in to see the Fat Lady, or they'd take the Ferris wheel, sitting straight as the farmer couple in *American Gothic*.

Rory had already liquefied enough of his assets and simplified enough of his needs to cushion the worst effects of the Depression, and he already lived as the Depression forced people to live—sitting inside in the space he could afford to heat, listening to the radio. After the stock market crash, the natives counted on things improving by the next summer and the next tourist season. Rory knew better, and didn't care. He liked the winters on the Atlantic best. The beach was still and the fish were plentiful. In the morning, they'd all bundle up to go out for sand crabs.

By the end of the Depression, they were all a little tired of seafood, especially when salt and butter grew scarce. But, children of potato-eaters, they could abide monotony better than most, and they never had to wait on a bread line. They never went barefoot. They were always warm. In 1931, Rory took some money out of his mattress and gave it to the town, an act of philanthropy that improved his image in Atlantic City some, but for the most part he still kept his distance.

Things went on like this for about five years.

Needless to say, in five years Katey and Frog got to know each other and despite the invention of Monopoly they eventually had to talk. And when they talked—unless Rory was there—they talked about their brothers. Katey usually instigated these conversations.

"We should have stayed with them," Katey said once.

The two women were sitting on a pier some miles from the house. It was almost summer again; cats and children were out; Rory was puttering in his garden; Katey and Frog had their shoes off outside for the first time since the previous September, although it was still too cold to swim.

"We could have stayed. We could have just not had children. Why didn't we stay?"

"I don't want to talk about it," Frog said.

"And why haven't we written? It wouldn't have done any harm to have written."

"Because of Rory."

"He knows I have a brother," Katey said. "He *thinks* I have a sister, too. If he'll believe that, he'll believe anything. You're allowed to have relatives. I think we should have stayed. I don't care what you say; I'm going to write. I'm going to track them all down, even Kitsa, if she's not dead of syphilis by now."

"Stop thinking about them."

"You're not going to convince me that you don't think about Casey."

"I don't."

"And how he was in bed."

"Stop!"

"I'm sorry. But I know that when the boardwalk is crowded you're looking for him. You half-expect him to be behind you in line for cotton candy."

"Please, Katey."

"Just admit I'm right. I imagine running into Gato in the strangest ways: I'm buying a refrigerator and he's the refrigerator salesman. Or I'm boarding a train and when the porter comes for my bags, it's Gato. Or Gato becomes our foreign correspondent in Paris."

"Don't hold your breath."

"I'm not, but I know we'll see each other before we die."

Katey would never see Gato. Before the next month was over, however, she'd see Klaus Frankovich.

Katey and Frog had been in a penny arcade. A fortune-telling machine told Katey, *Your life will be happy and peaceful.* Then it told Frog, *You are worrying about something that will never happen.*

The two women came out arm in arm. The sun was strong; they'd begun to get tan again. It was noon. Klaus was sitting on a bench on the opposite side of the boardwalk, across from the arcade. He was poorly dressed and unshaven; his hair and beard were almost entirely gray.

"Ladies," he called.

They thought he wanted a handout. Katey reached into her wallet for a dime.

He said, "You don't remember me."

Frog and Katey stared. He did a little soft-shoe, his hands outstretched. He doffed an imaginary hat.

"Klaus Frankovich," he said. "It's Dad!"

Frog and Katey ran down the boardwalk. He ran after them, catching up with them in a couple of minutes.

"Don't do that," he panted. "I'm too old to run."

They began to run again, but Klaus caught Katey's belt and dragged her back. He kept his finger hooked in her belt and took Frog by the arm. When Katey began to scream, he let go of Frog's arm and clapped his hand over Katey's mouth, whereupon Frog started to run again; he caught Frog's arm again, freeing Katey's mouth, and she screamed again.

"Ladies!" he said. "Please!"

They listened only because they thought he had information on Casey and Gato. He motioned to a bench and asked them to sit. The women sat. He stood above them.

"I owe you more apologies than I have time to give," he said, "but I do want you to know that I've turned over a new leaf."

"Let's go," Frog told Katey.

"I show you this creased and faded paper which is the postage receipt proving that everything I'd taken from the Louvre I sent to Tourisme as a donation. I've carried this receipt for six years to show you. I'm an American citizen now. I'm starving like everyone else and I ask for no pity. If you don't believe me, call Casey."

"Casey," Frog said. "How—"

"He's fine, fine. Misses you and won't let on. And your mother's fine, too. Sometime when we have the leisure I'll tell you what accounted for my change of heart. In the meantime, I need your help."

"Gato?" Katey said. "And Gato?"

"Haven't seen him, which is why I'm here. I must find Kitsa. Have you heard from her? Do you know where she is?"

Katey shook her head.

"Have you any idea who her clients were, who she might have stayed with if she left Paris, or even if she stayed in Paris? Or does Gato have any contacts that might know where they are? I'm assuming Gato and Kitsa stayed together—"

"No," Katey moaned.

"Let me give you a sense of the problem. It's very hard for me to get in and out of the country on my visa and loose change; and even if my skills were what they used to be, which they're not, I'd still need your help. I'm going to take care of Kitsa. I'm going to grow old with her—even older than I am. I'm old, but I'm in love."

Katey smiled. "Men have died from time to time, and worms have eaten them, but not for love."

"I get your drift. It's not that. I just keep thinking of a way she stood when she was relaxed, not that I often saw her relaxed. She could wear high heels and her feet would still hit the ground in this relaxed way, like she was barefoot and just out of the shower. Her hands were small and plump, and her fingers looked awful where she'd chewed them, but her feet were so wonderful—high arches, toes like toes on a statue, just the right size and thickness. I've spent hours looking out the windows of trains and thinking of Kitsa's feet. It doesn't do me much good, but it makes me happy."

"That's not the way we heard it from Kitsa," Frog said.

"She didn't know," Klaus said.

"I thought you had someone else," Katey said. "Someone in New York who was an accomplice."

Klaus grimaced.

"If you left her," Katey scolded, "you'll leave Kitsa."

"I can't leave her if I can't find her."

"I won't let you find her if you're going to leave her."

"I'm leaving," Frog said. "Let's go, Katey."

"Let's make lists of places we could look," Klaus said.

And surprisingly, Katey took a note pad from her purse.

Even with her back turned, walking away, Frog could feel the two of them there on the bench in the sun—a tension, like the pull of flowers in an unlit room. She didn't understand why Katey would comply with the villain's request. Klaus had probably found out that Rory was rich. Tomorrow their food would be gone, their clothes.

Rory, in the garden, was dressed entirely in white. His face was pink and he was squatting. When he saw Frog he stood, wiped his hands on a cloth, and declared accusingly, "You're not Katey's sister."

"What?"

"I can't believe five years passed before I thought of it. Katey doesn't have a sister. She has a twin brother. You're not Katey's sister."

"I'm her sister-in-law. I married Casey."

"Oh. You're—divorced?"

"Yes."

Rory looked embarrassed and annoyed. "Why didn't you and Katey tell me that?"

Frog shrugged, and offered her help in the garden.

Rory put his hand on Frog's shoulder, just as Gato had put his hand on Katey's shoulder, a decade ago. "Forget the garden," Rory said. "Tell me straight. What did Katey do in Paris?"

"How would I know? I was in Tourisme."

"I won't hold it against her. I just want to know. Was she—a prostitute?"

Frog laughed. "Whatever would make you think that?"

"She's hiding something."

Frog ruffled her friend's hair. "No, she's not. You ought to know better than that. She just acts mysterious."

"Are you sure?"

"Positive. She did just what she told you she did in Paris. She lived in the Louvre and chummed around with Kitsa and—and—with artistic types."

Rory looked doubtful.

"She'll never leave you, Rory," Frog said.

Rory handed Frog a shovel.

Frog prayed that Katey wouldn't bring Klaus back with her, and she didn't. She returned alone at about three o'clock, in a new straw hat. She spun around to model it.

Rory stood and leaned against his shovel. "I can't believe," he said, "that you bought a hat."

"Why not?" Katey asked.

"The banks are down, Katherine. We're in a Depression."

"So? You have your garden. You're *cheap*. Gato would never have denied me one hat!"

"Who's Gato?"

Katey looked at her shoes.

"Her brother," Frog lied promptly. "Our nickname for Casey."

"I never heard it before," Rory said. "You don't tell me anything. *I* never heard you call Casey 'Gato.' Why would you call Casey 'Gato'?"

"What are you doing, you two?" Frog asked, proud of the quick response that had just saved Rory from hearing about Katey's husband. Katey *wanted* to tell him, too. That was the pity. "You two don't argue."

"That's true," Katey said. "I'm sorry. That was a close call."

"I'm sorry, too," Rory said. "It's just that lately I've been feeling so left out. It's not anyone's fault. I'm not blaming you. Maybe I just miss working. Katey, let's get married."

"Don't be silly."

"Let's get married and have children."

"Children!"

"Please. Let's get married."

Frog glared at Katey. "What a wonderful idea, Katey. Why not today?"

"Why not?" Rory said. "We can do it right away."

"We can't get married," Katey said. "I'm already—"

"—his common-law wife, so what's the point?" Frog put in. Katey looked at Frog gratefully.

"Why not make it official?" Rory said.

"But we can't afford the license," Katey said hopelessly.

"Sure you can," Frog said. "Return the hat."

Frog feared that Katey would leave if she got any word on Gato's whereabouts from Klaus, but Klaus never came back. He never even wrote. He did, however, inspire Katey to write her brother, the family archivist. Casey told her freely what he knew about Gato and Kitsa. But it took Katey several months to get up the courage to write, and Casey several months to respond—by which time Frog had disappeared. Although Katey continued to correspond with her brother, she never followed up on Gato or Kitsa. Perhaps she'd finally settled into her second marriage, or perhaps she was still afraid of what she might do if she could communicate with Gato. Perhaps, too, secrecy had simply become a habit for her, just as quick exits had become a habit for Klaus. Casey would later complain to Mildred about how compulsively his relatives withheld information. Mildred said such reticence was understandable, given a father whose identity was a sleight-of-hand, given mothers who lied to themselves and abandoned their children. Still, Casey couldn't help but resent the fact that Frog never wrote, that after she left Atlantic City she sent pictures of herself to Katey and no pictures to him. What did Frog think Casey would do: track her down from various postmarks on letters to Katey, when her indifference to him was so clear? If his relatives ever felt the need for reunion—as they might have in old age—Casey never knew about it: he had long ago abandoned the prospect himself, had even stopped biking to Chamonix for the mail he received sporadically.

Katey, Frog, and Rory returned the hat late that afternoon.

Katey O'Brien Haggerty and Rory Kirn were married, bareheaded, late on a Thursday afternoon, right before the Justice of the Peace's office closed, with Frog Haggerty O'Brien as witness.

They couldn't afford gowns or cakes, but they did drop by one of the booths on the boardwalk where, for a nickel, you could have your picture taken, with your head sticking through a cardboard painting that showed the bodies of Revolutionary War heroes or sunbathers playing ball. They chose the sunbathers.

I have the picture. Katey sent it to Casey after Frog disappeared. Casey gave it to Mildred, who gave it to me.

Rory is happy in the picture, squinting a bit and grinning, his face open to the sun, a long shadow trailing his chin like a beard. He has the expression of someone who has just won a stuffed bear at a shooting gallery and doesn't want it, even feels stupid to be carrying it around, but is proud anyway.

Katey is expressionless, but under that mask you can see the odalisque's *angst*—the face she'd worn in the painting that would be stolen from the Louvre right before World War II and never recovered.

Frog's head is attached to the body on the painting that is twisted to throw a beach ball. When I saw that picture, I was almost willing to believe that Frog was my mother. Her face is a death mask. Her eyes are closed. Her mouth is stretched into a thin, impassive line. The disease must have been just setting in. To the left of the cardboard bodies they're standing behind, you can see a blur which is Frog's hand, clenched, moving toward her head.

# 15

Eight photographs of Frog Haggerty O'Brien, a.k.a. Lucy Werner Spell, were spread out on my lap, Mildred's lap, and the rest of the bench. In one of the photographs, a close-up, Frog wore my mother's diamond-and-ruby bracelet, or a similar bracelet. There was a picture of a woman who looked much like my mother, leaning against a car much like the car my mother was leaning against, in the picture she left for me, in a suit much like my mother's suit and many other Forties suits. Mildred, in fact, was wearing a similar outfit. She'd showered and changed. Her maroon suit had padded shoulders, wide lapels, a pinched waist, a slit in the narrow skirt, and a linen carnation stitched onto one pocket—it was exactly the kind of suit I'd have liked to buy myself, but I'd have worn it with some irony, and I'd have worn it in winter. It was a wool suit. It was hot and humid and there shouldn't have been a breeze, but there was enough of one to knock over a photograph balanced on Mildred's knee. The photograph fell face down in a puddle by the bag of evidence she'd brought me.

"Pick that up," she said. "I can't bend."

I picked up the photograph and dried it on the inside hem of my skirt.

"Have you no respect for property?" Mildred asked.

"It's dirty anyway. I need to do laundry."

I'd been crying all night and hadn't gotten much sleep. I'd gone to work in the same clothes I'd worn the day before, with my hair unbrushed, mascara from the day before in flecks on my cheeks, and a sallow taste on my teeth. My boss leered at me—he thought I must not have made it home after a big date. I was trying to rearrange chronologically the pictures Mildred had brought me by guessing at the progress of my mother's disease, which, by the last pictures, had made her bony and pale. In the better pictures, though, I could see that Frog, my mother, and I had the same eyes, and a certain hardness around the mouth.

"Where'd you get all these?" I asked.

Mildred had made me wait almost a week and listen to the Atlantic City installment of her story before she'd show me the pictures. She'd spoken much more slowly, much less vividly, than I was used to, as she would for the rest of the week; I thought perhaps she'd tired of her own family romance, but she insisted she was just tired.

"A lot of them were Casey's. Everyone sent Casey pictures. He was the Home Office. Some of the pictures of Frog are my natural mother's, which Casey found among her things in Tourisme. Some of the pictures of Kitsa I got from Kitsa in Hollywood. I visited her there in 1965."

"Is she still alive?"

"I doubt it. She was in a nursing home when I saw her."

"But why California? Did Gato know she was there? Did Frog? Did Klaus ever find her?"

"You ask a lot of questions."

"Actually, I can imagine Kitsa in Hollywood. I can even see her in a nursing home in Hollywood. There's something right about that. What did she do, marry some rich old film producer?"

"Never married."

"Did she live with Gato?"

"Until she got sick. Gato, who had never been kind to anyone but Katey in his life, refused to take care of Kitsa after her stroke, although she took care of him for decades—ironed his shirts, found him women and acting parts."

"So he's in Hollywood too."

"Was. Emphysema got him by now."

"They were lovers, I assume."

"Gato and Kitsa? Never. They were local color. He was an actor, your Uncle Gato, except he went under an alias which I can't recall now. Bit parts. You've probably seen him. He's the dark, aloof, melancholy extra the camera lingers on for a minute in Forties films—the bartender disdainful of the drunks."

"And Kitsa? What did she do?"

"A courtesan her whole life. She entertained the film people at bars and parties with her delightfully eccentric stories. They were always giving her things. When I visited her she gave me ten watches. Said she didn't need to know the time anymore. Gave away watches like butter cookies. The one I gave you Klaus stole for me, though."

"Why didn't they ever make a movie about her life?"

"They did. *The Wizard of Oz.*"

"No, seriously. Then Katey and Rory would have seen the movie, and they would have known Kitsa and Gato were in Hollywood."

"The Kirns didn't go to the movies much."

"But Klaus must have. Klaus would have recognized Gato."

"The only reason Klaus would have gone to the movies was to have a cool place to jerk off."

"I don't believe that Gato and Kitsa would have been in the States and not gotten in touch with Katey and Frog. You can understand Katey's desire to protect Rory from the whole mess, but Kitsa had nothing to hide. Why didn't Klaus and Gato meet in the Army? They had to get drafted, didn't they? If they took American citizenship, they would have been drafted."

"Klaus was too old to be drafted. The Army is large."

"Furthermore, I don't believe that Gato and Kitsa never made love. Neither of them had what you'd call a low libidinal drive. And whatever happened to Klaus?"

"Died."

"When? Did he ever come back to you?"

"I assume he died. He was a heavy smoker."

"Have you ever been to Atlantic City to check out Katey and Rory? When did my mother leave, assuming she is my mother as you claim? Can you explain why none of these couples ever had children? Not Casey and Frog, not Katey and Gato, not Katey and Rory, not Kitsa and Klaus?"

"Just lucky, I guess."

"With Pia so fertile, and those twin genes in Klaus? I'm the only offspring?"

Mildred yawned.

"You break my heart," I said. "You spring these cartoons on me as family, then you give me such a spotty account. I'm beginning to crave order."

"You've got more order than you can shake a stick at."

"Don't tell me what the weather was like on a Thursday in 1933 and then not tell me how Lucy turned into a Werner, or how and why she got to Cape Cod to meet my father, or who died when. There's a ten-year gap in Frog Haggerty's life!"

"I told you, I'd lost track of her."

"Mildred, I've got a vested interest now. I cried all night. I can't keep this up. Every time someone knocks me with his elbow on the subway I think he's going to whisper my name and announce he's my long-lost great-great something-or-other. I can't concentrate."

Mildred coughed. Her knees jerked and the photographs of Frog Haggerty went all over the place. As I picked up the pictures, she began to cough so hard that she couldn't breathe. A wad of pea-green sputum landed on my forearm. She raised her arms. I pounded her back with one hand. Her neck was bony and soaked with sweat. There were big veins in her neck.

"You okay?" I asked, when she stopped coughing.

She nodded. Her head was in her skirt again.

"Do you feel faint?"

She nodded yes.

"Do you want to go to my place?"

She raised two fingers in a weak V.

"Do you mean a woman who stops thefts with her bare hands is succumbing to a cough? You ought to see a doctor."

She said something I couldn't hear.

"What?"

"The heart will get me before the lungs."

Her head rose abruptly and fell on my shoulder. I stroked her hair. The contours of her scalp were soft as a child's.

"Let's go to your place," she said.

"Maybe we should take you straight to the hospital. I don't even know how to take a pulse."

"Your place. Call a cab."

I called a cab. I'd intended to confront her about how irritating it was that she kept her address a secret, but this wasn't the time. When we got to my place I fluffed some pillows for her and helped her prop herself up on the couch. She asked for bouillon. When I gave it to her she placed the mug down carefully on the end table and spent a long time searching in a canvas bag she'd brought until she pulled out a small gold goblet. She transferred the bouillon from the mug to the goblet.

"My only superstition," she said. "Casey's goblet. You know how children hold conch shells to their ears to remember the ocean? I drink from this goblet and it's like those masks the dentists use, full of nitrous oxide. I smell Casey's bourbon in there and I'm delirious with Casey. I want to have this goblet with me when I die."

"Will you knock it off with the dying already?"

"I am not seven with the chicken pox, Jennifer. I should have gone home."

"You have a 'home'? You mean you don't just sleep on park benches?"

"You're an idiot if you thought that."

"What do you expect me to think? You won't show me your place. Sometimes you're as bad as Argyle. You always want to have a card up your sleeve."

The lights went out.

"I don't have a fuse," I said. "I don't even have a key to the basement where the fuse box is."

I crossed the hall to my neighbor's. His lights were out too. He didn't have a fuse either. He was about to go back into his apartment to call the landlord, when another tenant came in and told us that the blackout was city-wide.

"Good," I said. "Maybe we won't have to work tomorrow."

At first I thought Mildred was asleep, because she didn't say anything when I told her about the blackout; but then I heard her slurping her bouillon. I went to the window. People on the street were laughing. The couple that liked to argue in front of their building had brought out a transistor radio, and people were gathering around.

I got my own radio, turned it on low, and lit a candle.

"Think of the people on life-support systems," Mildred said. "The people with artificial hearts. Eight million of us. I like this. Last time this happened, I was at a gallery opening. A hundred of us talked about art in the dark. If I could breathe, I'd be very happy."

I was happy that my apartment faced the street. The darkness, so long as I was so close to the life of the city, was almost comforting. The city had a grainy forest-green tint, like an old black-and-white photograph. My apartment had never been so dark. Usually some light from the streetlamps seeped back to my bedroom. Then there was the dial on my digital clock, the dial on my television. I wandered between my rooms a bit, my arms folded. I could just make out Mildred's outline by candlelight.

She was on her back, her head raised, her arms crossed mummy-fashion, and when the radio announcer paused I could hear her breathing shallowly, mechanically. I noticed a bad smell every time she exhaled. She'd showered, but she hadn't brushed her teeth. The smell seemed to be intensified by the darkness.

"This probably isn't much fun for people on elevators in the World Trade Center," I observed. "I wonder how long it'll take the frozen stuff to rot. Do you want me to talk and keep you awake, or stop talking and let you sleep?"

"Up to you."

"I knew a girl in college whose father found out he was going blind. They gave him about three more months. He'd already had all the operations with no success. For his last sighted months, he practiced being blind. Walked around his own house with a scarf over his eyes, memorizing the staircases and lightswitches—the lightswitches because he could still make out some patterns of light and dark. He learned how to touch-type, how to get a can under the can opener, how to crack an egg and get it scrambled. I always think about that. If I found out I was going blind, I'd see everything I could. I'd go to tropical rain forests and fireworks displays. I'd wear bright clothes—yellow rain slickers and magenta shoes—and visit gardens in full bloom."

"Shows how little you know," Mildred said slowly—so slowly that the "know" broke off from the rest of the sentence, and seemed to be "no," in connection with something going on in her body. "A common mistake. When the Americans liberated people in Auschwitz, they wanted to feed the inmates Napoleons—duck—steak Lorraine—when what they needed, those hungry people, was a nice piece of bread. Maybe a little butter. People who lose their sense of smell don't miss the Monkey House, don't miss the Botanical Gardens. Miss instead the smell of newsprint on the Sunday paper. The coffee brewing. You can remember how flowers smell. Garlic you can remember. But you miss paprika. Dill."

"I wonder if their eyes water when they chop onions."

"Miss cashews. The salt on the cashews."

"You can't smell salt."

"Ivy cut from the chimney. Licorice. Eucalyptus. Clean—clothes. The sulfur from—lit matches."

"Don't talk. It's too hard for you. Don't you think you ought to go to the hospital? I'm thinking maybe we should call an ambulance."

"Tea," Mildred said.

"Pia?"

"Tea."

Luckily, I had a gas stove. While the water was boiling I found the handle to my refrigerator and looked inside. I was confronted with the acrid smell of celery leaves that lets you know the vegetable bin should be rinsed out. There was yesterday's tuna fish and an old loaf of bread. I pressed my thumb into the side of an apple that seemed relatively fresh. On the fire escape, some of the tenants were playing guitars and singing.

Mildred sat up to blow across her tea. I offered her the apple, which I'd sliced and put on a plate.

"What are you," she said. "Kidding?"

"You've got to eat."

"Piece of bread, maybe."

"Only bread I have is maybe not so fresh."

"Soak it in water."

"Don't make me sick."

"It won't go down—otherwise."

She sucked the bread through her teeth. I ate the apple. The apple was good.

"I need to shop," I said. "Last time I didn't have anything in the house I had an apple, too. I remember because that was the night I called information in all sorts of cities, trying to track down old lovers. Most of them weren't listed and the ones that were, weren't home or were busy, except for one, who was having a party in Houston and was very stoned. I didn't even have a magazine. I was so lonely. For a while I read the dictionary, then I skimmed the phone book. Looked up my own name and all the strange names—the Orlandos and LaKisha Leatherberries. There really is a LaKisha Leatherberry. My favorite name, though, was Loveless. I was going to call all the Lovelesses in the city and invite them to a party. Maybe on Valentine's Day—pink crepe paper and big construction paper hearts."

"Take the tea away now."

"Mildred, when you feel better, let's have a party. Invite your friends and my friends. What do you say? I think it'd be an interesting crowd."

"Neither of us have friends. Anyway I won't—be feeling better."

"Sure you will, because tomorrow I'm taking you to the hospital. Hang in there, champ."

When she didn't argue about the hospital, I continued to talk, afraid of the silence. "Strangers are closer than family. You don't have to watch family. You think you know everything about your cousins, even if you only see them for a couple of hours a year, over a turkey in November, and all you've said to them since you played doctor together at age six is 'Pass the stuffing.' I don't have cousins myself. My Aunt Mara never married and my mother—well, as I've told you, Lucy wasn't exactly running home for the holidays. You didn't have a family either, if you were an orphan. Mildred? Mildred!"

I shook her hard. I thought she might be dying or dead. She wheezed and lifted her head. When I knew she'd fallen asleep on me, I was offended.

I still had some Scotch. There was no ice—just ice water. I took my drink, the candle, and the pictures of Frog Haggerty into the bedroom with me, undressed, propped myself up in bed, and examined the pictures for a while, but they didn't keep me awake for long.

Mildred jabbed me with one hand and offered me coffee

with the other. The announcer was still droning in the other room. It was still 9:35. The mug seemed heavy in Mildred's hand. She was disheveled, as if she'd been on a long bus trip; and I might have looked the same way. My sleep had been as gritty and bland as bus terminal food.

"You look better," I said.

She sat on my bed and nodded. "If I'm good, I have a week left. I've been trying to wake you for an hour. There's looting going on."

"What time is it?"

"9:35. How's that for symmetry? I just called time. They don't know when the power will be back on."

I picked up the clock and shook it as you'd shake a light bulb, then sighed. "Have you eaten yet?"

"Nothing to eat."

"We'll go out then."

"Nothing's open. I let your cats out on the fire escape."

"Hope they find their way back. I don't let them out very often."

"They're sitting on the fire escape. Don't worry."

"Are you hungry?"

"Not hungry enough to eat cat food. How about Leopold and Loeb?"

"What do you mean?"

"For cat names. Sacco and Vanzetti?"

"Nope."

"You're stuck with me now."

"My pleasure."

"I'm not leaving. Can't. Can't get down the steps. Too hot in the park. Soon it'll be bedpans and bedsores."

"Then it's doctor time."

"Why? I've been waiting for this for seventy-six years."

"Why are you so anxious to die? You don't like my company?"

"An extraordinary effort is what this conversation takes. I

have to be more thrifty with my energy. Pickpocket and piano took two months off my life. No more small talk."

"But Mildred, I don't know the first thing about dying."

"Deaths, like births, generally take care of themselves. Just fasten your seatbelt and watch."

"I don't want to watch."

"I thought you'd want to learn something. If not, I'll have to pay you for helping me. I'll call my lawyer."

"I don't want your money!"

"Got something against my money?"

"I don't want you to think—"

"You're right. Mustn't strain. You're off today. Entertain yourself for an hour or so while I take a nap. Then I'll tell you about more death, more desertion. Casey's face, smooth and calm. Sleep. I'd like to talk about Casey."

"Aren't you hungry?"

"It's not hunger. I have a tumor on my large intestine the size of a grapefruit. Can feel it sometimes, knocking like a fetus. Want to see?"

She unzipped her skirt, which was wrinkled from being slept on. I'd never realized how thin she was. Purple veins in high relief pointed to her hipbones. Her stomach was bloated. A thick scar ran down from her belly.

"What's that?" I asked, pointing to the scar.

"Oh, that." She got the dreamy look she always had when she thought about Casey. "Haven't had a uterus since before Pearl Harbor. Have you ever seen a uterus? Dime-sized. Smash one between wax paper, you could slide it through the coin slot of a washing machine. A scarlety blue they are, color of garnets, of insects' eyeballs."

"I wish the electricity would go back on," I said helplessly.

"The better to see me with, my dear?"

She smirked. She was trying to scare me—I was scared. I got a nightgown from my closet and handed it to her.

"Put this on," I said gruffly.

She undressed quickly, with her back to me. The night-gown, which was large on me, was enormous on her.

"You can sleep on the bed," I said.

"Thank you, but I've gotten accustomed to the couch."

"Why couldn't you have died last night, during the black-out, if you like symmetry so much?" I asked, to be flip, because I was scared, as she arranged herself on the couch. "That would have been pretty, don't you think?"

"Sober up," she said. "We don't have much time."

I was sober. I was sober and I swear to God, I didn't want her to die.

# 16

Pia Maginski and Helen Haggerty died within hours of each other in January 1933, from food poisoning caused by undercooked pork. It was the housekeeper's day off, and Pia had concocted a hasty rôti de porc provençale with what, so far as she knew, was Tourisme's last pig, recently slaughtered—its blood still swirled in the mushy snow out back. The beef had been gone for a year. They still had poultry, though, and occasional venison, if Casey or one of the two or three other able-bodied men left in town was feeling energetic.

The second doctor, like the first, had relocated in America. Casey stopped by Pia's house on an errand the next morning. When he didn't find them in the study, where they'd recently been spending most of their time, and when they didn't answer his call, he knew what had happened. He found them on the floor in the dining room and tried to induce vomiting, but Pia's and Helen's faces were already the telltale color of curdling blood. Their deaths were Tourisme deaths: clean in principle, messy in practice.

The house was cold, and the women were wearing almost

every article of clothing they owned, including their jewels, as if diamonds and rubies would keep their necks and wrists warm. Casey removed the jewelry, washed it off, and took it to Chamonix after the burials. He traded some of the pieces for two sides of beef, three pounds of Brie, a new refrigerator, and a red bicycle that went very fast. The rest of the jewelry he saved for future needs. The new goods he shared with the remaining denizens of Tourisme—at the time there were seventeen people left, mostly old and mostly women, so that the town resembled an old folks' home more than a resort.

Casey was known to dislike traveling, and part of the reason he left for Chamonix was to avoid visitors. Whenever someone died in Tourisme, a visit came from someone who tried to change the survivors' lives. This wasn't superstition; it was fact. The year before, Casey had buried Uncle Nose and returned to the inn, where he found the aging Klaus Frankovich. Klaus demanded Kitsa—as if Kitsa were Casey's to give. Casey knew from his childhood sweetheart's last letter that she was in Hollywood, but he didn't tell Klaus. The old man had deserted Casey and Katey as a father, deserted Pia, deserted Kitsa, killed Kitsa's father, stolen Kitsa, and scared away Frog. That was enough to produce a strong dislike of Klaus in Casey. Casey, not given to grudges, watched the old man eat stew and endured a story of rebirth, wanting the whole time to pour the stew over the old man's head, to watch the peas and noodles drip into his eyebrows and beard.

Pia and Helen, however, could not be induced to remember Klaus. Klaus tried, but even with his diligent prompting the two women would only smile and offer him tea, as they'd do for any tourist, especially with tourists so scarce.

The only visitor that death brought was Mrs. Haggerty's lawyer, come to settle Helen's estate. While he was at it, he settled Pia's. Both women had left their jewelry to Casey. Pia also gave Casey her house, including the museum. Helen's money went to a woman named Mildred Howell, whom the lawyer had never heard of, on the condition that she not be told the where-abouts of her mother's grave or anything of her mother's story.

The lawyer's wife offered Casey a pretty sum for several pieces in the museum. Casey refused. He hadn't thought about the museum in years. It was Tourisme's last asset and, as Tourisme's last citizen, it stands to reason that Casey gave the inn to a man ambulatory enough to handle its maintenance, and devoted his time—when he wasn't performing artificial respiration or burying someone—to renovating Pia's house.

In the women's twelve-year joint tenure, the house had fallen into critical disrepair. Like most eccentrics, the women had thrown nothing out, including their garbage. Insolent cats had free run of all the rooms. Stacked against the walls, some-times ceiling-high, were bottles, tires, pipes, cans, broken picture frames, newspapers, old shoes, the carcasses of fowl. The smell was so deadly that in some rooms Casey had to wear a mask to clear out the debris. He didn't know a thing about renovation. Mr. O'Brien had taken care of such work around the inn while he was alive, and until now Casey had let the other men worry about plumbing and wiring. If a fuse had blown at Pia's, the women had simply moved into another room. But now Casey wanted every room perfect. He wanted to feel as if he were seeing each room for the first time; he wanted to keep his op-tions open.

He enjoyed chopping trees and pouring concrete. The smell of wood and sweat was strong in the rain. He especially liked the fact that his heavy work was devoted to such a delicate end—the smooth union of two pieces of wood in a corner, the clean line of the pavement against close-cropped grass. He took his time. There was no rush. At night, Casey worked on the library. Its holdings stopped entirely at 1901, except for the *Britannica* that Rory had sent to Katey; even that, of course, was now out of date. So far as Tourisme was concerned, there was no automobile, Russia was still ruled by a tsar, and the radio would have been science fiction, had science fiction existed.

Casey ordered books from Paris and New York with money from the sale of the jewels. He was, by middle age, one of the most widely read construction workers in France. His Xanadu was finally completed in 1944.

Casey was forty-two. There were three other people left in Tourisme. Two of them, old women, lived in a room in his house. The other was a dim-witted son of a long-defected citizen. The boy operated the inn. Casey knew that when these people died, his wife would arrive.

One of the women died in July. Casey walked down to the inn to look for his wife, but she hadn't come yet. The second woman died in December. Casey had the flu and asked the boy at the inn to bury her. The boy slipped on some ice at the cemetery and plunged to his death.

Casey went to the balcony off his Portrait Gallery, confident that he would see a woman walking up the path.

He didn't expect her to be young. Beauty was not imperative. She didn't even have to speak English. She just had to have all of her limbs, most of her teeth, and be able to move her bowels without assistance. It would help if she were heather-scented, had green eyes and a good sense of direction, or knew something about art. Now that he had finished the house, Casey had moved all the art to the cellar. He planned to restore it, sell everything to buyers in Paris and America, buy a yacht, and spend the last years of his life with a woman on the flat blue sea.

The gallery had been the last touch in Casey's house. The small room was built in part of what had been Kitsa's bedroom, and Casey added the balcony, so he could look at the inn and the road from Chamonix. The walls of the gallery were papered with enlargements of snapshots he'd received over the last quarter of a century from Kitsa and Katey in Paris, Atlantic City, and Hollywood. Although Frog had never written him, hers was the largest picture. Frog had sent it to Katey (Katey never told Rory, which is curious, since there was no reason not to tell Rory that Frog was in Baltimore), and Katey had promptly forwarded it to Casey. It showed Frog in a light mood, blowing a kiss, outside a house in Baltimore. Casey also had a movie poster showing Gato in the background, wielding a gun.

Casey didn't get a wife that day. He had begun to think that she might not come, that he should perhaps go to Chamonix and pick a woman out. What came, the next day, was a German bomb, or at least Casey assumed it was German.

Tired of waiting in the Portrait Gallery, Casey had brought an apple into the cellar, where he was cleaning up the portrait of Maginski from the State Room. The cellar was solid. Casey felt the bomb only as a slight tremor in the foundation of the house. He went up to his balcony to see if it was raining again, for it had been raining heavily.

The bomb destroyed the inn and all of the other remaining buildings in town, which was fine—it saved Casey the trouble of razing them. It also ripped off half of his own house—exactly half. The house came apart at the center beam. One half of the house fell to the ground, flaming, clean as an orange section. Casey had run outside. From where he stood, he could see some of the rooms in the standing half, as if the house were an architect's cross-section or a doll's house—the gilded Master Bath (with Portrait Gallery and Study attached), his bedroom, the outer rooms of the Museum.

He stood on the hill and watched the other buildings in Tourisme burn. He did not scream *Fire!*; he did not cry. He knew it would rain, and it did, which was lucky, because he had no fire fighting equipment.

Most of the art was in the cellar, and safe. He salvaged what furniture he could, even the pieces that were soaked or charred, and moved them into the cellar. There he would spend most of his time for the next eighteen years, except in the summers, when he'd sleep in the exposed bedroom as he'd slept, for many of the first eighteen years of his life, in the treehouse.

Nothing in the library had been damaged, nothing in the Portrait Gallery. Those rooms, farthest from the flames, were not even ruffled, although for years they retained a roasted chestnut smell that surfaced in damp weather to remind him of Kitsa Maginski.

Casey didn't bother to rebuild.

The cleaved house, with its ragged line of falling stones like punk architecture, did well enough. In the upstairs rooms he was open to the elements as he would be at sea. He didn't report the bombing to the authorities. There was no point. What would he do, sue for reparations on a ghost town? They were unlikely to build for the comfort of one citizen; besides, even he wouldn't be there for long.

He hoped his wife would come soon, because if she didn't, he'd have to go to sea without her.

He kept the master bedroom clean, or as clean as he could, considering its exposure to snow and rain. He shaved in front of a mirror he'd salvaged. He was in perfect health. Mountain air kept his face muscles taut; exercise kept his body hard. White hair fell on his forehead, confident as snow on the Alps. His posture was good. He didn't hold his arms stiffly, away from his sides, as old men so often do. His eyes had the steady alertness of people used to solitude. He took care to keep from becoming odd. He washed his clothes weekly. He showered or bathed every other day. He swept the dust from the exposed rooms into the courtyard, now littered with ashes and broken glass; then swept it from the courtyard back into what had once been the garden, where strange and wonderful weeds, apparently receptive to the chemicals in the bomb, grew taller than Casey himself, even in winter.

The only change that Casey made in Tourisme after 1945 was the creation of a new sign at the bottom of the road leading to Tourisme, and the installation of an oil lamp there, so someone lost at that spot would head toward him.

When Mildred Howell came, Casey had just finished bathing. His hair, in fact, was not quite dry. He hadn't spoken a word to any living creature but deer, stray cats, himself, and the odd shopkeeper in Chamonix in twenty years, and he hadn't made love in forty.


Only in drama do lone men clench their fists and berate the stars. Women who sob into their pillows always hope to wake their husbands, are always aware of the camera angle, how the milligram of streetlight in the chandelier amplifies their trage- dies. But true hermits never cry. Thus Casey, alone for so long, should not be accused of heartlessness because he didn't howl at the moon, or run to Chamonix to tell his story to every bar- keeper who would listen. Nor should he be credited with excep- tional fortitude or insight. We have been told that the meek shall inherit the earth, and indeed the passive-aggressive can ap- pear quite strong. Why didn't Casey go somewhere to find his wife? If he wanted a boat, if he wanted to be at sea, then why on earth didn't he buy a boat and sail it on the Atlantic? It is hard for me to understand, just as it was hard for Mildred to understand, why Casey stayed on in Tourisme. If he loved books and art, he would have done better in Paris. If he loved the Alps, then he shouldn't have spent all his time in the base- ment with his books and his art.

Besides, he wasn't alone, not really. Even after everyone else in Tourisme had died, he kept company with his phantom wife. She was a combination of Kitsa and Frog, unlike any woman he'd ever known, an impossibility—she didn't exist.

But Mildred Howell existed and was good enough. Casey, after all, did not believe in fate. We must credit him for that. The first woman who got lost in the Alps and found herself in what had once been Tourisme would be his bride. That didn't mean she was meant to be his bride; that just meant she was the first woman who got lost in the Alps and found herself in Tourisme. It didn't have to be Mildred Howell, but it was. It had taken Helen Haggerty's lawyer three years to track Mildred down and give her a million dollars; it had taken Mildred another twenty-five years to unearth some spotty information about who her natural mother had been, and where she had died. Mildred had narrowed down the location of Helen Haggerty's grave to the Alps, and had actually stopped in a few towns on her vacation to ask after her mother, but had given up and gone to an auction. The way Casey looked at it, he'd saved himself a lot of trouble.

# 17

Mildred borrowed my tooth-
brush, allowed me to brush her hair and sat up very straight,
trying not to cough—she cleaned up for the doctor as people
clean up for their maids. She even put on some of my lipstick.
Despite her efforts, she still looked ragged.

The intern was a grandson of an old friend of hers, a
woman to whom she'd sold art. "Jack," the doctor said, extending
his hand, when I met him at the door. Within seconds he had
me pegged as a steno or a candy-striper. He was just old enough
to have practiced the gentle-but-firm gaze doctors so pride themselves on, but I was sure he already had a wife on East Seventy-
ninth Street. For the duration of the handshake I imagined his
wife at her bridal shower, gurgling over salad spinners and
Dansk flatware; Jack was on the porch with the guys, drinking
bourbon and reading the *Times*.

"You shouldn't have let them do that to Greenie," Mildred
told him. "How is she?"

"Much better. She's walking about and using her arms."

"I'd never let them do that to me," Mildred averred.

"Mastectomies are peanuts," Jack said. He sat down, the
beeper awkward as a gun against his side, and opened his black

case so clandestinely that you'd think it contained cocaine and pistols. "What's bad is end-stage congestive heart failure. You been taking the Digoxen?"

Mildred shrugged.

"How often does she go to the bathroom?" Jack asked me.

"I didn't really notice."

He glared at Mildred. "You haven't been taking the diuretics either."

"My heart's the same," she said. "It's this new tumor I'm worried about."

He pushed her shirt aside—but not far enough to see the tattoos—and listened with his stethoscope. "Fine? Want to hear the Grim Reaper chopping timber in your chest?"

"Not particularly."

"You're going to have to come back to the hospital."

"I just want something to help me breathe, that won't make me foggy."

"If you haven't been taking the Digoxen, it's a little late."

"I *did* take it."

Jack sat back and sighed. "My home treatment program was canceled, you know. I almost lost my internship. This is just a personal favor, and I'm taking a risk. The home treatment program wasn't a good idea. They're people like you who want to be treated at home, too set in their ways, more afraid of pain than of death."

"What about my tumor?"

"You expect me to take a peek at the skin and give a diagnosis? What, I go to school for seven years and I'm a crystal ball?"

"Can't you give me a rough estimate on how long it's going to take the heart to give out, and whether it's more likely that anything in the stomach or intestine will get me first?"

"You know I do coronary. I don't know shit about stomach tumors. But let me tell you a little story about hearts. I had a patient who insisted on home treatment. She had rheumatic fever as a child and her valves were damaged; naturally by the time she got scared enough to go to the hospital, we couldn't do surgery. She was old and her heart was three times the normal size. This was a strong woman, no whiner. Her heart was so big it couldn't pump; she couldn't move from her bed. We had a crateful of her medical records by the time she was gone. Her veins were so wiped out we had to give I.V.'s through the groin. The groin got infected. She had labia like an ape's, like a black bear's. Everyone was worried she'd die on his shift."

"Lovely," Mildred said.

"Then there was the angina case who had both legs amputated and an alcoholic husband, and lived in a fourth-story walk-up, and she was deaf. She couldn't hear us knock. We had to do a forcible entry. She had so much fluid in her chest you could have bred fish in it."

Jack looked mournful.

"You should have been a dentist," Mildred said.

I could imagine Mildred's records in the crate full of grotesque anecdotes. *This lady could have bought Bermuda, but she was too cheap to fill her prescriptions.*

"I'll give you two days," Jack said. "Die. Fine with me. But not on my record." He was writing prescriptions furiously. "I'm going to have my mother hit up your friends now and get them to come over here and hound you with their senile babble until you get your tail to the hospital. Try to get down those steps and you'll have a seizure. You want to die in the middle of a sentence? Fine. I don't mind. But in two days I'm going to put you into a ward of cripples and kvetches."

He turned to me. "What's your relationship to the near-deceased?"

"I'm a friend."

"A friend. You been listening to that cough, pal? You been looking at that sputum? For all we know she could have adeno-carcinoma now as well. She hasn't been in for tests in over six months."

Mildred started to say something that came out as a cough. The doctor, packing his things, watched triumphantly. "Two days," he said, as she went to open the window for air. He beckoned me into the hall.

"End stage is end stage," he said, "but she hasn't even given us a chance. Think this'll photograph well against your beige carpet?"

I was indignant. Mildred wasn't a mother I'd packed off to a nursing home. I'd helped a stranger; I didn't deserve to be rudely spoken to, and told the doctor so.

"I know," he said. "She's stubborn. Spoke to my mother about her this morning. Mom wanted a blue painting once, to go with a new couch, and Mildred refused to sell her anything unless she bought this wooden pinball machine that didn't even work. But if you want to help, get her to the hospital. Just get her to me at Bellevue."

Mildred was still at the window.

"He's right," I said, standing with her to watch Jack look at his watch and hop into a double-parked BMW. "You should go."

"I'd counted on more than two days. I need a week. I'll have to talk fast, make an effort."

"I'll visit you in the hospital every day." She didn't answer. After a while she fell asleep, and I went into the kitchen to balance my checkbook and pay some bills. I was just about to start a letter to my father when Mildred began to cough in her sleep—it didn't sound too promising. I went out to fill the prescriptions.

As I was heading back, I saw a gargoylish woman in the middle of the intersection, a shopping bag hooked over her arm, brandishing an umbrella at each passing car that splashed more mud on her mauve wool coat. Why do old women wear wool in summer? When the pedestrian light changed and I approached, the old woman grabbed my sleeve and said:

"Please. Groceries."

We got to the corner just in time to avoid getting hit by rush-hour traffic. Her eyes were pale blue, and she was short, even shorter than Mildred. She stopped to pant for several minutes, still clutching my sleeve, before she spoke again.

"The PR's help me. The blacks give me their seats on a bus. I love the minorities. I need groceries with no ingredients. At my age you can't fool with ingredients. Ice cream will do for now. I eat only Häagen-Dazs. Coffee is my first choice, carob next. Don't buy it if it's more than forty-five cents—they try to hike the prices after a blackout. The orange rind has all of the vitamins and all of the chemicals. What's an old woman to do? I almost ate a can of the vichyssoise with the botulism. You young people think the botulism is over? It's not."

"It's been nice talking to you," I said, "but I've got to run."

"Me too. I'm visiting my friend Mildred. She's sick. Jack just called. Jack is Greenie's grandson. We're all worried about Mildred. You're welcome to come. A young face might cheer her up."

I went into a corner market for ice cream, feeling defeated.

The grocer was out of Häagen-Dazs—I bought Breyer's butter almond. I also bought a can of chocolate syrup and some bread and soup for Mildred.

"That's great—perfect!" the old woman proclaimed, opening the bag. "I'd bake you a cake if you bought me the mix but it's too risky. BHA, MSG, and sodium nitrite which you can't even feed to a rat. Eating chemicals is why Greenie has long hairs growing out of her moles, why Doris Gardner got the paranoid schizophrenia. Only disease the blacks get is sickle-cell anemia so they don't have to worry what they eat. They just drink orange juice from Florida to keep away the scurvy. They don't get arthritis—play banjos on their deathbeds. How lucky it's so close. Well, young lady, you have been an angel for walking me here."

"I live here," I said. "Mildred's staying with me."

"You have her nicely set up there?" the old woman asked, not the least surprised.

Mildred was propped up on the couch, watching the TV, which at the moment was spinning vertical and horizontal malfunctions. A game show was on. The sound was up too loud.

"Hello, Harriet," Mildred said. "How nice of you to stop by. Did you meet Jennifer?"

Harriet was in my kitchen, searching for a spoon. "You can take off your coat," I called, but she didn't. Her hands and face were sweating.

"Mrs. Magershack is coming soon," Harriet said, "and she's going to bring the Countess."

Mildred gave me an apologetic sigh. Harriet sat in the chair facing the TV and was eating her ice cream, so I sat down on the floor. The intercom buzzed.

"Mrs. Magershack and the Countess," a voice said.

I let them up. Mrs. Magershack wore a cherry-colored wig and a girdle over her dress. Like Harriet, she was very short. Other than the mandatory shopping bag, she carried a small black patent leather evening bag and had a black coat thrown over her arm. The Countess was tall. Her stole was a string of multi-colored socks linked together with safety pins, and though she had an overbite which revealed a spitting space between her two front teeth, you could tell that she was once very beautiful. She had long wavy auburn hair. Her skin was freckled. She cleared her throat but said nothing.

"Out of the woodwork we come," Mildred observed.

"She's not going to share the ice cream," Mrs. Magershack observed, still out of breath from the steps. "Make her share the ice cream. Make her save some for Jack. I left the downstairs door open in case Jack comes back."

Harriet had found a can opener and was drinking the syrup out of the can. The ice cream appeared to be gone.

The Countess, who wore a very strange dress—chartreuse

silk with a train and a bustle—stood in front of the TV, block-ing Harriet's view. Harriet told her to move.

"You could have stayed with me," Mrs. Magershack told Mildred. "What's wrong with my place?" She sat down next to the Countess on the piano bench. My cats circled them cau-tiously.

"The Countess is a mite rock-happy," Mildred confided to me, as the tall woman drew some wool from her bag and began to knit. "She was turned down for Anne Baxter's role in *All About Eve* and has been some combination of Anne Baxter and Marilyn Monroe ever since. She knew your Aunt Kitsa. Believe it or not, most of these women are very accomplished."

"So how are you?" Mrs. Magershack asked Mildred.

"Could be worse."

"*Arbeit Macht Frei.*" Mrs. Magershack laughed, showing bad teeth. "In China they wake up at dawn and sweep the streets. There isn't a bubble gum wrapper in sight. In Russia there are no telephones, so they have to bug your box springs. Here you get mugged."

Mrs. Magershack slapped her arm across her other arm, squinted at me and asked, "What's my number, young lady?"

"Excuse me?"

"4389," Harriet said smugly.

I thought she'd been imitating one of the game shows, but she was talking about her concentration camp tattoo. She showed it to me proudly.

"Stop showing off," Mildred said. "We've all had hard times. How's your quilt, Countess?"

The Countess pulled from her bag a patchwork quilt that was only a quilt in name. The only materials were a square of mauve wool from the hem of Harriet's coat and several squares of striped cotton pajama; the rest was newspaper, yarn, parts of wigs, with the most dominant theme being parts of a pink plastic shower curtain. This implausible mix was somehow bound to-gether with gaudy gold thread.

I crouched beside Mildred. "These people are bonkers," I whispered.

"Don't worry. They'll leave soon. They're my friends."

"Friends! But they're mad."

"Very nice, Countess," Mildred said. She was trying to breathe.

"They don't even care if you're sick!"

"Of course they do," Mildred assured me. "You'd behave a little strangely too, if you had to live off Social Security."

"But they're so *old*, and they're all shouting. They're so much older than you."

Someone knocked. I didn't want any more harridans in my apartment. The place already stank of old age. I was tempted to pretend that I wasn't home. Even though Mildred was sick, I was a little angry with her for entertaining her hags at my apartment.

Argyle was at the door. He wore a pale blue suit and old-fashioned gangster shoes in exactly the same rich brown as his hair, which was getting too long.

"How nice to see you," I said. "Why are you wearing a suit?"

"I'm looking for a job."

"What happened to New Zealand?"

"Fell through. May I come in?"

I'd closed the door to my apartment behind me to meet him in the hall. The thought that Argyle may have suspected there was a man inside pleased me. "So what have you been up to?"

Argyle sat down on the steps in the hall. My building was clean and the steps had been recently washed, so there was no reason for him to sit down with a show of bravery, as if there were a risk of dirtying his suit.

"I'm between interviews. I'm trying to be a stockbroker now and I only have a second. I just haven't seen you for a while. You look tired."

"A *stockbroker?*"

His smile was cold and bitter. He was delighted by my surprise, as he'd been delighted when people asked why New Zealand. "I'd like to be a pole-vaulter in the Olympics but somehow it didn't seem like fast bucks, and since no show at the Met is forthcoming, I do what I can."

"But Argyle, you were doing fine before, weren't you? It relaxes you to paint apartments. What do you need so much money for?"

"The usual—cadmium yellow, travel."

"Ah." He couldn't afford the trip, so until he earned his ticket he would come to me. I imagined his honey wore a delicate gold cross. By focusing on his shoulder, I could almost imagine our intertwined arms shiny as bone in the light filtering through my fire escape, pretty to look at; but the thought of touching him stuck in my throat.

Harriet opened the door. Bad air and "Bowling for Dollars" filled the hall. From where Argyle sat, he could see the piano, the Countess, and Mrs. Magershack. But he didn't comment on the piano, which he hadn't seen before. He was too shocked by Harriet, who held a bottle of Mildred's pills in one hand and one of my shirts in the other—an embroidered Indian shirt, armored with purple and green birds and flowers.

"The Countess likes this," Harriet said. "May she have it for her quilt?"

"No, she may not."

"How many of these should Mildred take? She isn't breathing so good."

I charged into the apartment. Mildred was kneeling in front of the window. I brought her a glass of water and fed her the right number of pills. Harriet and Mrs. Magershack were running back and forth from my bedroom with articles of clothing, which they were presenting to the Countess.

"Get out of here," I screamed.

"Calm down," Mildred said.

"Out!"

They ignored me. Argyle was cringing in the doorway. Argyle liked to shock people, but he didn't take too well to being shocked himself.

"Argyle, help me get them out!"

"Don't worry," Harriet said haughtily. "We're just leaving."

"What's going on?" Argyle asked me.

"Help me carry Mildred into the bedroom."

"No, no, I can't lie down."

"Who are these people?" Argyle demanded. "You start an out-patient clinic? You rehearsing the witches from *Macbeth*?"

"Don't do us any favors," Mrs. Magershack said, leading her friends out the door.

"Pick up her feet. Get the feet end, Argyle."

Mildred's head was tilted back, her eyes closed. When she opened her eyes, she was looking at Argyle at the door, upside down.

"How cute he is," she said. "Who's that, Jennifer?"

"That's Argyle, who's not cooperating."

Mildred manufactured a grin. A clump of hair had fallen in one of her eyes; she was blinking convulsively. I moved the hair, but it didn't stop the blinking. One contact lens was visibly dislodged, eclipsing the paler green of her iris.

"Take the contact out," I said.

"Can't lift my arm. You."

I took out the lens. I'd never removed one before, and it was difficult, like braiding someone else's hair or tying some-one else's shoelaces. The lens immediately fell off my finger onto the rug. "Don't move," I said.

"Don't worry."

After a couple of minutes I found it, cupped symmetrically on one shag of the carpet, like a mushroom cap.

"I'm glad it's green," I said, putting the contact in a clean ashtray.

"You'll sit with me," Mildred said. "You'll let me talk."

"Of course, after you rest. Argyle, get her feet."

"He just left. You can't blame the boy. Some people don't cotton to death and decay."

My apartment door was open. One strand of dusty light cut across the hall. I couldn't possibly move Mildred alone. The empty carton of ice cream was on the floor beside the orange chair; Freud was licking it. So Argyle had beamed himself out as suddenly as he'd come.

I closed the door and lay down on the floor, diagonal to Mildred, my arms crossed behind my head. I found myself thinking about an episode of "The Outer Limits" or "The Twilight Zone" I'd seen as a child. I must have been four or five, but I've never forgotten. A man tosses a coin into a shoebox to pay for his morning paper. The coin stands up on its side and the paper boy says that only happens once in a million times. Sure enough, the man discovers that the coin-toss was magic, and that now he can read minds. The supervisor at the bank where he works feels threatened by him; an attractive secretary has a crush on him and is rooting for him to stand up to his boss. Later in the day, he becomes a hero by reading the minds of some bank robbers, telling the police where they plan to hide out; but then he's implicated in their plot. Actually, I'm not sure if the robbery part isn't from another show. His secretary is thinking of another man when she kisses him and his clients are plagued by landlords, cancers, balances due, until the avalanche of thoughts on a rush-hour street are giving him a migraine and, when he buys his evening paper and his coin once again lands on its side, when the same paper boy looks at him in amazement, he's glad to lose his mind-reading skill, to live alone once more in his own uncluttered mind.

I was terrified. I wasn't worried that I'd know what other people thought; I just didn't want anyone reading my mind. People on the show had such wholesome, reasonable thoughts— nothing you couldn't guess from their faces or say out loud. I was sure my thoughts weren't that likable. But what worried me more was that I had no thoughts at all—not even a brain wave.

No little beep, no tickertape. Just space. Like Dracula's corporeal form, my mind wouldn't show up in a mirror.

Skinner was sitting on the soft pedal. Freud jumped onto the keys and played, with his left front and hind legs, the first interval of Beethoven's Ninth. With the soft pedal down, the notes rang through the apartment. I couldn't help but laugh.

The TV was still on—a commercial for a new candy bar named after a basketball star; the ad's song was recorded at my studio. I could hear my own voice in the chorus: a cheerful refrain about caramel and hazelnuts.

"That's me," I told Mildred. "Hear those caramels? Hear those hazelnuts? That's Jennifer Spell, suburbanite and prodigy."

But Mildred was asleep. I reached my leg out, pointed my foot, and turned off the TV with my toes. The screen flickered green for a moment, like the tracing on a cardiogram.

# 18

Mildred and Casey were lying at opposite ends of the bathtub. The water was very cold. The house no longer had plumbing, and Casey had boiled water outside and carried it upstairs to the bath. That had been hours before. But if Mildred shivered, it was because she was happy. Her comfort with Casey was deep, real, and immediate. She knew him instinctively as Eve knew Adam. Though her hair was thin, though she had a scar on her belly thick as hemp, she could look Casey in the eye without embarrassment. His eyes were portholes revealing an internal life of sky and water—uncomplicated, but not shallow. Moods were weather on his weathered face. Now, for instance, he looked slightly overcast.

"They're all the same to you," he said. "For all you care Katey could be Kitsa, I could be Gato. You couldn't tell us apart."

"That's true," Mildred said. "I could point to the different people in the Portrait Gallery, but you're right; they all sound alike."

"Kitsa was the way gold flashed on her wrist. Gato was the deliberateness of his walk, a caution in the way he set one foot down in front of the other. If you're going to be my wife, this has to be real for you. Even as old ladies, Pia and Helen weren't quite alike. Helen was blue, and Pia was a shade of pink between rose and salmon—the color red velvet turns when it fades. Katey was green, of course, and Kitsa was red; I was pale yellow and Frog was something like mauve. Gato was blue like his mother, but he was a much deeper blue than Helen."

"Helen what?"

"Helen Haggerty. I told you."

"Helen Haggerty, did you say? Was that the Irish tourist's name?"

"Yes."

"The other one that Kitsa's lover impregnated?"

"Yes. Pay attention."

"Where was she from?"

"Detroit. And Klaus Frankovich was always gray to me. An invidious tenement gray."

"Klaus Frankovich? You're not serious."

"You can understand why the Grand Progenitor chose to use an alias. Did I call him Jim O'Brien before?"

"I believe you did."

"O'Brien is faster to say."

"Good Lord. How do you spell that? Klaus Frankovich? Are you sure?"

"Why are you dwelling on that?"

"I'm going to faint."

"You already fainted."

"You did say Helen Haggerty. You did say Klaus Frankovich impregnated her?"

Casey studied Mildred carefully.

"Howell. Howell. Howell, right?"

"Right."

"You said it days ago. I didn't pay attention."

"I didn't pay attention to Haggerty."

"Are you the Howell—"

"Indeed."

"The other child. The natural one put up for adoption who got the money?"

"I'm the natural one?"

"Right."

"There's a relief."

"You got the money?"

"Right. Before you is the Mildred Howell who has made a concerted effort not to find out her natural mother's story, not to track down her natural brother and sister, and not to find her mother's grave. Who decided not to dwell in the past. Who speaks this calmly only because she doesn't believe you."

"I'll be. So you knew Klaus Frankovich."

"He picked me up in a New York bar in 1919 and put me to work. I'd just left home. I was his art pimp. He loved me for long enough to put me through college. So you're my brother. I sleep with two men in my life and they're father and son. What does that make me, the Holy Ghost?"

"You slept with him? But Lord, he's a monster."

"To put it mildly. I suspected another woman. When I inherited the money, he took a hundred thousand to invest in art, then disappeared. Very on-the-level he was claiming to be in those days. I never saw Klaus or the money again. Still, I felt grateful. If it weren't for Klaus, I probably would have returned to Detroit like the prodigal daughter and worked in a factory my whole life until I wound up in the suburbs with a crushed velvet sofa and a husband in plaid shorts."

"If you were lucky."

"If I were lucky, yes—a dog begging to be let out and the neighbor's dog crapping on our azoysha."

"I'm jealous."

"Of Klaus? You're a little old to expect a virgin."

"I love you, Mildred."

"Sorry, brother."

"I'm not your brother. That's the beauty."

"Beauty? Like a Rube Goldberg cartoon of a better mouse-trap!"

"All I know is that we're the only two offspring of the century's biggest chain-birth who could conceivably marry."

"Hush."

"I'll hold you. You're cold."

"Probably because I died of shock."

"I'm not Klaus. Be thankful for small—"

"Don't say it."

"All right."

"Just hold me."

Both leaned forward to meet at the center of the tub. Their embrace was a wrestling hold. Eventually Casey helped Mildred shift so that she was in between his legs, her back against his chest. They shared a small, tight sleep—cozy but hard to maintain, like Jonah's in his bower. Both of them dreamed about rooms and rooms opening into quicksand and forests, quicksand and forests closing into more rooms. But the dreams were vague and slow enough not to disturb their sleep; and their transitions from landscape to room were effortless, seemingly without consequence.

The next several weeks were spent cataloging Casey's art.

Mildred gave him estimates on his paintings, statues, and curios. He gave her the pieces she particularly liked. Mildred guessed that his holdings were worth just over three million, not counting the pieces he'd given her (which were worth another half million—Mildred had good taste), or the forgeries. More than a few of his paintings were forgeries.

Every time that Casey tried to return to the story of Tourisme, Mildred cut him off to talk of her own past. She told him things she'd never told anyone, not because the stories were so personal or even so unusual, but simply because she'd spent a good number of years trying to forget them. She told him about the working conditions in Detroit factories and about having her head shaved for lice. She told him about her battle for admission to Yale, an arduous process that had gotten her name in the papers briefly and helped Helen's lawyer to locate her. She told him how bad she'd felt going to college to study the world's riches, her tuition paid by funds from stolen art, when she'd seen the country starved and spiritless, the country and herself with it. Each stray cloud that passed over the house reminded her of something else she simply had to tell Casey, and he listened, because the sound of her voice was enough, just as the fact of her skin had been enough when he'd first touched her. But Mildred was edgy. When Casey mentioned the boat, Mildred would laugh or change the subject. Finally she said:

"I'm not marrying you. I'm not getting married and going on a boat."

"Why not?"

"I have to get back to New York."

"You don't mean that."

It was dusk in the master bedroom, the only bedroom. From the bed they had a view of most of the Portrait Gallery. Frog wasn't watching them. In fact, no matter how Mildred moved around in the bed, she couldn't get Frog to smile at her.

"I assume there's public transportation from Chamonix," she said.

"Yes, but none to Chamonix."

"Doesn't your car work?"

"I got it going after the bombing but it died in the winter of '59."

"Do you think you could get mine going?"

"I don't know much about cars."

"May I ask how you were planning to get your art to Paris? Were you going to walk there with two tons on your back?"

"I was going to walk to Chamonix and rent a truck."

"How long is the walk?"

"Depends on how fast you walk. I'd estimate five days to a week."

"Charming," Mildred said.

She put on the robe Casey had lent her and walked to the edge of the bedroom. She toed some dust and dead leaves off the second story. The robe was red satin hemmed with emeralds; it had been Pia's.

"Why don't you want to marry me?"

"I couldn't stay here. I'm not the least bit interested in living on a boat. You wouldn't want to move to New York, would you?"

"New York? Not at all."

"You see?"

"But you love me."

"I think I may well love you, for what it's worth."

"Not much?"

"Depends on whether or not you think love entails giving up the world."

"I don't think you're used to staying with people."

"I've been single for quite a few years," Mildred admitted.

"But you love me."

"I love New York, too. I love art."

"There's art here. If you want, we won't sell all of it. We can buy a smaller boat and have a gallery on board."

"It's not the same. You can't hang art in a boat. You can't hang art in a shelled building; you can't hang art in a forest."

"Why not?"

"You just can't."

Their lovemaking that night had the desperation of last rites.

The next day was sunny. The engine of Mildred's car turned over; the condenser was the problem. The car was going to stall on and off to Chamonix, but it would make the trip if it didn't rain.

"You were beautiful fixing the car," Casey said. "I enjoyed watching you. You'd be perfect on the boat."

"The boat again?"

"Only God would send me a woman who knows how to fix a car."

"I don't know how to fix cars, Casey. I just know cables, condensers, and filters. And I don't know a thing about boats."

"You could learn."

"Casey. Please."

Mildred was looking around for something on which to wipe her hands. Casey took her hands and put them around his waist.

"You'll get grease on you," Mildred said. "This is hard."

"A kiss?"

Mildred gave him one.

"I'm not going to get sad," Casey said, "because you'll be back."

"You're sure of that."

"Positive. Is everything in the car?"

"Yes. I'll write."

"Don't. I don't go to Chamonix for mail anymore. Just hurry back. I'll give you a year."

Mildred smiled.

"Okay," he said. "A year and a half."

Mildred rode to Chamonix with the grease from the car still on her hands. Only when the stewardess served her cocktails on the flight did Mildred realize she still hadn't washed her hands. The grease smudged the champagne glass. There was grease in the pores of her tweed skirt, in her knuckles and cuticles. Maybe you *could* hang art in a shelled building, just as you could serve potato chips in a thousand-dollar faïence dish. As she lost view of the ground on the plane, Mildred finally understood Tourisme. Her understanding, when she returned to New York, made her a prime target for Pop Art. The customers Mildred had so carefully prepared for Abstract Expressionism were now talked into Oldenburgs and Dines. But as soon as Pop and Op began to sell—and they sold quickly— Mildred tired of them, turning instead to Minimal Art. When the customers who had just been talked into Rauschenbergs were ready for pink "installations" in their guest bathrooms, Mildred gave up and returned to the Baroque and Rococo work she'd specialized in all along. Pop and Op and constructions, she told her clients, were jokes which everyone at the party had already heard. But it was too late, or not late enough. With masking tape still rampant on the museum floors, the world wasn't yet ready again for kitsch angels. So after a little over half a year, many of Mildred's clients had dismissed her as hopelessly old-fashioned.

Furthermore, New York was noisy. Food was expensive. The garbage collectors went on strike and the streets stank. Women's skirts were so short that their panties showed when they bent; they wore huge bowls with live goldfish in them for earrings, and through open windows in summer Mildred heard music that sounded like the assembly line where her adoptive father had worked. Laundry that had been hung out to dry got filthy from the polluted air. Suits she sent to the dry cleaner's never came back, and people were constantly trying to take her purse.

Mildred's itch to get back to New York, she decided, had been nothing more than the vacationer's longing to be settled again. She wasn't attached to the city—she was just fond of clean sheets and towels. Casey, like the south of France, had seemed too pretty and peaceful to own for life. Mildred had lived in New York for too long to believe in the free lunch. But Casey wasn't free. In order to have him, Mildred would have had to give up time and place. That was the final step. She would no longer have to be anywhere by any particular time. Casey had been at peace that way; he wanted to share peace with her on a boat, on the ocean, going nowhere. Mildred had claimed she wanted her freedom, but the fact is that her life was always framed. And now the frame around her life had gotten too ornate, dwarfing whatever delicacy of thought and touch she might have shared with Casey O'Brien. If she really didn't know Casey, all the better. She'd known Klaus, or so she'd thought. She'd known her job at the factory. She knew the view from her twelfth-story window. But now it was time to forsake security for strength.

Seven months had passed. Mildred sublet her apartment overlooking Central Park and moved her art into the basement apartment that she and Klaus had used to hide their stolen art. At the time that they rented, of course, Greenwich Village was not yet a village, and their hideout was as safe as Tourisme had been in the Alps—at least as safe as it had been, before Klaus and the ax murders.

She flew to Paris, rented a car, stopped in Chamonix for a late dinner, and arrived in Tourisme by daybreak.

Casey didn't seem to be around.

The house was tidy enough but wet. The rugs and furniture were covered with leaves and soaked in snow.

"Casey," Mildred called.

The portraits were still up in the Portrait Gallery. There were none of Mildred. The bed was made. In the basement, the art was crated and stacked in a corner. The large desk that had been in Parnell's study was in the center of the room. Mildred wondered how on earth Casey had moved it. On the desk was a catalog of Casey's holdings in Mildred's hand, and a note in Casey's hand:

By the time you read this I'll be around the world. I'll pull into port on New Year's Eve, 1965. Wait for me at the Statue of Liberty. The art is yours to dispose of as you see fit. I love you.

Mildred went back to Chamonix to rent a truck and seven strong men.

"This must be where the lunatic lived," one of the men told Mildred, when he saw Tourisme. "Are you looking for the tall hermit? He's dead. He had an appendectomy and tried to escape from the hospital, but he couldn't have gotten far, with the stitches so fresh and all that malnutrition and frostbite."

Mildred said, "Put the crates in the truck."

By the time the shipment of art arrived in New York, Mildred had packed up most of her own art and quit her job—she merely notified the clients she hadn't already alienated that she would no longer be available. She closed her bank account, put money in a Grand Central locker just in case, and was on the ferry first thing in the morning on December 31, 1965, hoping that Casey would show up in time for her birthday at midnight, but vowing not to be cross if he were a little late.

A police officer came by around dinnertime and said she couldn't stay on the island after dark.

"But I'm expecting my husband back from sea," Mildred said.

"Sorry, lady. We close at dusk."

He tried to strong-arm her onto the ferry. A crowd of tourists watched the old lady at the base of the statue try to fight the officer off. He took out his club.

"You're not going to hit an old lady," Mildred said. At that time, she was still a lady—elegantly dressed, wearing an outdated diamond brooch, and a bright suit in the latest mainstream fashion. She slipped the officer a fifty and promised him that she'd leave on the first morning ferry.

The next dusk, she was still there, and she had to give the officer a hundred dollars to let her stay another night.

By the next day she was more than a bit ruffled. She hadn't eaten. Her stomach was complaining, and she would have liked to brush her teeth, but she felt the intoxicating freedom she hadn't felt for a year, since the time she noticed the grease on her hands. She had no intention of leaving. She didn't believe that Casey was dead, and she wasn't going to lose him twice.

But there was a different officer that day. This one was overweight; his face had no character.

"He may not come," Mildred told him, "and in a way you're right: it's silly for me to stay here. If he comes, he'll track me down. Casey wouldn't be scared of New York. He waited all those years for me; the least I can do is wait another day for him. I'm starting to like the idea of a boat. All I need now is Casey. If he's dead, I'm not sure what I'll do. I certainly can't stay in the basement; the crates take up the floor space and besides, it reminds me of Klaus."

The officer called other officers, who called a special unit, who straitjacketed Mildred and took her to a state mental hospital.

None of the patients at the hospital could swallow right. They paced back and forth like people waiting for a train that would never come. One patient anointed Mildred; another did an Indian war dance around her; but most of them just stared with mouths that didn't close. The psychiatrist was upright and affected—Mildred detested him. She gave the psychiatrist a thousand dollars, passed every test of sanity with flying colors, and was sent back to the police station; there she was fined for defying an officer and sent home on her own recognizance.

She found it difficult to sleep on the floor in her apartment. She vowed to unpack in the morning and sell enough things to make the apartment habitable again. In the meantime, as a tribute to Casey and freedom, she'd sleep in the park. The park was cold, and as she fell asleep, she could almost imagine herself in Casey's house, open to the sky.

The next day, in a fit of grief, Mildred got herself tattooed.

She'd narrowed her dislikes to money, Klaus, doctors, and chic; her likes to Casey and art—real art. She did all of her traveling in those first few months. She went to Hollywood and spoke with Kitsa. Kitsa was already senile, but her eyes were, indeed, green and brown; she was hospitable and had some fascinating stories to tell about her childhood with Casey and Katey. Mildred felt that Kitsa's senility was a calculated attempt to remember nothing but the good times.

Gato was not hospitable. He didn't want to talk to Mildred, and was only interested in finding out if she had any information on Katey.

Mildred found Rory in Atlantic City. He told her how sweet Katey had been, how accommodating. She'd died in childbirth, along with the child. He told her how the bank in Atlantic City had stayed solvent during the Depression thanks to his generosity, and how disappointed he was that Frog had disappeared. Rory still didn't know about Katey and Gato, and Mildred saw no reason to tell him. She flew back to Hollywood and told Gato that Katey was dead.

"I should have gone to her like Heathcliff," Gato said. "Shot Frankovich in the mouth and gone right up the stairs to her bedside."

"You couldn't shoot anyone," Mildred said.

"Maybe not then. But try me now. Give me Klaus Frankovich and a gun."

Mildred could see more of Klaus in Gato than in any of the other Frankovich offspring. Gato had Klaus's brooding criminality, the veneer of strength like a five o'clock shadow. Katey must have been fooled into thinking that tough people have tender hearts, which is not the case; their hearts are brittle and crack rather than break. Mildred couldn't love another Klaus after having loved Casey. Besides, she didn't have room for another tattoo, and she was tired of traveling.

Let the other children of Tourisme get buried alive. Mildred Howell intended to keep moving—but not too far. That would betray Casey's legacy. She would be true to him by not forgetting, but moving on. She would go only far enough.

In New York she bought a pocketknife to protect herself and to slice the watermelon which she bought from a street vendor and ate in the park. She spat the seeds into the grass. Before she spat each seed, she rolled it around against the back of her teeth until she could feel it, smooth and whole, in the center of her mouth. Sometimes she spat out a seed at the very instant that a traffic light changed and a dog lifted its leg against her bench. Such synchronicity pleased her, made her think of Casey, made her think that she didn't have to think of Casey, because she was finally living the kind of life that Casey would have wanted her to live, and that was enough—that and the watermelon and the sunset, pink and gold, in the temperate park.

There is one thing that troubles me about all this, that still bothers me.

At the moment that Mildred ceased to be a working woman in January 1965, she still had half a million dollars in a locker and another half a million dollars worth of art in an apartment, not counting the money from Helen Haggerty's will in a bank in Detroit. In the twelve years before she died, she managed to smuggle most of the money she'd earned as a dealer to Detroit, tax-free. Why didn't she give the art to the Met, the money to the American Heart Association—or, if she hated doctors so much, to the Committee to Restore Venice, to revolutionaries working to overthrow the Shah? If she lived as she did because she was cheap, then her history is not remarkable. In fact, it is reprehensible. Mildred then seems mindless and dated as the children of the Sixties who, with their parents' money, bought marijuana, copies of the *I Ching*, and vans to travel to Woodstock. The fact that Mildred had once been poor doesn't exonerate her; it only makes her love of money understandable. For I do believe that Mildred loved her money intensely, maybe even more intensely than she loved Casey. I think she knew that only money made her more appealing than Harriet or Mrs. Magershack, and I think she felt guilty about this, however unconsciously; I think that guilt, not love, made her live for so long in her story.

I could be wrong. I *hope* I'm wrong, because I have lived for a long time in Mildred's story as Mildred lived in the story of Tourisme.

Before I'd met Mildred, if someone in a red satin robe hemmed with emeralds whined to me that she didn't know what to do and demanded pity, I would have told her to go fly a kite. Or I'd have told her to sell the robe and buy some time to practice the piano, because at the piano she wouldn't have to think about herself so much. I don't ask for praise for having followed my own advice. I don't ask for praise for having moved on with my life, because I had no choice.

# 19

At work we were recording a public announcement about activities for senior citizens. The man they'd sent over to do the commercial was a cuddly seventy-year-old with soft white hair who was obviously glad to have something to do. My own father had retired from the symphony years before and was now amusing himself with his coin collection and a quartet composed of other senior citizens. I hadn't seen him since March. He could still hold his liquor, but his movements were slower and he had the taut sadness in the neck and shoulders that makes old people look short-waisted. I'd talked to him on Father's Day. The cellist from his quartet had been going in for surgery that afternoon—I'd never even called back to see how she did; I hadn't even sent a card. To compensate for my lousy daughterhood, I was very kind to the man doing the commercial. I brought him his coffee and adjusted the air-conditioning for him, prompting my boss and co-workers to tease me that maybe I'd missed a calling as a nurse.

I had a brief fantasy about fixing Mildred up with my father before I remembered that Mildred wasn't the marrying kind.

After work, right outside the office, I almost collided with a timid blonde woman pushing a stroller. You don't often see babies in this part of town. I excused myself. The woman smiled; I knew right away that she was not American, that she spoke little English, and that the child wasn't hers. The baby was dark, and in its hands was a rather large clock with no face and no hands. "A *clock?*" I said. The baby smiled. The woman smiled and shrugged. We walked in opposite directions.

This incident seemed particularly portentous, although it was no more unusual, after all, than the mother and teen-age son I saw several blocks later who were exactly the same height and had exactly the same features, the same look of aimless anticipation. I resolved that as soon as I got home, I would discuss New York with Mildred Howell. I was so looking forward to her observations that I forgot she was sick, but I remembered at once when I saw her sitting on the couch, holding a glass of 7-Up, breathing carefully.

"Hospital time," I said.

She said, "I'm fine."

"Walk to the hospital while you're fine and just check in for a few minutes with Jack."

"I'm not that fine."

"He'll come for you tomorrow, you know. He said he'd huff and puff and blow your door down."

"Pshaw."

"If you're going to stay here, I suggest you take a shower, as I'm about to do."

"Don't worry. I won't be here much longer."

"That's right, because you're going to the hospital."

"That's right. The big hospital in the sky."

"You wish."

"Actually, I wish nothing of the kind. I plan to go straight underground and be converted into worm food."

"Wouldn't you rather be cremated? I'm going to be cremated."

"Cremation is tacky."

"Never showering is tacky. On that note."

In the shower, I let the steam be a dissolve that moved me into the future, when I'd be trim and relaxed, reading a French paper at an outdoor café in Paris, looking up occasionally at Frenchmen or at the chunks of Roquefort in my salad. I had the studious calm of a jazz musician savoring every minute of the break between sets. Nothing in my manner indicated that I hated eating alone, that I was mortified to ask where the bathroom was, that since I was ten I'd been dying to live at least one day of a charmed life and that, at least so far, I hadn't.

I came out of the shower wrapped in a towel to find Mildred gesturing to me energetically from the couch.

"Sit down," she said. "I almost forgot."

She pressed a key into my palm. Attached to the key was a piece of costume jewelry—a peacock fashioned out of big fake diamonds, emeralds, rubies, and sapphires.

"Sure is ugly," I said.

"You don't like it? Sell it. That isn't costume jewelry. Get yourself a nice condominium or take a couple of years off to think in Paris."

"I was just thinking about Paris."

"I wore that brooch the New Year's Eve that Casey didn't show. The key is to my apartment on Christopher Street. I'm about to tell you the number of the building and you should remember it."

"Lord, Mildred, your breath is torture," I objected, as she whispered the number in my ear. "What's there?"

"Enough. Slip the rent in cash under the landlady's door on the first floor each month. It's only fifty dollars—the building's rent-controlled. Jennifer, you're not in my will."

"I didn't expect to be in your will."

"I left my lawyer's number behind the nutmeg on your spicerack. The minute I die, call him in Detroit and let him know. He'll take it from there. Don't mention the art to anyone. You're going to have to be very careful about how you move the art out of the apartment. I suggest that you take the peacock to Karl Weldon. Tell him you knew me and demand cash. Don't take less than $400,000. If he says he can't pay that much, or insists he can't get cash, tell him you'll go to Gus. It would help if you found a friend with a gun. You'll have to use New York as a base for moving the goods, so get an unlisted number. Don't try to sell anything abroad because you'll never get through customs. Take the brooch money to Maine or New Hampshire and put it in a safe deposit box under a false name. Don't try to open a savings account—you'll never get away with it. Try to keep moving the money around. If it gets too complicated for you, you may need to get an unscrupulous accountant."

"It's too complicated for me already. How much money are we talking about?"

"I'd say a couple million."

"Funny. I wouldn't have the foggiest what to do with a million dollars."

"You'll think of something."

"The Government will probably want some of it."

"Not if you play your cards right."

"Actually, I'd like a roll-top desk."

"It's yours."

"Or I could go to China. I've always been something of a Sinophile."

"I'm going to sleep now," Mildred said.

"Have you taken your pills?"

"Yes. Good-night, Jennifer."

After a couple of minutes I said, "Don't you think you'd be more comfortable if you lay down?"

"Can't lie down anymore."

"Would you like to rest your head on my shoulder?"

"No thanks."

"More pillows?"

"Good-night," Mildred said.

I sat with her in the living room until I was sure she was asleep. She snored jerkily. It wasn't yet dark. I went into the kitchen and called my father. He said his cellist had recovered fine. He said he was glad I'd called, and asked if I'd come to visit soon.

"Soon," I said. "Very soon."

We chatted. When I got off the phone, Mildred called me.

"Don't go to the morgue," she said. "Let Harriet or Mrs. Magershack identify the body. Or Jack. Jack might be best."

"Anything else, cheerful one?"

"Yes. You may want to get in touch with Rory Kirn. Take a couple of days at the beach."

"Do you want to go to the beach? Maybe that would help."

"You're a good person."

"How nice of you to say so."

"I mean it. You should believe that much. When you wake up in the mornings you should look at yourself in the mirror and say, 'I'm a good person.' Where did you put the brooch?"

"It's in my pocket now, but I'll put it in a safe place."

"Put it in the box of cornstarch in the refrigerator."

"Okay. Now get some rest."

"Another thing. About the watch. Don't sell it. Promise me."

"Ever?"

"Ever. I'd rather you lost it at the beach than sell it. Promise?"

"Promise, but Mildred, why are you so attached to the watch?"

"I've had it for fifty-seven years. It has been ticking for fifty-seven years. I have never misplaced it or overwound it. Old people get very attached to their watches."

"You're taking a chance, giving it to someone who goes through ten pairs of gloves each winter."

She squeezed my hand. The phone rang. It was Argyle. He wanted to apologize for how he'd been acting. He knew he hadn't been nice. Freud sat in my lap as Argyle told me how confused he was, how he wasn't utterly convinced that he could make it as a painter, how he didn't enjoy earning a living. I tried to think of him as he was when we first met. It was still winter then. One morning after I'd spent the night at his place and overslept, when I got done dressing, Argyle stood at the bathroom door with a cup of coffee. As I was putting on my shoes, he brushed my hair. And as I put on my coat he was wrapping my scarf around my neck and handing me my gloves. He was so warm. But now he sounded drunk, and I kept thinking about his Seattle sweetheart. He asked me if I'd like to have dinner later in the week. I told him I'd see.

For some reason, I was still thinking about my father: how his glasses sit on his nose and the way his face scrunches up when he plays the violin; the slight smile he has when he has been playing the same passage over and over and finally gets it right. I remembered in particular the way he sat on my bed the night Lucy died: how his grief went straight into his bones, into the defeated way he sat; but how his grief went so deep it was entirely mute.

When I got off the phone, Mildred was asleep again, one hand tucked under the pillow, relaxed as the model in a Sealy Posturepedic ad. I felt like playing the piano, but I didn't want to wake her, so I spent the rest of the evening in bed, doing a crossword puzzle and thinking about my father.

My theory about people, which I never had a chance to check out with Mildred, is that in your first interaction with anyone—the first time you chat in line at the grocery store or shake hands at a party—you know everything you will ever know about that person. You know exactly what will happen between the two of you. Time may rarefy that knowledge, but consciousness is mostly used to suppress knowledge, for if you were conscious of all you know you'd be paralyzed. Confronted by how much would go wrong, you'd simply cry. If I'd paid attention to the way Argyle held his beer can at the party where we met, I'd have known exactly why we wouldn't get along. Everyone else was drinking out of a glass. Not only did Argyle insist on the can, but he wouldn't use a coaster—wouldn't, in fact, even *put down* the can, even when we were dancing: I felt its coldness on my neck, along with Argyle's infamous two-fingered stroke. I'm sure that his mother got him to clean his room by commanding him to go out and play.

Mildred was still asleep when I left for work in the morning. I didn't have to listen to her heart to make sure she was alive because she was breathing noisily. I bent down to stroke her sweaty hair, to kiss her near her eye. She shifted. The texture of the couch was imprinted on half of her face. I turned down the air-conditioner and covered her with the quilt from my bed.

Outside, the humidity had been somehow sucked out of the air—the day was embalmed, almost too pretty. All of the drunks and cripples were hibernating, replaced by an uncanny number of young men. One, in a white suit and jogging shoes, was straddling his briefcase, waiting for the light to change, reading the paper. Another, with an ass like marble, walked a Great Dane. But the man I liked best was struggling with a large, flat box which was obviously too much for him. I saw him first from behind: his back was distinguished by the luscious oval of sweat on his shirt. He put the box down and rested. I flanked his side and asked if I could help. He wore round pink glasses. His eyes were a startling green when he turned to me, even greener than Mildred's; and when he said "No thanks, but thanks for asking," I was blessed with a zoom shot of his tongue, the same shade of pink as his glasses. I was tempted to suggest he leave the box right there and come home with me—we'd be quiet, we'd close the bedroom door, we wouldn't wake Mildred. He might have done it, too. But I left him there with his box— a painting, perhaps, or a mirror for over his bed. When I got to work, I was sour in that scintillating way you can become when you're in love with someone you'll never see again.

# 20

Mildred Howell died of natural causes on a bench in Washington Square while I was at work.

The policemen who took her body to the morgue that Tuesday morning found on her person a black plastic comb, a telephone number written on a piece of newspaper, and a photograph of a man in old-fashioned clothes posing in front of the Alps.

They would have found more, but her purse and bag had been stolen before the police arrived, which means that someone in New York City is now in possession of a seventeenth-century gold goblet worth about twenty thousand dollars and all of Mildred's pictures of my alleged relatives, except for the ones of Frog I'd been examining in bed the week before.

The telephone number was Jack's at Bellevue. He identified the body and ordered an autopsy. Mildred had been beaten when she was mugged; Jack wanted to see if the black-and-blue marks on her abdomen had contributed to the cause of death. Perhaps if she'd died of a mugging, Jack would have felt less guilty. But the autopsy showed, not surprisingly, that Mildred had died of a seizure due to congestive heart failure, probably aggravated by the mugging and by the swallowing of a large labeled key, which turned out to open a locker in Grand Central Station.

The locker contained approximately three hundred thousand dollars in cash and coins, neatly sorted and stored in socks. Most of the coins were silver, adding several thousand dollars to the total.

I found all this out in half a minute from the six o'clock news on fifteen or twenty televisions in a store window, on a corner where I'd been waiting for the light to change.

I'd called Mildred from work at around ten and she hadn't answered. I figured she was still asleep. When she still didn't answer at noon, I told Leland that I'd lost a filling and that my mouth was killing me. Mildred wasn't at my apartment. I spent the day looking for her in the park and the outlying area without success. I knocked violently on the door of her apartment on Christopher Street, but didn't have the courage to return with the key—she'd instructed me not to find her dead. I called all the hospitals and gave a description of her, but they said she hadn't checked in. After that, when I didn't know what to do, I heard about her death on all of the televisions.

They had no pictures of her. They hadn't bothered to photograph her corpse in the park—she wasn't newsworthy until the money turned up, and until the writers decided it was a slow day for World Events. As the announcer talked, the footage on the screen behind him was of bag ladies, chosen at random, in rapid succession—a sort of bag lady pageant, multiplied on all of the screens. Apparently they assumed Mildred was a bag lady because she had been sleeping in the park. They showed a woman with a purple wig like a space helmet trying to cross a street and someone I was almost positive was the Countess, her back to the camera, checking out a trash can in Central Park. The longest footage, though, was of the ugly, gum-chewing bag lady with long gray hair and pale green pedal-pushers who hangs out at Grand Central Station. I was outraged that they would make a correlation between this monster and Mildred Howell.

They interviewed Jack for ten seconds at Bellevue. Jack looked the way doctors always do on TV—sympathetic yet brisk, because so many living patients in the wings need attention. "I don't know why she'd swallow the key," Jack said. "She didn't have all of her marbles. Since she had my number in her hand at the time of death, it's possible that she was going to call me as I'd told her to, but then it's hard to understand why she swallowed the key."

No it wasn't. She hadn't expected to get mugged. She had no idea that anyone would do an autopsy. She wanted Jack, not me, to identify the body. She wanted the money in the locker to stay in the locker.

The announcer closed by remarking that there was a lead on a young girl who might be able to provide more information on the cause of death or the source of the money. Fifteen or twenty of him looked straight at me as he talked.

Then all of the televisions switched to a commercial about hair conditioner you could use every day, and another commercial about a deodorant so good you didn't have to use it every day. After the commercials came the rest of the local news—a baby rescued from flames, a twelve-year-old shot by his younger brother during a game with their father's gun—and more commercials; then the sports and the weather (hot). I was so numb that I stood there until a man switched off all the televisions, let down an iron bar over the front of the store, put his hand on my shoulder and asked if I was all right.

I turned back to the street and was trying not to look at the headlines at the newsstand when a huge, bad-complexioned black man wearing a gold power fist on a chain and a rayon shirt depicting the Moulin Rouge grabbed my arm and said:

"You. You know. Who's the chick who gets turned to salt?"

"What?" I said.

"She's in the Bible. She looks back and gets zapped into a salt statue."

"Lot's Wife?"

"Lot's Wife!"

He let go of my elbow and slapped his thigh. "I *knew* it." He disappeared into a clump of commuters, turning to blow me a kiss. I stood very still for a moment, then began to walk home, crying.

Only when I rounded the corner to my street did I realize that I couldn't go home. They'd be looking for me. Sure enough, there was an officer in front of my house, in a marked police car, reading the paper and drinking coffee from a styrofoam cup.

I needed the peacock brooch and the key out of the cornstarch box, plus the number of Mildred's lawyer in Detroit. I braced myself and walked to the police car.

"Waiting for me?" I asked.

The policewoman looked up from her paper. She was a husky woman with thin arms, broad shoulders, and a voice much too high for her size. "Should I be?"

"I'm Jennifer Spell."

"What's wrong?"

"I'm the girl Mildred Howell was staying with."

She was puzzled.

"The lady who had all the money in the locker?" I said. "The one who died this morning in the park?"

She drew a cigarette from the pocket her badge was pinned to. "Just heard about that on the radio. Actually, I'm a traffic cop. Lot of people have been speeding around here. Pedestrian was knocked over on this street yesterday."

"I didn't know that."

"Girl around your age. Still in critical. Hit-and-run. Hey, are you all right?"

"It said on the TV they were looking for me."

The officer smiled and blew smoke out of the corner of her mouth, away from me. "On TV, everyone's looking for everyone, at least until the unemployment rate goes up. Don't worry. If you have reporters on your tail, check in at headquarters."

My cats were hungry. I fed them, ran cold water over my

eyes, and concentrated on not crying again. The only way not to cry was to find some domestic activity to perform. But the apartment was clean. Mildred had even put the pillows from the couch back on the bed before she left. So I dusted the piano. I dusted the piano and didn't cry. While I was dusting, the phone rang. I let it ring for a long time before I picked it up.

"Jennifer," Argyle said. "You know that hag who was in your apartment the other day? That isn't the one who died, is it? I just saw it on TV and it occurred to me."

"No, it wasn't."

"Are you sure? She seemed pretty sick when I was over. Also, I thought I recognized some of the other bag ladies they showed—"

"Mildred wasn't a bag lady!"

"They said they were looking for a girl—"

"I know. I saw the show. I've got to go now."

"You don't sound good."

"Yes. Well. I just lost my job."

"Really? Why? That's awful. I called your office a little past noon to see if you felt like getting lunch and they said you were off to the dentist, and to try in the morning. Why would they fire you?"

"They didn't fire me."

"But you just said they fired you."

"They didn't."

"So why would you say that?"

"I really have to get off the phone now, Argyle."

"You're in a great mood. What's the matter with your teeth?"

"Nothing."

"I was going to invite you over for linguine al pesto and an old movie."

"Some other time."

I got the brooch from the cornstarch and put it in my pocket. I dialed Detroit and let the phone ring three times before I remembered that I was supposed to call from a phone booth. The lawyer's office was closed for the day. I left a message after the beep that Mildred was dead. The line uttered aloud in my apartment—*Mildred is dead*—sounded like something the chorus would say in a Greek tragedy, or a parody of a Greek tragedy. Then I looked in the phone book and found a home listing for a Karl Weldon. I was amazed that I'd remembered the name. A woman answered the phone and said, No, Karl wasn't in; she expected him back in a second, though, and maybe she could help me. Karl Weldon came in just as I said I didn't think she could. He sounded either very old or annoyed to be bothered at home.

"I think I may have something for you," I said.

"Yeah? So big you couldn't call the office during working hours?"

"I think so. Mildred Howell told me—"

"You say Mildred Howell?"

"Yes; she told me you might be interested in something I have."

"Terrible news about Millie. You the girl they talked about?"

"Yes I am, and I have the brooch—"

"The peacock?"

"Yes. She told me—"

"Let me pick this up in the other room," he said.

When he picked up the line he said, "That woman should've never left the business. How'd you get that piece?"

"She gave it to me."

"Know how far back I go with Millie? Close to forty years. Of course I haven't done business with her since she flipped. How much you asking?"

I knew they weren't friends. A friend wouldn't have called her Millie. "Five hundred thousand in cash, tonight," I said.

I couldn't believe what I was saying and neither, apparently, could Karl Weldon.

"You don't watch your movies carefully," he said. "See, that piece was stolen. All I have to do is make a couple of phone calls and you'll be in jail before you finish high school."

I felt silly to say what I was about to say, but I said it. "Very well. I'll call Gus."

There was a pause.

"Gus is out of town."

"Think so?" I said.

"You win. I can get you three hundred thousand in cash by tomorrow morning. Then, of course, we can be sure all the stones are the stones they're supposed to be."

"Nope."

"Honey, I don't know about your bank, but my bank closes at night. I can't pull together that kind of money tonight. Four, maybe."

"Okay, four."

"I'll give you three hundred thousand in cash tonight and a check for the rest."

"Nope."

"I see you're Mildred's prodigy. I'll see what I can do. Give me until midnight. What's your address?"

I almost gave it to him, but I thought twice and gave him Argyle's. It was the only address I could think of offhand, other than Mildred's on Christopher Street and my father's in Baltimore.

"Mr. Weldon?" I added. "No guns."

"Deal with Gus you get guns. Deal with me you get a sales receipt."

I walked to Argyle's.

He answered the door with wet hands. The water was on in the kitchen; he'd been doing the dishes. He smelled of turpentine and Balkan Sobranies.

"Shit," I said. "I forgot to get a gun."

He thought I was trying to be clever and ignored me. "Have you eaten?"

I was examining the canvas Argyle was working on. It had too many browns on it and looked like the tar on the roof of a house. Argyle put his arms around me from behind. He'd been into the kitchen to dry his hands and to give me time for his painting, but I could still feel the dampness through my shirt.

He'd expected me to come over. He thought I was being coy over the phone. This irritated me. I broke his embrace, walked to my purse, and got the brooch to show him.

"Woolworth's Special," he said.

"A man's coming over here at midnight to give me four hundred thousand dollars for this. You're the gun moll. Look tough. I'll give you—what sounds fair? Ten thousand?"

"Get serious, Spell."

"Do you mind if I use the phone?"

"Go ahead. I was painting."

I think I was in shock. I think efficiency was a temporary screen. I took the phone into the bedroom and called the police. In muted tones, I told the officer everything I knew—except, of course, about her apartment, her lawyer, and her brooch. I gave him my phone number and told him to please not give my name to the press, because I didn't want to upset my father. He said not to worry, the press was fickle, they'd have forgotten by the morning. I called Jack at Bellevue and thanked him for all his help. He said not at all, and that between the two of us he was sorry we couldn't have saved Mildred. He said that the next time I found a lady in distress I shouldn't play doctor, and I said I wouldn't. I asked him to please not give my name to the press. He got offended, and said he wouldn't dream of it. If anyone did, it would be Mildred's friends in the park. Then I called my boss and told him I was very, very sorry but I had some kind of virus and wouldn't be in in the morning.

Argyle brought me a beer. It wasn't cold enough and there was some unappealing slime around the pull tab. I went into the kitchen to wipe off the tab and to get a glass. When I came back, Argyle's shirt was thrown on the chair where I'd been sitting. Though it was hot, I didn't see why he had to paint bare-chested. I sat and watched him paint, trying to decide whether or not I liked his back, until the nine o'clock movie came on; I didn't move except for several trips to the bathroom, where I was disturbed to have to look at the reproduction of Leonardo's *Ginevra Benci*, hung over a backdrop of American flag. It was too late in the decade for that. Ginevra's five-hundred-year-old eyes blinked idly, like an iguana's.

Only three hours had passed since I'd found out Mildred Howell was dead.

The movie was one of those stock intrigues set on a tropical island, where all of the strong men run nightclubs and all of the women are expatriate daddy's girls who talk tough but bawl at the first sip of their Margaritas. The movie was not old enough for its sloppiness to seem quaint. I watched intently, however, because I have trouble getting my checks approved at the grocery store and I hoped to get some information about how people pull together huge sums of money in cash in the middle of the night.

Argyle and I engaged in some perfunctory foreplay during commercials. After the movie, he took my hand rather carefully. The line of his hand moving toward mine was clean and thin as the lines made by the Etch-A-Sketch toy I'd had as a child. In the kitchen, when I'd gone for a glass, I'd seen a picture of his girlfriend in Seattle. He hadn't bothered to hide it. The snapshot, curled around the edges, was standing up against the sugar bowl. She was tall and blonde; her grin was impish and meek at once, a smile that said he brought out the tigress in her. She wore shorts, a polo shirt, and hiking boots—I could imagine their children laughing at her preposterous outfit when they saw this picture in a scrapbook.

I wasn't jealous. I just felt very distant from the Pacific Northwest, which I have never seen, but imagine as a watered-down version of Tourisme.

I could almost like Argyle if I tried to remember him coming out of the black truck in a white suit with a bunch of daisies in his hand. From my window I watched him park the truck illegally and smile down the street at something I couldn't see— a pretty girl, an afghan hound chasing a cat. His short attention span had made him seem airy and spontaneous. But now, as he turned off the TV and began to make love to me, I knew that our relationship was not old enough, or fresh enough, to have any depth. It was not heavenly or hellish enough to be divine or painful. I wasn't proud of this. With my head against Argyle's shoulder, I could see the clock and the shadow of the chair. I thought, This isn't me doing this; I also thought, Classic case of dissociation; then I thought that, although it didn't *feel* like me doing this, those were my legs wrapped around Argyle's back, this was my pleasure I could intensify by clenching the muscles in my upper thigh. But Argyle was cardboard. What wasn't cardboard was the fact that, for half a second, my spine was inclined toward Argyle's chest in precisely the same way that Mildred's back curved when she coughed, and for that half second I was *in Mildred's bones* and couldn't breathe, and I shouted as I came and as the doorbell rang.

We dressed quickly. Later I discovered that my shirt was on inside out. The room smelled of sex.

"You're early," I told Karl Weldon, a pleasant middle-aged fellow in a nice tweed suit and wide orange tie.

"You look like you just woke up," he said. "That your husband?"

"No, that's Argyle Lovett, my—lawyer."

"Mr. Lovett," Weldon said, and shook Argyle's hand. Argyle glared at me. Weldon put his briefcase down on top of the radiator. Inside were piles and piles of bills, stacked the way they're always stacked on television. They must come that way from the bank.

"Three hundred thousand," Weldon said.

"But you said four—"

"I tried. God knows I tried. I'll pay you the rest next week. You must know I'm a nice guy if I can pull together this kind of money from friends. If you knew how hard it was to get this, you'd elect me president. I haven't eaten a thing since lunch. My wife had something special in the oven, too. You'll excuse that some of the bills are a little crinkly. Where's the brooch?"

"Don't I get some kind of promissory note for the other hundred thousand?"

"You get Karl Weldon's word."

Although I felt like I shouldn't give him the brooch until I saw the rest of the money, I withdrew the fist-sized monstrosity from my purse and unhooked it from the keychain. The jewels flashed like a twenty-one-gun salute.

"How do I know these are the real stones?" Weldon asked.

"How do I know I'll see the rest of my money? For that matter, how do I know that's not Monopoly money?"

"Got a plant light? You know, the kind that's ultraviolet? Hold the bills under the bulb and look at the watermarks. Is that a beer? Got another?"

I brought him a can of beer. He was examining the brooch under Argyle's pole lamp, a jeweler's glass hooked over his eye.

"Look at this," he said. "See this diamond that's supposed to be the peacock's eye? Take a look. What do you see?"

He hooked the glass onto my eye. "Nothing," I said.

"Look careful. Nothing like the initials LL?"

"Well, there's something like the initials LL carved into the, into the, whatchamacallit—the facets."

"That's right. Lorenzo Lotto, who designed this thing in 1883."

"I thought he was a Venetian painter."

"Different Lotto. Say, do you have a scale?"

Argyle, who had been standing by the door in shock since Weldon came in, looking much like a gun moll despite himself, hopped to and went for the scale he'd used when he dealt marijuana. The brooch weighed in at a pound. Weldon sighed.

"Mildred would have never parted with this thing," he

said. "Ten years from now, if she'd lived that long, she could have bought Malta with it and set up a pretty little sanitarium for herself and for all of her harpies. How does it feel to have this kind of money?"

"I don't know yet. It'll feel better when you give me the rest."

Actually, I was less worried about the rest of the money than I was about Mildred's harpies. I hadn't really thought about them yet. They knew where I lived.

After Weldon left—I gave him my real address—I gave Argyle ten thousand dollars and put on my shoes.

"I can't believe you," Argyle accused.

"What can't you believe?"

"Who do you think you are? I'm having a quiet evening. You meet criminals at my house. Then you hand me ten thousand dollars."

"If you don't want it, I'll take it back."

"I want to know what's going on."

"So do I," I said. "If you find out, will you let me know?" And I took the money back from him.

I began to feel sick—just a queasy feeling that might have been from something I'd eaten, if I'd eaten; or maybe it was from not eating.

I was not mugged walking home.

Weldon had thrown in the briefcase with the money as part of my payment. It was a very nice leather briefcase. I went into the bathroom and got out the forty-count box of Tampax I'd recently bought, and went into the kitchen for a trash bag. I broke the outside wrappers of the Tampax very carefully, threw out the tampons, stuffed the inserters with the bills, put the wrappers back on, turned the Tampax open-end down back in the box, put what money didn't fit in the inserters back in the briefcase, and then put the briefcase at the bottom of the box in the closet where I keep my diaries.

I got the month's dial-pack of birth control pills from my purse—I'd just started a new series of them—and dropped them, one by one, down the kitchen sink.

Then I sat down on the couch with my cats.

The couch still smelled of Mildred Howell.

The smell seemed to be confined to the couch and to the area surrounding the couch, but in that vicinity, the smell was nauseating.

I went into the bathroom to vomit convulsively for what must have been an hour.

The next morning, I left for Atlantic City.

# 21

What had Mildred Howell lived for? Had it been worth her while? For the five hours after I woke up on Wednesday, July 20, 1977, I didn't think about that at all. I had too big a lump in my throat to concentrate. I was driving a car, something I hadn't done in seven years, since I got my license in Baltimore. Renting the car had seemed the right way to celebrate new wealth and its intimations of freedom. I had no idea where Atlantic City was, but hoped to arrive before dark, because I couldn't find the lights or the windshield wiper button on the dash of my subcompact. If it rained, I'd be finished. But I was happy. Driving was what practicing the piano had been for me: a divine attention. The roads were notes I was sightreading. I thought, if only driving could stay new and challenging like this; if only love could.

I arrived in Atlantic City in time for a lunch of crab cakes at the restaurant nearest to the parking place I could pull into front-end forward. I brought my tampax box in a paper bag into the diner with me, along with the newspapers I'd bought in New York. They'd sat on the front seat next to me for the duration of the trip, tempting as unopened letters. But I wasn't in either paper. The *News* had a little note about Mildred in the local section; the *Times* didn't mention Mildred or me at all.

I'd be lying if I said I wasn't disappointed. I'd enjoyed my brief notoriety the night before. Afterwards, I could better understand why people would hijack a plane or bomb a convention hall for a glimpse of themselves on the eleven o'clock news. Even to see your name in print must induce a satisfying sense that you live outside the limits of your own life in something much like history. If there's distortion, it's the distortion of your voice on a tape recorder—wrong, maybe, but close enough to fascinate. Everyone knows how you feel, and the fact that everyone knows enhances the pleasure, because you're comfortable to know you're feeling the way you're supposed to feel. Fame is like any ritual—birthdays, weddings, funerals. Like any ritual, it replaces uncertainty with a code. I was fairly uncertain right then.

Rory Kirn wasn't hard to find. His name was in the phone book, and a gas station attendant directed me to the street, a cul-de-sac a distance from the end of the boardwark, only yards from the beach.

It was a private beach far enough from the main drag so that there were no families or hoodlums, not even on the periphery. The house was an enormous Victorian structure with rounded upstairs windows which looked like cartoon eyes, giving the whole house from a distance the face of a jack-o'-lantern. There was no one in view, no movement inside. I walked to the beach.

The water was so pretty. I was at the beach and I hadn't even brought a bathing suit. A blimp went by, congratulating someone on a marriage. A pinpoint up the beach was flying a kite; the kite was a red pinpoint in the sky, much smaller than the gulls. It was too sunny to look at the sky for long.

A middle-aged woman answered when I knocked at Rory's door and told me he was around back. She told me to walk around, so I didn't see the inside of the house. She was a nurse or a maid—she couldn't be a wife; she wasn't interested enough in who I was or what I wanted.

Right away, I saw the Japanese garden. It was so breathtaking that for the minute I stood at the side of the house, looking at the garden, I even forgot to feel ridiculous, which I was, holding my paper bag. Then I saw Rory in the back of the garden, squatting near a small plant, examining one of its leaves. Mildred hadn't lied. Rory was just as Mildred had described him—just as he was the day in 1936 when he proposed to Katey, who was conceivably my aunt. He was still gigantic. He still wore white pants and a white T-shirt, just as he had that day in 1936; and although he was standing in soil, his white clothes were spotless.

But he was bald. I hadn't expected that. Not even a crown of white encircling the hairless top of his head; he was completely bald. He was also tan and trim—even the top of his head was tan. He looked like Picasso in his later years. His head was round and shiny, and he carried himself like someone who was meant to be bald, who had expected to be bald all along.

I introduced myself.

"Miss Spell?" He offered his hand. He put his hand out slowly, because age had slowed him, or because he didn't know who I was, or because he was used to people being shocked by the size of his hands—I swear the fingers were as long as my feet.

"Mildred Howell's friend," I added.

"Mildred Howell," he said. "She came to see me in—'sixty-five, I think. Casey's friend."

"Yes," I said. "Your garden's beautiful."

"Thank you. Can I help you?"

"Mildred's dead," I said.

It was the first time I'd said that out loud.

"I'm very sorry," he said. "She seemed like a lovely woman. Are you also delving into the family tree?"

"Not exactly. I'm—I'm, well, I thought I should introduce myself. I'm Frog's daughter."

"Frog's daughter," he said.

"Lucy Haggerty? The woman who stayed with you and Katey? I'm not sure she's my mother, but Mildred's sure."

He just stared at me.

"You haven't forgotten, have you?" I asked.

"It's just a surprise. Your friend told me she couldn't find Frog. It's been so long. Please. Sit down."

He beckoned to some lawn chairs. We sat.

"Frog. I'll be. How is she!"

"She's dead."

"I'm so sorry. How long ago?"

"1959."

"So young! Oh, I'm so sorry."

"She killed herself."

"Is your father still—"

"He's alive."

"I'm sorry," Rory said. "Frog Haggerty. Oh, I'm so sorry."

I started to cry.

It was the old story. I'm allergic to discussing my mother. My eyes just water. I don't feel any particular grief; it's a physical reaction. But this time, I was crying for Mildred too. Rory offered me a slightly muddy handkerchief.

"I'm glad you came," he said. "I always thought there had to be some reason that Frog didn't stay in touch. I didn't even know where she was. I couldn't even write to let her know when Katey died. Was she—very unhappy?"

This took Rory a long time to say. He spoke slowly. In between his words I looked at the garden. It was so lovely.

"No," I said. "She had this rare brain disease."

"She'd already begun to get sick before she left. I don't think she was quite right in the head from it."

"They still don't even have a name for the disease."

"You were raised in—"

"Baltimore."

"And you are how old?"

"Twenty-three," I said.

"I'm glad to know you," he said. "Very glad."

Then it appeared that we had nothing to say to each other.

I didn't want to pry, but I'd hoped that he'd tell me more, tell me things about Katey and Frog and Tourisme; I'd hoped that if I could get submerged in Mildred's story again, I wouldn't have to think about Mildred. I asked him if he missed Katey; he said "Sometimes," and didn't elaborate. I asked him if he got lonely in the big house. He said "Sometimes." He wasn't hiding anything; he just didn't have much to say. His face had the serenity of a man who had done nothing wrong, who regretted nothing. It occurred to me that I could ruffle him pretty fast by telling him about Gato, but of course I wouldn't do that, so there was little left to talk about except his garden, the heat, or how gamblers and outsiders were ruining his city. So I talked about myself. This was awkward at first. His nurse brought out lemonade, and I talked, tentatively, about how I'd met Mildred. Rory's face was expressionless as a psychiatrist's would have been. Occasionally he'd inject an "I'm sorry" or "That's too bad" as I told him how I didn't like my job, how I wished I'd kept up the piano, how I had never recovered from my mother's death, how I had no luck with men. I only stopped talking to eat a sandwich and have coffee. Perhaps he saw a bit of Frog in my face, or maybe he was just too polite to interrupt, but I talked until it got dark, and mostly what was visible then was the gleam of his white clothes, his shiny scalp.

"You never met my wife," he said. "You would have liked her. Your mother liked her very much. They were very close. I could never understand why Frog didn't write. Was she very much in love with your father?"

"I suppose. I was too young to know."

"Were they comfortable? Did he provide for her?"

"They didn't have a private pool or go to Europe much, but they were comfortable enough."

I felt a little offended. After all my talk, the questions Rory thought to ask were: *Were they in love?* and *Was she provided for?* But perhaps those were the questions worth asking. Perhaps love and comfort were the things that mattered.

"Did she leave you money?"

"Mildred? In a way. I have to work for it, sell a lot of art."

"I assume it's more money than you've had."

"You kidding? I don't know what to do with it. I feel like if I try to open a bank account, I'll get arrested."

"Do you like the idea of having money?"

"I don't know. It's still an *idea* to me. I feel aimless. Is it true that the minute you have money, you cease to want it?"

"I'm the wrong person to ask. Like Mildred, I've never been fond of money. But in general I'd say that people like having money better than they like not having money. Mildred gave me some money, you know, in '65."

"No, I didn't know that."

"A lot of money. Couple hundred thousand."

"That was nice of her."

"She didn't give it to me to be nice. She gave it to me to save for you."

"But she didn't know me then."

"She knew there would be someone like you."

"Is that what she said?"

"I don't recall. She just said that if anyone ever came to me who knew her, to give the money to that person. Do you want it now?"

"What am I going to do with it? No one will believe it's mine."

"You can leave it in my account if you'd like, the other money you've gotten too, and when you're ready for it, you can call for it."

"That's a good idea. I'll take a little money and leave the rest with you."

"And anything I can do, let me know. I'm like family, remember that. I knew your mother."

I wanted to go somewhere with no TV and no papers.

I drank my coffee and watched some more news on a different channel—plane crashes, violence in third world countries. I took a shower, dressed, then carried my cats and the kitty litter box to the car. I returned the car to the rental place. The workers there saw the cats, kitty litter box, kitty litter, and bags of cat food on the back seat and looked at me as if I were crazy. My cats looked at me as if I were crazy. Maybe I was, but I don't think so. I got my cats into a taxi and went straight to Mildred Howell's.

There I began my official mourning on July 21, 1977. I mourned until August 22. But after a while, I wasn't mourning very well. I was out of cat food, and I really had to do laundry.

I looked at the stars during the ensuing silence. Stars are one of the things we've learned to do without in New York. We live underground and overground, without air or light. Except for Mildred Howell—Mildred lived in the park.

Rory said I was welcome to spend the night, but I felt anxious to get back. I took two Tampaxes out of the box, made sure they contained five thousand dollars each, and then gave the rest of the Tampaxes to Rory. He smiled at how I'd hidden the money. It was the first time I'd seen him smile. He wore false teeth. I gave him my address and he walked me around to the front of the house. There may have been pictures of my mother in the house, but I was never invited inside. Rory embraced me at the car so tentatively that afterwards I wasn't sure he actually did it.

It was only about nine. I was home before one. I parked the car illegally; even with my much-reduced stash, I could certainly afford a parking ticket. I washed up and went straight to bed, where I had a dream in which a cat was giving birth to kittens. The kittens were far too small—a litter of runts, all fingernail-sized—and poured from the cat, who licked placenta from herself effortlessly. The cat was in a box that was shorter than her body. She had to contort herself to fit into the box, and in the dream I wondered if perhaps the kittens were so under sized because the box was so small. The cat, however, seeme perfectly comfortable.

When I woke up, I found myself sleeping on the couch.

I wasn't in bed. I was on the couch, which *was* too short f my body (if not for Mildred's); my head strained against t armrest, and my neck was sore. Sometime in the middle of night, I'd gone to the bathroom and walked the wrong way ba as children do; or I'd sleepwalked to the couch. In either cas found the experience unsettling.

It was ten o'clock and just as well that I was up, bec I had to return the car. I made coffee and turned on the The news was on. Nobody said a word about Mildred.

# 22

I felt like a character from a Russian novel, except that characters from Russian novels don't feel like characters from Russian novels. They have better things to do, like get epilepsy or frostbite.

Mildred's basement apartment was enormous—four huge rooms running the entire length of the building. But it was without furniture except for a huge metal desk, a file cabinet, and a single mattress on the floor. The windows faced west on an alley; the apartment was completely without light. The bathroom had no light fixture at all, nothing but rusty water in the sink tap, and no shower, so I had to go to my place to clean up. These excursions gave me some air and the opportunity to open my mail.

If anything, my little jaunts into the outside world only intensified my sense of isolation. New York was bright and fast but transparent, without weight. I'd watch the confident hands of the girl at the grocery store as she rang up my sale (I was eating only sandwiches and things I could cook on a hot plate), and I'd feel that I couldn't at all understand her, had no idea how she lived, what she cared about; in her distance from me she'd seem terribly self-possessed. I began to feel that living any life at all required genius and passion, and that I clearly had neither genius nor passion. Even my job now seemed beyond me. I was astonished that I'd once sang about candy bars and automobiles, for these things had no meaning to me—not even the old certainty that they had no meaning.

I called Leland to officially quit my job the day I got the check from Karl Weldon for the balance on Mildred's peacock brooch. (Actually the check may have been in the mailbox for several days. I felt about time as Casey O'Brien must have felt after the bombing, biking to Chamonix for supplies.) The check looked legitimate. Afraid to cash it, I put the check, along with Mildred's watch, in a safety deposit box under the alias of Frog Haggerty. I deposited the ten thousand dollars of Tampax money and the rest of the briefcase money in my savings account until I decided what to do, and called my father to explain that an old woman I'd helped for a month had died, leaving me some money—did he want some? He said of course he didn't want any money, but I should get a lawyer to tell me about windfall taxes and money markets. He said he wished I'd visit, and I said I would.

My boss said that the least I could have done was to give two weeks' notice. He said I was irresponsible, and I knew he was right. I wouldn't be moping in a basement apartment if Mildred hadn't left me the money, or if I didn't have a place of my own to return to. But Mildred had left me the money and I'd worry later about how that would change things. Meanwhile, I moped and went through Mildred's collection of art.

There was tons of art, millions of lists and catalogs. Most of this didn't interest me. I had no idea what any of the art was worth; most of the pieces were drawings or curios I'd walk right past in museums. There were engravings of men in tails and gleaming shoes, indifferent still lifes of oranges and dead fowl. When I came across a catalog for the work of an artist whose name I recognized, I'd feel the seedy satisfaction of seeing my own name on a dean's list or in a yearbook. I rearranged the papers in chronological piles on the desk, throwing out nothing, not even the scraps scrawled with times or figures. I restacked the paintings and engravings against the wall according to size, then color, then an amateur's estimate of period. The only piece of art I really liked was a small unsigned portrait of Mildred from the waist up, modeling her faraway look. It's a curious portrait because her clothes and hairdo are distinctly 1962, but the pose and style of the painting are eighteenth-century. I took this painting home in a paper bag and hung it over my dresser, along with the undated, yellowing newspaper clipping that I'd found taped to a piece of legal paper under a pile of show announcements:

> Mildred Howell, art dealer, was arrested last night for refusing to leave the Statue of Liberty after dark. Howell, 64, claimed to be "awaiting a ship." She was fined $1,000.

Someone had dated the paper "1/6," circled the article in red ink, and written underneath in sepia ink:

> M: Good work! A living construction. Knew we could count on you. See you at the opening—C

That one note was more intriguing to me than all of the art. I spent days thinking of artists whose names began with C; I ransacked the apartment for Casey's Statue of Liberty note, for a short note from Kitsa thanking Mildred for her visit, or a canceled check in Mildred's hand to the car-rental place in Sallanches. But there was none of that. All of that—what of it Mildred had kept—had been in the bag of evidence the mugger took.

I called Karl Weldon, because I didn't know who else to call, and asked him what I should do with the art. He said that he wasn't an art man. He was a jewel man. If I wanted to dispose of art, I'd have to call an art man. But he gave me an opinion. Much of the art was probably stolen. If I auctioned off one piece that had a legal owner still searching for it, I'd be in trouble. Furthermore, if Mildred didn't explicitly will the art to me, it wasn't my property, as the law doesn't function under the finders-keepers theory. If the law didn't confiscate the goods outright, they'd get me in taxes, or they'd get me in lawyer's fees to avoid taxes. The best thing was to get rid of the pieces very, very slowly, saving the most valuable ones for later, getting just enough money to live on from year to year; but I'd have to start following auctions, because there was no way to tell what would sell ten years from now. He explained all this to me slowly and loudly, as Mara had talked to Jeremy the night of Lucy's suicide. I'd never needed to fill out the long income-tax form before.

"You understand," he said, "that wealth is a full-time occupation. You don't skip off and play. You grind your teeth and worry about your money. Even if you have accountants and lawyers and agents, you still have to worry about your accountants and lawyers and agents, because when you're at that height you fall hard."

I agreed and changed the subject to my Prodigal Son watch. I'd suspected for a while that if Klaus had given the watch to Mildred, it probably wasn't very valuable. In fact, I thought it might even be a forgery.

Weldon laughed. "You can't forge a watch. A watch is a mechanism. You can't forge a car—not even a Rolls—any more than you can forge a toaster oven. I've seen that piece. It's very nice, but I've seen dozens—it's not worth nearly as much as Mildred thought it was. You know, when I met Millie I was twenty years old. She broke me into this business, but it's changed. Some pieces that were worth arms and legs in her time aren't worth pinkies today."

He paused. "Let me ask you something. Do you love the art?"

"You mean art in general or Mildred's art?"
"Mildred's."

"Not particularly," I admitted. "Most of it's garish."

"That'll be a handicap. Mildred loved her art. I don't know what to tell you. One other thing. You happen to hear of a red satin robe with emeralds on the border?"

"Heard about it. I wonder where it is."

"Me, too. You'll let me know?"

I thanked him and promised I'd keep in touch. I walked back to Mildred's (she had no phone, so I'd called from my place), where I spent the next several hours mulling over the phrase *Mildred loved her art*. It was another fact about her, something else to assimilate.

And I obsessed about the robe. Surely Mildred wouldn't have left it in Tourisme. She hadn't; she'd left it at my apartment. I found it three and a half months later. I was having company for dinner. I was cooking spaghetti sauce and discovered that I had to go out for bay leaves. I went into the very back of my closet for a heavy coat I hadn't yet worn that winter. The robe was stashed at the bottom of the garment bag. Mildred had planted it there as a practical joke, or as a practicality, to make sure that no one but me got the robe. I never told Weldon. I still haven't even had the jewels assessed. I'd keep the robe no matter what it was worth—I plan to wear it on my honeymoon. If I never marry, I can always wear it on some weekday when I need to commemorate ordinary happiness.

I certainly couldn't have dealt with a jewel-laden robe that August. Mildred had been right to hide it. Too many things still didn't make sense. Why had Mildred tattooed Klaus's name on her nipple if she hated him so much? How had she rented a car in 1964 with a driver's license that had expired ten years before? How had she been privy to Pia Maginski's thoughts, to know about her dream of the white house? Where was the house Pia dreamed of, the white house with the balcony she'd remembered so fondly? What had happened to Marcel, to Étienne? Was Frog my mother? Why did my mother kill herself? How on earth had she gotten pregnant at fifty-one—was there some hor-mone being secreted, some quirk of the disease, that made her madly fertile? After Katey died, why hadn't Rory gone through her things and found the letters from Frog? Why hadn't Rory suspected a Gato earlier? Couldn't he have guessed what Katey was doing for all those years in Paris? Or maybe he *had* known about Gato, and just didn't want to discuss it, so long after Katey's death?

Some of the uncertainty would have been easy enough to clear up. At least I could have decided finally whether or not I bought Mildred's genealogy. In Mildred's apartment I dreamed detective dreams. I could have called New Haven to see if a Mildred Howell had, indeed, graduated from Yale. I could have checked City Records and orphanages in Detroit for birth certifi-cates. I could have dug up 1883 newspapers for mention of Tourisme; I could have looked in old Hollywood phone books for Kitsa and Gato. I could have called Mildred's lawyer. But I did none of this. Perhaps I will someday—after all, I waited seventeen years before opening the box my mother left me.

I spent most of my time pondering that August. I spent hours watching my cats against shadows on the wall, wondering whether or not it was time to sleep, trying to remember if I'd dreamed anything important the last time I slept.

A month is not, by anyone's standards, very long. My month hardly competes with Casey's decades in Tourisme, with my father's decades in the big Baltimore house, with Rory's decades alone in Atlantic City. Still, it wasn't easy to fill the time. I had no vocation. There was no lover to make a huge fresh salad for—cutting the vegetables slowly, planting black olives and artichoke hearts. I couldn't read in soft light with Bach and a plate of brie. Mildred's things—dusty, demanding, imperious—oppressed me, but I wasn't sure what I could call my own. I missed the few friends I'd managed to make, mourned them almost as somberly as I mourned Mildred. Most of them had moved away: one to the Foreign Service in Thailand, one to law school out west, one to a husband in Vermont. I tried to write letters:

> Other than quitting my job, forgetting about Argyle, and inheriting enough money to live on for a while from an old woman claiming to be a relative who died and left me to mope, not much has happened. How are *you*?

But I was so out of touch with these women that they hadn't even heard of Argyle. Most of them wouldn't have believed that I'd been in the same apartment all these years, that I was wearing my hair in the same blunt cut. Besides, writing letters at all seemed a decided breach of my mourning contract. The point of being at Mildred's was to confront the fact that I could disappear for a month without making the slightest ripple in anyone's life.

My biggest pleasure that month was stealing time, when I went home, for playing the piano. With Mildred sick I hadn't yet treated myself to the glee one registers over a car, a Cuisinart, or any major new possession. My piano, of course, was much more than a thing. The reason it looked so massive and solid in my living room was not so much its size as its capacity to restore me to myself. I dug my music from the same box where I kept my diaries, assuring myself that I couldn't have forgotten how to play the piano any more than I could ever forget how to swim or to make love. While I was in no shape to play the "Scarbo" section of Ravel's *Gaspard de la Nuit* or Liszt's B Minor Sonata, and while my rendition of the Chopin Ballades for Mildred in the Waldorf turned out to have been an unrepeatable lucky stroke, I could still vaguely play the *Appassionata*. Even when I scolded myself for hitting a wrong note or playing a passage flatly, I was hooked into the infinite sadness and order of music, the supreme order that is not always immediately discernible to the untutored ear. If my ear was rusty after eight years of bad rock and Musak, at least I could posit a future in which my ear would improve. I could feel it happening already. I wasn't just getting back what I had; I was getting more. I may have been playing Beethoven's *Hammerklavier* at the age of fifteen, but I'd played it badly—I hadn't understood the beauty of very simple progressions being milked for all of their possibilities, had viewed the opus simply as a virtuoso exercise. When I played it now, I'd play it with heart. At night, as I fell asleep, my brain was printed with scores, at least until the dense black notes were replaced with the black squares of crossword puzzles.

I did an insufferable number of Double-Crostic puzzles before beginning to construct my own. I went home for a dictionary, a thesaurus, and a book of famous quotations. Anyone who saw me on the basement floor, filling the letters spelling *diaphanous* and *Last Tango in Paris* into little numbered squares, would have undoubtedly found my concentration most comical, especially when I ran out of *U*'s and *L*'s and began to comb the dictionary for the name of a Nobel Prize-winner whose first name began with *E* and whose last name contained as many *C*'s and *W*'s as possible. The whole process more resembled a sensory deprivation experiment than civilized pleasure. I finished about ten puzzles in a week. The trapped feeling I got from the failed puzzles—the ones that stalemated after three hours with three homeless consonants and no vowels—was so perfect a model of my life that I became most self-righteously obsessed. A commitment to word games seemed no more arbitrary to me at that point than a commitment to politics, or art, or music, or another person.

Of course, I hadn't lost *all* perspective. It was the crossword puzzles that finally got me out of the basement. I was in the final stretch of the eleventh puzzle, with paper letters sprawled out before me; I was just about to assign the letters to the grid of numbered squares when Freud and Skinner—quite intentionally, in unison—sat on the letters, scrambling them hopelessly. I cried. I actually cried: not because of Mildred, or even my sadness in losing her; not because of the foul way I'd been treating my father, but because my cats had sat on my letters. Then I asked myself what on earth I was doing. Mildred, I think, would have asked the same thing.

I brought my cats and their kitty litter home. I opened the windows and read the mail—mostly bills; Mara's annual birthday letter, always several days early or several days late; and a note from Rory, thanking me for my visit and assuring me that my money was safe. I realized that Rory would probably leave me his money, too; this pleased me, and I chided myself for being pleased. As it turned out, though, Rory didn't leave me anything but trouble.

Mildred had apparently willed all of her money to Rory, which is about the same as willing it to a locker in Grand Central Station—Rory didn't need the money, was too old to use it, and had no one to will it to. This was just under a million dollars that had been in a safety deposit box for over forty years. Not a penny had been paid in taxes on either the money from Helen Haggerty or the money Mildred had earned as a dealer. Mildred's lawyer in Detroit, who had co-signed for access to the box, was unscrupulous enough to aid Mildred in this scheme; it therefore isn't surprising that he was unscrupulous enough to be dipping into the million all along, and to have no intention of giving money to any Rory Kirn. Mildred, he was sure, would not be traced back to Detroit. But the lawyer was over eighty himself and not spritely enough for the perfect crime. He tried to use the money in cash for a house and was almost immediately caught. What was left of Mildred's money was attached to the settlement of her estate. (This lawyer was so on the ball that he didn't even think to destroy Mildred's will, or to forge another will leaving the money to himself.) The lawyer would have been promptly disbarred for cooperating in a felony if he hadn't retired twenty years before.

Now all of this happened very quietly in the dusty courtrooms of the Midwest. It might not have touched my life at all.

I continued to slip fifty dollars a month under Mildred's land-lady's door until I could decide what to do with the art. But two things backfired.

First, the landlady raised the rent. Her son visited from Colorado and informed her that fifty dollars in rent was low for the Village. She slipped a note under Mildred's door notifying her of the increase. I hadn't been in the apartment—it was still too painful for me—so I didn't pay the increase. The landlady couldn't find Mildred and called the police. The police broke into the apartment and found the art; some of the art was identified as stolen and confiscated; the landlady had the rest of the things moved and rented the apartment to someone else but continued to accept my fifty dollars under the door; and in March, when I finally gathered courage to return to Mildred's apartment, I found that the lock had been changed.

After several days in the library with microfilm, I found a brief story about the art confiscation. The landlady knew she'd rented the apartment to a Mildred Howell, that Mildred Howell was found to be dead, and it was still unlikely that they would bother tracing Mildred to me.

I would have been right, perhaps. I could easily have gotten away with my $500,000, watch, and emerald-trimmed robe; I had no intention of fighting for the art. My deal seemed fair enough, and I'd use the money quietly. There was only one other problem.

Rory Kirn died. He left most of his money to the American Lung Association, but he left my $200,000 to me, plus the $200,000 that Mildred had left him, in case anyone materialized who cared for her. This was very thoughtful of Rory, but the $400,000 was taxed and I now had some visibility with the IRS, an organization that strikes such fear into my heart that I panicked.

It was April 1978. I still hadn't tried to cash Karl Weldon's check. I wrote him an apologetic letter, asking him to reissue it. I still hadn't filed my 1977 return, but it wasn't too late, so I waited for Weldon's check and told the whole story (or almost the whole story, minus the watch and the robe) to an accountant, asking him to file a return on the whole amount.

It's 1981 now, and Mildred's and Rory's estates still haven't been settled. My accountant told me to get a lawyer; my lawyer told me that these court orders can take upwards of six years. He has suggested more than several times that the amount of money I see in the end won't last forever.

After a month, when I still hadn't heard from Weldon, I asked my lawyer to look into that, too. Between 1977 and 1979, Weldon went bankrupt, then died of a heart attack. I still suspect that the bankruptcy had something to do with the peacock. More than once I've been tempted to call Mrs. Weldon and ask if I can help her with anything, but I've controlled myself.

The sense of loss about the money was mostly ticklish, like the sense you have when you search your shelves for a book and realize you lent it to an acquaintance years ago, in a different city. The sense of loss was nothing like what I'd felt about Mildred or, for that matter, about the photographs she'd had with her when she died. The photographs would have given me something to look at for the month in her apartment, other than so much art.

Even now, as I'm unpacking clothes or digging into the back of the cabinet for a pan I don't often use, I expect to find something of Mildred's. I'm both relieved and disappointed when no gold comes up in the pan. I'd especially like mementoes of Mildred's adoptive parents, of her life before Tourisme took her in its thrall. It took me a long time to understand that Mildred had used Tourisme to distract herself from her childhood in Detroit, much as I'd used Mildred to distract myself from Baltimore. Now that I'm on good terms with Jeremy and Mara, I know that neither of them could have been for me what Mildred was, or what I wanted her to be: a Zarathustra, a verbal Uncle Nose. I'd wanted to revere Mildred as I'd revered my eleventh-grade English teacher, who didn't believe in war or drug regulation. I'd been determined not to acknowledge that my gorgeous, brilliant teacher had a paunchy husband, a brother who taught gym, and an ugly row house which she drove to in a Camaro without a muffler.

Mara understood, as soon as she heard about Mildred from my father. As a P.S. to her birthday letter—about my father's house, the weather in Boston, some movies she'd seen, trouble with her car, her hopes for my future—she'd written *Hear you've been playing nurse. What's wrong with the old folks you've got?* I was thinking about that, in my first hour out of mourning, when the phone rang—my father. "Where have you *been?*" He wanted me to come home. He wasn't a demanding person, but this time he was asking. Mara would be coming the following week; could I take off work? Was I all right?

The calendar taped to my refrigerator was still set on July. I flipped the page and found the date. The calendar seemed arcane as a tax table. "I'm fine," I told Jeremy, "and very, very sorry. I'll be home by August the twenty-ninth, at the very latest. Are you angry?"

"Not angry. Just at sea. What *is* it with you? Are you in love? Don't you think you might bring the boy home to meet your family?"

I laughed. "No boy, alas. I'll see you within the week. Thanks for worrying but there's nothing wrong—there are just some things I need to get into focus."

"Do you need train fare?"

"Train fare," I told him, "is one of the few things in the world that I *don't* need."

If my attachment to Mildred still hadn't come into focus, neither had my new wealth. It wasn't much more real a full year later, when the financial repercussions began. The full effects won't be known for a while. I'm sometimes tempted to believe that Mildred had been sloppy, but I know better—she planted her clues meticulously, to guarantee that I would continue to live in her story. And I have, to the extent that I've written all this down. But her loving ruse didn't entirely work, because a year after her death I was playing the piano again, learning to cook with a wok, making love, looking for a job and a new apartment, meeting women whose boyfriends could spare them for a movie or a walk, and dreaming quite happily about a future with Daniel Stern, whom I met on August 22, 1977, in a laundromat.

# 23

Outside of the laundromat, a man photographed his daughter in the dark. The child was around three, blonde as an ad for lemonade. He took her from the basket attached to the back of his bicycle, laid down the bike, and posed her under the laundromat's floodlights, beside a large vat of plastic geraniums. "Stand up straight," he said. "Look at the sky. Now look at Daddy." The man took only one shot, and as the flash went off I realized I'd be visible, already half-cropped, at the right edge of the photograph—against the wall, bored as a hooker. The daughter, in contrast, looked like someone who had died in a canopied bed during the Renaissance and gone straight to Heaven. Yet there was something coy about her. You could tell that she'd posed before. She could probably already envision a future in which this grainy photograph would join a collection of photographs, all slightly better than amateur, showing her growth into a photogenic woman with a husband just as kind and responsible as her father, only slightly more exciting. I felt sorry for her. She thought she was the center of her father's attention (and even, perhaps, of mine), whereas her father only wanted a chronicle of his own growth: how, on a night in some summer of our Lord, he had an urge to go for a midnight bike ride with a creature whose bones hadn't even hardened yet, who would remember the night in some inchoate form, would remember him as vague as sky. He got on his bike and waved to me as he drove away with the child. I didn't wave back. I was angry with the man for fixing me, badly dressed, in his history. But I knew I was just jealous because he wasn't my father, because I wanted to be a child again—and barring that, I wanted a child of my own, or at least a man.

It was after midnight. I was crazy to be doing laundry that time of night. I was apparently the only person in New York with dirty sheets at midnight and alone in the laundromat, I was an easy target for anyone interested in stealing dirty sheets. But no one came to steal my sheets.

Who came was Danny Stern.

He had a carload of laundry. He had more white T-shirts than anyone I'd ever seen. He had one of those faces—brown eyes, brown hair, straight nose, mouth—that sounds like every other face, but is like no other face when you see it.

Oh, did he have laundry. He filled eight machines—two just with jeans—a whole row, except for the three machines I was using. He had rolls of dimes and quarters and went down the aisle with soap and coins, systematic as a factory foreman. Then he disappeared and came back in a minute with *Time*, *Esquire*, *Newsweek*, *The New Republic*, *The New Yorker*, *The New York Review of Books*, and *Science*. I knew the titles because he threw the magazines on a table with such force that they fell on the floor. He looked at me.

"You're smiling," he said. "At least you didn't laugh."

"I'm sorry. I couldn't help it. Are you a speed-reader? The wash cycle is only a half hour."

He looked at me for so long that I started to get uncomfortable. That's all I needed—a rapist who read *The New York Review*. He stood. I was sitting on a table at the opposite end of the laundromat, some distance from him; I'd had to talk louder than I was accustomed to, after my month of solitude.

"Are you busy?" he asked. "Do you want to talk?"

"Sure, if you don't want to read."

He said he'd be right back, half a second, he just wanted to get something from his car, but it wasn't half a second—it was more like ten minutes. He came back breathless, carrying a bag that contained a bottle of champagne, plastic cups, Fritos, and a store-bought onion dip.

"What?" I said. "No flowers, no candlelight?"

"I'm sorry," he said. "They made me move the car. The champagne, I am sorry to report, is not quite cold. Will you help me celebrate?" He opened the bottle and poured the champagne. "Danny Stern. You are?"

"Jennifer."

"Your glass, your glass. A toast. To Jennifer—Jennifer—"

"Spell."

"Spell. Nice name. To Jennifer Spell."

"What are we celebrating?"

"Sit. I'm going to talk your ear off."

"Why do strangers always talk my ear off?"

"Because you look like you can't defend yourself."

"All that has changed."

"Good. Don't defend yourself now, though, because you'll enjoy this. I just quit my job."

"Did you! Congratulations."

"Thanks. I'm a psychiatrist—was. I'm done. Started waving good-bye to my patients last Tuesday and finished today. I was the Great White Ape, swinging through the unconscious with the greatest of ease. But the picture of Freud in my study at home has a sleep mask over its eyes. I no longer embrace the notion of depth. Oedipus, Freud, Sherlock Holmes: all were convinced you could peel off the skin and penetrate to the heart of darkness. But all you find sometimes is bone. They believed in innate heroism—the born genius, the born lover. But there isn't a fighter in every weakling and there isn't a siren in every schoolmarm. There isn't a Martin Luther King in every black heroin addict any more than there's a chicken in every pot. Some pots are empty. They believed that man is born free, and everywhere he is in chains. I now find this a boyish illusion of manifest destiny."

"You should have been a Behaviorist, then."

"No, I haven't the heart for it. Or rather, I have too much heart. I realize I'm contradicting myself."

"You do speak with forked tongue."

"True. Like every good nihilist, I'm a good romantic. I like to be bowled over by the wonder of it all. I'm still astonished by the amount of craziness packed into one hit of blotter acid, the amount of itching in one mosquito bite, the amount of expression in one face. Just because everything isn't a mystery doesn't mean you can measure everything."

"So you sneer at Kurtz but you still believe in the horror, the horror."

"You got me pinned. I'm squirming, I'm squirming. Smart girl. Anyway, I've always wanted to quit just the way I quit, but I never thought I'd get up the nerve. I was trained to do everything right, not to take any chances—"

"So your eccentricity is calculated to offend your family?"

"Probably, although now that you point it out, it sounds weak to me. Has to be somewhat more original. In any case, I'd already alienated a lot of colleagues by getting argumentative at conferences, so I had to be very sure I wanted to stop. Well, I stopped."

"Good for you."

"Thanks. I had my usual Monday morning lineup. First thing, eight in the morning, before I've even finished my first cup of coffee, there's Edward. Now Edward—you realize I'm betraying confidentiality—has his butler warm his watch each morning, so the cold gold doesn't shock the skin. The truth is I've never liked Edward. He walks in, sits down. I say, 'Tomorrow you won't warm your watch, Edward. You've been coming here at eight in the morning five days a week for a grand total of about $50,400; the least I can do is to stop you from warming your watch. It's summer; your watch will get warm all on its own.' Would you like more champagne?"

"Please. So what did he say?"

"Of course he tried to change the subject to Sophie. I told him to forget Sophie. I told him that Sophie was a money-hungry little birdbrain."

"You didn't," I called from the dryer. I'd just finished loading my clothes. I sat down.

"I did. Then I asked him if he'd ever talked to his butler. I have. His butler is amazing. He comes from a polygamous tribe in Haiti where the children are raised collectively, and he doesn't even *know* his mother. She could be one of any number of women who have slapped his ass and patted his head. After this butler is done warming Edward's watch and fixing Edward his germ-free meals, he goes to night school to study Business Administration. He'll return to Haiti, manage a laundromat or a Burger King, and be accorded the respect of a Poet Laureate. Furthermore, he's utterly happy. He doesn't have a single problem. I tell Edward all this. Dismissed!"

"Edward was shocked?"

"Shock is what he needs. Nine o'clock and time for my forty-year-old virgin who follows eclipses. He has been to Zanzibar and to Sweden to watch eclipses through special glasses and expensive equipment. That's all he would talk to me about is the sun, the properties of the sun. He doesn't want to talk about the fact that he's forty years old and still living with his parents. Forty years old, still living with his parents, and for two years he tells me that something's wrong, he can't quite put his finger on it. 'Son,' I say. 'Stop with the eclipses. The one in Seattle next year is going to be a big disappointment and the next one won't be until 2017. Just stop. Dismissed.' My frustrated agoraphobic housewife canceled, so I had my fifty-dollar hour to drink coffee, pack some books and talk to my secretary. I don't have to feel bad about her; I got her another job. But I do feel bad about Cynthia. Cynthia was my favorite patient. She's a fine woman and the only thing wrong with her is that she can't hold down a job, because she keeps sleeping with her bosses and then crying about it to everyone. Actually, I'm not even sure if it's a problem. Cynthia has had many jobs; she knows so many things and she has such a nice detachment from what she knows, nice especially in contrast to her passion for cold men. You learn to live with someone's faults, don't you? Cynthia's as happy as she could be; now all she has to do is admit she's happy. I told her that if I didn't have someone else, I'd ask her out. I might yet."

"Think you're cold enough for her?" Silence. He wasn't unflappable. "Sorry," I said. "Overkill. So what's your someone else like?"

"She looks her age, except when she plays the flute. Then she looks like a child. She's not very sensual, but at least she didn't ask me to interpret her dreams—she didn't have any. What I did over lunch was break off with Christine. That wasn't easy. I'd stay with her, but she wants to get married. Now there's nothing wrong with marriage; I might even try it myself. But I don't want to marry Christine, and I felt I was being unfair to her."

"How old are you?"

"Thirty-five. How old do I look? Don't answer. Have more champagne. At one o'clock comes Sy Pepperman, who's in the wholesale office furniture business. I told Sy that he was a fine, warm, perceptive human being. The only reason he was coming to me was that his wife took a couple of adult-education classes and decided Sy was boring. At two I told Frank to shut up already and be gay. At three I told Mrs. Howe that there was no reason for her to stay with her lush of a husband if she didn't want to—what's wrong?"

"Did you say Howell?"

"Howell? No. Howe. You don't know her. She hasn't been outside her house in six years, except to get groceries and see me. What did I say? You're so pale."

"You don't sound like you were helping these people much."

"Of course not. And they weren't helping me either. You get pretty tired of other people's nightmares. For a while I toyed with the idea of breaking the codes, just telling everyone straight out like I did the last day what I thought was wrong, and what I thought they should do—a sort of truth-shock therapy. But it's in vogue now and it doesn't work. Anyway, I didn't know what they should do anymore. And I was beginning to be plagued by the old dictum that if you make a face long enough, it'll stick. I was becoming as bad as my patients. I folded my tissues after I used them. Unless I'd read every item in the paper, even the obituaries, I couldn't sleep. At dinners, I had to question my motivation every time I thanked someone for seconds. What are you looking at?"

I was looking at my clothes spinning in the dryer, and getting a bit dizzy.

"So do you think I did good?" he asked.

"You don't like women much, I'll tell you that."

"Really, I'd like a second opinion. You're the first person I've talked to since it happened."

"You're the first person I've talked to in a month."

"Literally?"

"Almost."

"So you'll make a good judge. What do you think, ignoring my putative misogyny?"

I shrugged. "I'll try. Sounds okay, assuming you can support yourself and spend your time happily."

"Time and money I've got. I was thinking of going into politics."

"Hah!"

"Why not?"

"You talk too much."

"I'm sorry."

"No problem. I think your clothes are done."

"Thanks." He put them in the dryers sloppily and sat down again. "You're already drunk," he told me.

"True."

"Then stop drinking. What do you do?"

"I'm a professional mourner. A keener, as the Irish say."

"Does it pay well?"

"It seems to. Lately, it has paid very well."

"Feel like supporting me?"

I must have looked at him oddly, because he said "Just kidding" and put his glasses on as, I suppose, a nervous gesture. He scrutinized me in a way that made it very clear he'd been a psychiatrist. I was glad I'd showered before doing my laundry. He was lovely in glasses. They made you want to touch his eyes.

"I can see how you wound up with female patients," I said.

"A compliment?"

I smiled. It was a real smile—I could feel it on my face, the way you feel the beginning of a suntan.

"What do you do, really?"

"I just quit a job myself. I worked at a recording studio." He looked disappointed, so I added, "I'm a concert pianist."

He lit up. "Really!"

"No. You're going to have a hard time slumming it, Dr. Stern. You're still impressed by them diplomas."

"Right again. Is that why you don't want to tell me what you do? You make porn movies? You a librarian?"

"I can't tell you what I do because I don't do anything, except attract strange strangers who tell me their life stories, die, and leave me money."

"You should be a psychiatrist."

"It's more fun as a hobby."

We sat looking at each other until my drying cycle was done. It was a funny kind of looking—shy but lazy, more the way you'd look at a wall or people passing.

"So what will you do now?" I asked him.

"Help you fold your laundry," he said, and he did. He folded the towels and shirts while I worked on the skirts, pants, and underwear. I could tell he was examining the underwear peripherally, but all he could sniff out about my predilections from my clothes was that I was rather conservative and not fond of bright colors.

"What are these?" he asked, disentangling a pair of Argyle's underwear from a towel. That's how long it had been since I'd done laundry. "You know guys who wear boxer shorts?"

"I think it's best," I said, "to be evasive at this point."

"Why? We all have dirty laundry."

"Clean now," I said, doing my best not to blush.

While we were folding my sheets, a couple came in with their laundry and the evening paper. Without even acknowledging Danny and me, or the comedy of laundry at this hour, they crammed their clothes into washers and sat down to divide up the paper. The man took the front page and business sections; the woman took everything else. You could tell that their paper-reading ritual was immutable and that they weren't mad about each other lately. The woman was of the dark school of beauty that I'd enroll in if I were given a choice—she was far too beautiful, in fact, to be with a man in so world-weary a fashion. She must have sensed me taking her in, for she looked at me briefly, dismissed me, dismissed Danny, looked at the bottle of champagne and the Fritos with mild disdain, then turned back to her paper. I wanted to back out of the laundromat, so sorry was I to have offended her. But I'd simply been in the basement for too long. When I unstuck myself, I saw that for a while I'd been holding my end of a sheet instead of folding it. Danny Stern was at the other end, the sheet between us like a hammock; he was tugging on the sheet to get my attention.

"Lost in thought?" he asked uneasily.

I smiled and shrugged.

When Danny and I were done folding the sheets, we checked his drying cycle, which was not quite done.

"Do you want to tell me more about yourself?" he asked.

"Not at all."

"A *Last Tango* routine? No names?"

He said this in a competent Brando voice, puffing out his cheeks. I remembered who he reminded me of. He wasn't tall enough, and he certainly wasn't Irish, but he reminded me of Casey O'Brien.

"You spend a lot of time alone in the mountains?" I asked. "You remind me of someone named Casey O'Brien."

"An old lover."

I laughed. "It wouldn't do to share a lover with my half-aunt and my mother. He's an old person, dead, whom I never met."

"Lot of inbreeding in your family?"

"I'm not sure yet. You don't happen to be related to anyone I know, are you?"

"Let's see," Danny said, in a Viennese psychiatrist voice, stroking his chin. I could see that his imitations were going to be a problem. We folded his laundry then, although some of his jeans weren't quite dry, and there was no reason for us to be in the laundromat, except to eat the Fritos and finish the champagne, which we did, at which point Danny Stern said:

"I assume it's too late to invite you over for a post-laundry drink."

"Right. I have a big day tomorrow."

"What's up?"

I thought a moment. "I'm going to Paris," I said, "to celebrate my birthday."

After I finished saying it, I thought it was a great idea. *I am going to Paris to celebrate my birthday*. Not exactly original, but perfect, in fact, for just that reason.

"Great," he said. "Drop me a postcard. How old will you be?"

"Twenty-four."

"Shee-it."

"I look my age," I said, "except when I play the piano. Then I look like a child. Don't worry. You'll be the youngest friend I've had in years."

"You think we'll be friends, then?"

"We're off to a good start. Maybe *too* good."

"You don't think we'll be lovers?"

I raised my eyebrows. Mildred's gesture. Mara's too, for that matter. I stood. Danny stood, too. We were standing on opposite sides of the table.

"You mean you'll leave it open?" he said. "I'm glad. I see a danger of us getting silly together, but we may, as they say, be able to work that out."

He said the last three words in a Southern drawl. "Only if you knock off with the accents," I said, in a Yiddish accent.

"I'm sorry. It's because I'm nervous. You know, I've been working so hard that I haven't *met* anyone in months. I'm not sure quite what to do."

"Me either."

"I can call you, though? You're listed?"

"Absolutely."

"When you getting back?"

"Friday."

"Friday! You're going to Paris for two days? You're going to be jet-lagged right off the globe!"

"I love jet lag," I said. "I love flying. Landings always get to me. Always the chance that the plane will spin into space like the toy cow in the tornado scene from *The Wizard of Oz* and I'll die with my head jerked into the lap of a drunk accountant in hound's-tooth."

I stopped talking, embarrassed. Danny Stern smiled. "You're drunk," he said.

"Maybe a little."

"You have very blue eyes. And you're sway-backed. I like that."

"*You're* drunk."

"No I'm not." He leaned across the table to whisper. "Don't worry. You're prettier than *she* is."

"But my eyes aren't blue. They're hazel."

"Look blue to me. Must be the shirt."

"Something I wanted to ask you, Dr. Stern. Don't you have a washer and a dryer in your building? I mean, you're rich, aren't you? Shouldn't you have your own machines?"

"Yes I do. But I felt like getting outside tonight. I wanted to, like, get in touch with the people. And meet you."

"Cute."

"Not cute."

He thanked me for listening. I told him he was welcome, and thanked him for talking. We were still standing across from each other, the table between us. No no, he thanked me for listening. But no, I thanked him for talking. The couple, shifting their laundry to dryers, did a couple of eyerolls. It was an old routine, and both Danny and I knew it was old, but that was all right.

He asked if he could drive me home. I refused. No one would have dared to hurt me—I could have killed them with my laundry bag. He asked if I needed a ride to the airport. I considered.

"Are you trying to do something for me?" I asked.

"It'll be 'for' you only in the narrowest sense. It's to assure further contact."

"I see. Well then. If I decide to stay in Paris longer, or if I go to Baltimore straight from Paris, will you feed my cats?"

"Sure. How long are we talking about?"

"I don't know, but there's plenty of cat food. If you went over, say, day after tomorrow? Then I'll call and tell you how long I'll be?"

"Do you have a spare key?"

I tore a bit off the edge of the newspaper the couple had

thrown in the trash and wrote down my address and phone number. Danny did the same.

"The mailboxes in my building," I said, "don't lock very well. They're all warped. There's a mailbox marked 'Basement' that no one uses. Inside it at the top is one of those metallic Hide-a-Keys."

"If you have the key there, then why don't you just give me the key now and use your Hide-a-Key to let yourself in tonight?"

"Good thinking, but my key isn't in the Hide-a-Key yet. It's the second-floor front apartment. Freud will especially want to be petted, just for a second or two."

"Freud?"

"Sorry."

"How many cats are we talking about?"

"Two."

"Is the other cat named Jung?"

"Skinner."

"How did I ever get mixed up with you?"

"Your mission, should you choose to accept it."

He bowed. We shook hands at the door of the laundromat. I liked his hand. It was strongly veined and warm. Up close to him, there was a delicious smell—some combination of soap, sweat, and testosterone.

My laundry bag was so full that it blocked off my view, but I could see lights on in some third- and fourth-story windows along the street. The weather seemed cooler than it had in weeks.

It wasn't just Danny Stern. It was everything. I knew that when I got home, I was going to play the piano, no matter what my neighbors thought, and that the next day, I was going to Paris. My shoes made a wonderful sound against the pavement.

# 24

Money doesn't have to talk. Money is the loudest dumb show, the only true Esperanto. If I hadn't already had a passport (from the proposed December jaunt to London with Argyle that had never materialized—he'd gone to Seattle instead), I'm sure that I could have gotten one in a minute by flashing a couple of bills. But I would have felt like a flasher, and I'd doubtless be exposed enough, as a New Yorker seeing Paris for the first time in her adult life. Frog Haggerty O'Brien Spell's diamond-and-ruby bracelet flashed on my wrist. I was pale from spending all of August in a cellar, and loud noises still made me jump. In my purse were the credit cards that Mildred Howell had confiscated from the pickpocket, and my watch, which I'd retrieved from the safe-deposit box that morning. I'd forgotten all about the credit cards until I found them on the plane as I searched for a pen to fill out a postcard of the Empire State Building which I'd bought at Kennedy and planned to mail to Danny Stern as soon as I got a French stamp. In a different life, perhaps, I might have used one of the stolen credit cards to buy alligator shoes.

As I looked at the sky from the plane, I kept thinking about Danny Stern's neck—how his neck emerged from the collar of his plaid shirt and met, in one efficient sweep, his chin and ears. Perhaps Danny's astrological sign is the one in which the neck is the chief body part, for even now that I know him better, I can still tour his body beginning at the neck—upwards to the head, slightly too large; downwards to the perfect chest and legs. His body is exciting and safe at once. I knew right away that I'd love him. I may never tire of the underside of his tongue, his sly look masked by directness. The summer was almost an embarrassment of riches so far as love went. I still have no idea what love is, but having admitted as much, I don't have to know. I just let myself alone. In one recurrent fantasy that first entered my mind while I was somewhere over the Atlantic, Danny and I stow away together on an island, where we are not tourists but neither are we natives; our life together is bound by an ardent refusal to define any one life. The trouble is that the refusal can become its own definition. Both Danny and I like to think of ourselves as more than we are. Basically, we're both underachievers. But Danny likes to believe that when his eyes fog up and he goes inside himself to browse, he's going somewhere. As often as he denies the interior, he likes to think that his insides are something like Australia, mostly unexplored, populated by aborigines and dotted with dry underbrush. And me: I believe I know other people's fatal flaws. I believe that by loving other people's failures, I dissolve my own. As I write that, I can hear Mildred's voice in the back of my head: *If you think your fatal flaw is your attention to other people's fatal flaws, you're wrong. Your fatal flaw is that you never think about other people at all. You think about yourself. Danny, me, Casey, your mother—we're all shadow selves.* She's right. That isn't her voice. I wish she'd come back to life, so I could take her to the beach in the back of Danny's car. So I could listen better.

I had no luggage. My reservation back to New York was for the following evening, so I wouldn't have time to sleep. The reason I made the trip so short was to make sure that I didn't enjoy myself too much. If I was tired and hurried, I could assuage my guilt about the extravagance of the trip. I was like the good Christian who drinks Martinis because good Christians shouldn't drink and he hates Martinis.

One of the first orders of business in Paris was to buy a suit to wear to the Louvre—a suit that would make me look leggy, audacious, and unassailable. But I arrived a little before midnight and the stores, needless to say, were closed. At midnight I was looking in the window of a shop that appeared to specialize in sexy lingerie—the Parisian version of Frederick's of Hollywood. Behind me, people in a café were drinking absinthe or whatever it is the French drink now that absinthe is illegal. The street had a luscious simplicity. All of the buildings were four stories high. I remembered that I'd just turned twenty-four and was so startled by this fact that I sang, out loud:

> Happy birthday to me,
> Happy birthday to me,
> Happy birthday to me-eee,
> Happy birthday to me—

Then I had a brief fit of mortification. Granted, I sang quickly and not all that loud; still, singing to myself without luggage in Paris so late at night made me feel a bit too much like Mildred Howell. I had no friends. I was dressed like a Catholic schoolgirl before the window of a candy store: superimposed against the baskets of chocolate and marzipan, I must have looked so out-of-date and awkward that you'd think I'd just been released from prison. I decided I'd better check into a hotel.

But it was the tourist season and most of the rooms, at least in the fancy hotels (I had to have a fancy hotel), appeared to be booked. One hotel did have a room that they thought would probably be a little too expensive for me. It was available by a fluke. I scratched my ear with my braceleted arm and assured them it wouldn't be too expensive; I managed not to gasp when they told me the price. After some repetition (my French was rusty), the desk clerk finally explained that it was their honeymoon suite. I said that was fine, and told them to wake me at six.

The room was purple and gold, commanded a view of the entire city from the balcony, and had a *heart*-shaped bed, O Lord, the size of my kitchen in New York. The bathroom was a Hollywood set. I tried to make a joke to the man who did not carry up my luggage about being married to myself, but I must have gotten a pronoun or a preposition wrong, because he merely looked puzzled. He smiled, however, at my mime requesting toothpaste and a toothbrush. After he returned with toothpaste and toothbrush, I had the hotel put through a call to my father.

"Hello?" Jeremy said. "Hello?"

"Jeremy?"

"Hello? Jennifer?"

Fifteen hundred miles away and I could hear Mozart from the living room, Jeremy's cocktail Mozart.

"Jennifer? The connection's crackling. You're not calling from home? Are you at the train station?"

"No, I'm in Paris."

"At work? I can't hear."

"No, I quit work. I'm calling from Paris."

Jeremy didn't respond.

"It's wonderful," I shouted. "I don't think I appreciated it before. Right now I'm looking out the window of my hotel. Remember in the third grade, Jeremy, how we made those Easter eggs with cut-out scenes inside? You squinted into a peep-hole and there was a whole world in the dome? That's what Paris is like. All the details are just right and utterly useless, like the squiggly lines in a postage stamp."

"How long will you be there?"

"Until tomorrow. Then I'll be in Baltimore."

"Jennifer, I didn't want to tell you."

"You're selling the house."

"Mara told you?"

"Yes. That must be a relief for you."

"True. It went on the market today. A nice young Chinese couple has already expressed an interest. I bought a condominium. I'm sorry."

"Why are you apologizing? I think that's great."

"The memories."

"Hey. Don't worry about *them*. You're okay?"

"Fine. It's about time you came home. I could use your help packing up the house. I've been going through the closets, the basement, the attic. Thirty years of junk. I've found some things of your mother's you might want."

"Diaries? Letters? Pictures?"

"Nothing like that. You'll see yourself. Some nice clothes that might be back in fashion. Her wedding dress. She packed it in the attic. No veil, though. Do you have the veil?"

"Sure do."

"That's good. We'll go through everything when you get home?"

"Where the heart is," I said.

"What?"

"Dad?"

"Let's not burn up your money."

"Right. See you tomorrow, or shortly thereafter. Do I have to tell you I miss you?"

"Show me," Jeremy said.

"You've been taking guilt lessons from Mara."

"No, dear. It'll be good to see you."

"I *will* show you," I said. "No kidding."

I went to sleep. That was good. I'd been too excited to sleep on the plane, too excited by Danny Stern and the thought of Paris to sleep after the laundromat. I was glad I had no luggage, for then I would have had a nightgown. As it was, I slept naked on lilac satin sheets and was idiotically, reprehensibly happy. It was easy to be happy in Paris with so much cash; knowing this made me feel guilty, and increased my joy.

They woke me up at six and I told them to try again at

eight. My sleep was buttery, light, and decidedly French, like the croissants. As soon as I tasted the croissants they brought, I could no longer pretend any nonchalance. They made for a sublime breakfast.

Outside, even the pavement seemed to be a richer, more even gray than any pavement I'd ever seen. There were windows full of pastry in front of which flowers were being sold and slim, sexy Frenchmen passed on their way to work—even Parisians work. It was Thursday. My decadence went unnoticed.

I bought a suit—a peacock blue raw silk suit. Never in my life had I owned anything in silk, and certainly not in so rich a blue; even my bath towels were beige or maroon. The shop was one of those salons you see in Forties films with fitting rooms big enough to have dinner parties in, with fresh daisies on a table and polished mirrors. I was sure the salesgirls would laugh at me when they saw my clothes (wrinkled from the long flight over the Atlantic), but they smiled charitably. They didn't even laugh when I chose the suit, which was the most conservative thing there (everything else was in a gypsy style, with enough material in each skirt or sleeve for a bedspread). They even suggested a blouse that might brighten things up, and when I came out of the fitting room for inspection, three sleek Parisian women nodded approval. I left with my old clothes in a bag.

Over lunch at an outdoor café, I indulged in a long-winded fantasy about being accosted by an articulate young French couple that wanted to get married, but not in the usual way: they wanted to exchange vows in the Louvre, and they wanted the vows witnessed by a total stranger—would I help them, please? But except for several admiring looks from men and a compliment from the American woman at the table next to mine about my bracelet, no one bothered this birthday girl. I went to the Louvre alone.

I saw the Venus de Milo. I tried to see the Mona Lisa over the other tourists' heads and the glare of the glass. I saw corridors full of gruesome crucifixions and a Vermeer so peaceful I wanted to sleep beside it for the rest of my life. Then I got a museum headache—a subtle but persistent headache like the one from too much monosodium glutamate in Chinese food. Actually, I don't enjoy museums. In the Louvre I thought about Baltimore, about how pleasant it would be to take Jeremy and Mara to an Italian restaurant along the harbor, a tacky place with watery red sauce over a single meatball. I could take them to Haussner's for stuffed shrimp, or, better yet, to Marconi's. If the old couple who ran Marconi's was still around, Jeremy could show me off—not that I'd accomplished much since I left home, but at least he could say that I was his daughter who lived in New York, who had just returned from Paris. And Mara! I couldn't wait to watch her fidget against the faded Montmartre wallpaper. I could spend a month, two months with Jeremy if he needed me.

As it turned out, I spent three weeks in Baltimore. There were some tense moments, especially going through things to pack. Jeremy wanted to be nostalgic. I was entirely willing to reminisce about my childhood with my father in that house: tending to the roses, or even the time that Jeremy, furiously embarrassed after a tame late-night movie, tried to explain menstruation to me. But I wasn't at all prepared to reminisce about Lucy, and certainly not the way Jeremy wanted to reminisce. The most innocent objects—napkin rings, bath mats, a stray playing card—would call forth reveries of domestic bliss from him. He'd pick up the garden shears and say, "Lucy used to hand these to me when I trimmed ivy from the chimney. She'd steady the ladder." Or he'd rattle a keychain in his fist and announce that once, on a Saturday, he and Lucy had just picked up the Chevy from the dealer and were on the way to the grocery store when the horn began to go off—they couldn't get it to stop. He didn't say a word about the suicide. It was as if Lucy had lived forever, buying cars and playing with the back yard. Confronted with Jeremy's eerily tranquil memories, I was afraid that I'd come upon some conclusive evidence that Lucy was Frog and not be able to keep the information to myself. Although Jeremy was in good health, I didn't want to be responsible for a big shock. But either Lucy had had the good sense to trash the evidence, or people who marry so late in their lives don't bother with the usual paraphernalia of remembrance, for there was no new evidence. I unwound, as people are supposed to do at their childhood homes. And luckily, Mara shared my distaste for turning the house into a shrine to the dead. *She* was still changing. To celebrate her excellent grades in a recent check-up, she'd bought a sports car, which she drove to Baltimore at top speed with the top down. She was dating a retired judge in Boston and had discovered several new restaurants which we'd have to try when we finally got off our butts to visit her. It amused me to see a seventy-five-year-old librarian carrying on like this, as it amused me to watch Jeremy's face get hot and soulful when he played the violin. It was a comfort to remember that I had energy and health in my genes. I wouldn't be at all ashamed to bring Danny Stern home, if it came to that. Trying to sleep in my narrow little bed, in a room still containing a Scrabble set missing half the letters and a Carnaby Street poster, I even regretted that Mildred Howell hadn't lived long enough to meet my family. She was very much like my father, happy in a mausoleum; and she might have learned something from Mara about embracing the new without forsaking the old.

On Thursday, I decided that I couldn't possibly leave Paris in five hours.

I blundered onto a street of fashionable shops where I bought a week's worth of underwear, clothing, and toiletries. I needed the underwear anyway. Then I went back to the hotel to see if my suite was still available. It wasn't. A couple was arriving that evening—from New York, in fact. But they did have another room available for the next few nights, also with a view but much smaller and less exotic, more befitting the pocketbook of a girl who had spent a thousand dollars between lunchtime and dinnertime.

Had I known that I wouldn't see a chunk of money that great at one time again for years, if ever—that, in a year, I'd be almost as cash-poor as I was before, still haggling with the IRS and in debt to a lawyer—I think I still would have spent the money in exactly the same way. I might have even spent it more joyfully.

I canceled my reservation back to New York, made another reservation for the following Thursday to Baltimore, called Jeremy to tell him when my plane would arrive, and ate veal for dinner.

By the next afternoon, I'd begun to get uncomfortable.

Paris is too pretty. Although Parisians undoubtedly pay taxes, get divorced, and die, the city itself is such a Shangri-la that the rest of your life feels slummy in comparison. Even if you can stay happy in full knowledge of how temporary such happiness is, you still can't help feeling that it's unfortunate to be alone. In Notre Dame, everyone feels alone in the face of so much history. You can survive in the public places—the tourist shopping streets or the Île Saint-Louis; but in the Tuileries, despite the noise of traffic and the other tourists, you feel that you've stumbled into an Impressionist painting that hasn't quite dried, and you crave an accomplice. Even if you have a newspaper to distract you from all that green, you can't help noticing how much more fun the couples are having. Or you pause on a bridge over the Seine to absorb yourself in the rhythm of light on the water and suddenly a barge passes underneath, full of chickens—you're so surprised that you need to exclaim, but there's no one about, and your mood shifts.

I found an American Express office and put through a call to Danny Stern, who was actually home.

"Danny," I said, "this is Jennifer playing Audrey Hepburn in Paris. Will you join me?"

"I can't," Danny said. "I'm cat-sitting."

"How are they treating you?"

"I went over this morning. I like your piano. The cats are

okay, but I tried to play the piano and they sat on my hands—
they're company-starved."

"So am I."

"With all the Americans there in August, you ought to be
able to find some company."

"But why don't you come? You're not working."

"What about the cats?"

I gave him a list of acquaintances who might oblige. "I
know it's an odd request," I said, "and of course the whole
scenario is a little too light, considering the fact that my father's
dying to see me in Baltimore—"

"Your parents are divorced?"

"Mother's dead. Notice how calmly I say that? It's a sham.
But I don't need a shrink. A week in Paris'll cure anything. I'm
flying back to Baltimore on Thursday so my father and I can get
reacquainted. Will you think about meeting me?"

"I don't have much time to think if you're leaving Thursday.
Why didn't you suggest this before?"

"I hardly knew you."

"I see."

"Danny? One other thing I just thought of. I don't have
any birth control."

"Why not?"

"I threw it out in an unshining hour."

"That settles it. I'll see you when you get back."

"Aw, c'mon."

"I was just kidding. Okay. If I come, you can be surprised."

"Surprised and gratified. I'm at the Hotel Meurice. They
give you terry cloth robes instead of towels, and the shower has
*seats* in it."

"But if I don't come, which is more likely, you won't be
disappointed?"

"Sure I will, but I won't leap from the Eiffel Tower. If you
don't come, the kitty litter's in the hall closet."

"Jennifer, I think you're fine."

His voice stayed with me for the rest of the trip.

I got back to the hotel in time to shower, nap, and watch the twilight from my balcony. I've never felt utterly at ease during twilight. In the second grade we saw a time-lapsed version of the tide rising in the Bay of Fundy. It scared me that the sea did such violent things every day. Something as normal as the tide rising can make vast quantities of land disappear. During twilight, the clouds do their floorshow, and soon the sky is darker than the grass. Twilight is even more frightening if you've just woken up for it, if you haven't had a day of activity to fortify you for the change. When you're a child your parents wake you from a nap and tell you what to do: it's dinnertime, or time to wash up, or time to say hello to the neighbors. Someone has made cookies and washed the floor; the television is on, and while it's unpleasant to think that the world has had the audacity to go on without you, at least you can tell exactly where it has gone. This is not the case when you're an adult and fall asleep in Paris. People were loitering outside my window, and you could tell they were tourists—Parisians leave the city in August, so as not to be gawked at by foreigners or have photographers ask to take a picture.

Still, I knew exactly what to do. I was going to be a tourist, with or without Danny Stern. I had to see the Sacré-Cœur, the Eiffel Tower, Versailles, the Arc de Triomphe, Napoleon's Tomb, and the construction on the Pompidou Center. I had to send postcards to my father and to Mara. The Louvre, once I got over my initial dread, would require at least two days. I had to get a map and a French-English dictionary; I had to go somewhere on the clean French subway.

It didn't occur to me to check City Records for the marriage certificate of Katey O'Brien and Gato Haggerty. Nor did I check customs for information on when Frog Haggerty O'Brien left the country, or the Louvre for information on their stolen art. At the Louvre, I almost woke up an old guard who was asleep by a sculpture of an Egyptian cat to ask him if he knew

Marcel or if he could help me locate the basement apartment, but I didn't. The truth is I hardly thought of Mildred Howell, sweet dead Mildred Howell who had taught me how not to mourn. I was a well-dressed American in Paris with a diamond-and-ruby bracelet and a pocket watch of the Prodigal Son, still set on Eastern Standard Time. I could barely walk in my high French shoes, but I was as giddy as a schoolgirl and not ashamed. I was a citizen of the heart; I could afford to be a tourist.

# A Note About the Author

Lisa Zeidner was born in Washington, D.C., in 1955, and was educated at Carnegie–Mellon University, Johns Hopkins University, and Washington University. Her poetry and fiction have appeared in a number of small magazines. She lives in Philadelphia and teaches at Rutgers University.

# A Note on the Type

The text of this book was set on the Linotype in Fairfield, the first type face from the hand of the distinguished American artist and engraver Rudolph Ruzicka. In its structure Fairfield displays the sober and sane qualities of a master craftsman whose talent has long been dedicated to clarity. It is this trait that accounts for the trim grace and virility, the spirited design and sensitive balance of this original type face.

Rudolph Ruzicka (1883–1978) was born in Bohemia and came to America in 1894. He has designed and illustrated many books and has created a considerable list of individual prints—wood engravings, line engravings on copper, aquatints.

Composed by Maryland Linotype Composition Company, Baltimore, Maryland.
Printed and bound by The Haddon Craftsmen, Scranton, Pennsylvania.

Typography and binding design by Karolina Harris.

KALEIDOSCOPE

# THE CONSTITUTION

by
Suzanne LeVert

***BENCHMARK BOOKS***

MARSHALL CAVENDISH
NEW YORK

Benchmark Books
Marshall Cavendish
99 White Plains Road
Tarrytown, NY 10591
www. marshallcavendish.com

Library of Congress Cataloging-in-Publication Data
LeVert, Suzanne.
The Constitution / by Suzanne LeVert
p. cm. - (Kaleidoscope)
Includes bibliographical references and index.
ISBN 0-7614-1452-5
1. United States. Constitution-Juvenile literature. 2. United States-Politics and government-1775-1783-Juvenile literature. 3. United States-Politics and government-1783-1865-Juvenile literature. 4. Constitutional history-United States-Juvenile literature. [1. Constitutional history-United States. 2. United States-Politics and government-1775-1783. 3. United States-Politics and government-1783-1865.] I. Title. II. Kaleidoscope (Tarrytown, N.Y.)
E303.L48 2003
342.73'02-dc21

2001007571

Photo Research by Anne Burns Images

Cover Photo by The Granger Collection

The photographs in this book are by permission and through the courtesy of: The Granger Collection:1(title),5,25,26,34; North Wind Picture Archives:6,9,10,13,14,22,38; Superstock:17,18; Jay Mallin:21; Corbis:29,33,37,41 Bettman,42 Jerry Tobias; Getty Images:30 Mark Wilson

Printed in Italy

6 5 4 3 2 1

# CONTENTS

# THE PREAMBLE

"We the People of the United States, in Order to form a more perfect Union, establish Justice, insure domestic Tranquility, provide for the common defence, promote the general Welfare, and secure the Blessings of Liberty to ourselves and our Posterity, do ordain and establish this Constitution for the United States of America."

*One of the oldest and shortest written constitutions in the world, the U.S. Constitution has provided the United States a strong base for political stability, personal freedom, and economic growth.*

# We the People

of the United States, in order to form a more perfect Union, establish Justice, insure domestic Tranquility, provide for the common defence, promote the general Welfare, and secure the Blessings of Liberty to ourselves and our Posterity, do ordain and establish this Constitution for the United States of America.

## Article. I.

**Section. 1.** All legislative Powers herein granted shall be vested in a Congress of the United States, which shall consist of a Senate and House of Representatives.

**Section. 2.** The House of Representatives shall be composed of Members chosen every second Year by the People of the several States, and the Electors in each State shall have the Qualifications requisite for Electors of the most numerous Branch of the State Legislature.

No Person shall be a Representative who shall not have attained to the Age of twenty five Years, and been seven Years a Citizen of the United States, and who shall not, when elected, be an Inhabitant of that State in which he shall be chosen.

Representatives and direct Taxes shall be apportioned among the several States which may be included within this Union, according to their respective Numbers, which shall be determined by adding to the whole Number of free Persons, including those bound to Service for a Term of Years, and excluding Indians not taxed, three fifths of all other Persons. The actual Enumeration shall be made within three Years after the first Meeting of the Congress of the United States, and within every subsequent Term of ten Years, in such Manner as they shall by Law direct. The Number of Representatives shall not exceed one for every thirty Thousand, but each State shall have at Least one Representative; and until such enumeration shall be made, the State of New Hampshire shall be entitled to chuse three, Massachusetts eight, Rhode Island and Providence Plantations one, Connecticut five, New York six, New Jersey four, Pennsylvania eight, Delaware one, Maryland six, Virginia ten, North Carolina five, South Carolina five, and Georgia three.

When vacancies happen in the Representation from any State, the Executive Authority thereof shall issue Writs of Election to fill such Vacancies.

The House of Representatives shall chuse their Speaker and other Officers; and shall have the sole Power of Impeachment.

**Section. 3.** The Senate of the United States shall be composed of two Senators from each State, chosen by the Legislature thereof for six Years; and each Senator shall have one Vote.

Immediately after they shall be assembled in Consequence of the first Election, they shall be divided as equally as may be into three Classes. The Seats of the Senators of the first Class shall be vacated at the Expiration of the second Year, of the second Class at the Expiration of the fourth Year, and of the third Class at the Expiration of the sixth Year, so that one third may be chosen every second Year; and if Vacancies happen by Resignation, or otherwise, during the Recess of the Legislature of any State, the Executive thereof may make temporary Appointments until the next Meeting of the Legislature, which shall then fill such Vacancies.

No Person shall be a Senator who shall not have attained to the Age of thirty Years, and been nine Years a Citizen of the United States, and who shall not, when elected, be an Inhabitant of that State for which he shall be chosen.

The Vice President of the United States shall be President of the Senate, but shall have no Vote, unless they be equally divided.

The Senate shall chuse their other Officers, and also a President pro tempore, in the Absence of the Vice President, or when he shall exercise the Office of President of the United States.

The Senate shall have the sole Power to try all Impeachments. When sitting for that Purpose, they shall be on Oath or Affirmation. When the President of the United States is tried, the Chief Justice shall preside: And no Person shall be convicted without the Concurrence of two thirds of the Members present.

Judgment in Cases of Impeachment shall not extend further than to removal from Office, and disqualification to hold and enjoy any Office of honor, Trust or Profit under the United States: but the Party convicted shall nevertheless be liable and subject to Indictment, Trial, Judgment and Punishment, according to Law.

**Section. 4.** The Times, Places and Manner of holding Elections for Senators and Representatives, shall be prescribed in each State by the Legislature thereof; but the Congress may at any time by Law make or alter such Regulations, except as to the Places of chusing Senators.

The Congress shall assemble at least once in every Year, and such Meeting shall be on the first Monday in December, unless they shall by Law appoint a different Day.

**Section. 5.** Each House shall be the Judge of the Elections, Returns and Qualifications of its own Members, and a Majority of each shall constitute a Quorum to do Business; but a smaller Number may adjourn from day to day, and may be authorized to compel the Attendance of absent Members, in such Manner, and under such Penalties as each House may provide.

Each House may determine the Rules of its Proceedings, punish its Members for disorderly Behaviour, and, with the Concurrence of two thirds, expel a Member.

Each House shall keep a Journal of its Proceedings, and from time to time publish the same, excepting such Parts as may in their Judgment require Secrecy; and the Yeas and Nays of the Members of either House on any question shall, at the Desire of one fifth of those Present, be entered on the Journal.

Neither House, during the Session of Congress, shall, without the Consent of the other, adjourn for more than three days, nor to any other Place than that in which the two Houses shall be sitting.

**Section. 6.** The Senators and Representatives shall receive a Compensation for their Services, to be ascertained by Law, and paid out of the Treasury of the United States. They shall in all Cases, except Treason, Felony and Breach of the Peace, be privileged from Arrest during their Attendance at the Session of their respective Houses, and in going to and returning from the same; and for any Speech or Debate in either House, they shall not be questioned in any other Place.

No Senator or Representative shall, during the Time for which he was elected, be appointed to any civil Office under the Authority of the United States, which shall have been created, or the Emoluments whereof shall have been encreased during such time; and no Person holding any Office under the United States, shall be a Member of either House during his Continuance in Office.

**Section. 7.** All Bills for raising Revenue shall originate in the House of Representatives; but the Senate may propose or concur with Amendments as on other Bills.

Every Bill which shall have passed the House of Representatives and the Senate, shall, before it become a Law, be presented to the President of the

G. Washington Presd.
and deputy from Virginia

John Langdon
Nicholas Gilman

Nathaniel Gorham

Rufus King

Wm. Saml. Johnson

Roger Sherman

Alexander Hamilton

Wil. Livingston

David Brearley

Wm. Paterson

Jona. Dayton

B. Franklin

Thomas Mifflin

Robt. Morris

Geo. Clymer

Thos. FitzSimons

Jared Ingersoll

James Wilson

Gouv. Morris

Danl. St. Thos. Jenifer

Danl. Carroll

John Blair

James Madison Jr.

Wm. Blount

Richd. Dobbs Spaight

Hu. Williamson

J. Rutledge

Charles Cotesworth Pinckney

Charles Pinckney

Pierce Butler

**6**

THE SIGNERS OF THE CONSTITUTION.

FAC-SIMILES OF THE SIGNATURES OF THE LEADING
MEMBERS OF THE CONVENTION OF 1787.

Those words—called the Preamble—precede a document known as the United States Constitution. The rights and regulations found within the Constitution created the model for the government of the United States. The U.S. Constitution remains the oldest written constitution in the world that is still in effect. Originally written on four pieces of parchment, the Constitution creates a government that is strong yet flexible. It has been able to adapt to the changing needs of Americans for more than two centuries.

*Thirty-Nine men signed the U.S. Constitution on September 17, 1776. The oldest person to sign was Benjamin Franklin of Pennsylvania (81) and the youngest was Jonathan Dayton of New Jersey (26).*

# THE FOUNDING OF A COUNTRY

In 1775, the thirteen American colonies rebelled against their mother country, Great Britain. This rebellion was known as the American Revolution. The Revolution began because the colonists no longer wanted to be ruled by Great Britain. Great Britain's system of government, a monarchy led by a king, did not allow the colonists to have a say in the way their leaders ran the country. The colonists wanted to form their own independent nation, with a government made up of men who represented the views of the people.

*Here, colonists are tearing down a statute of the British monarch, King George III, in New York in 1776. The American Revolution began in April 1775 and lasted until the Treaty of Paris was signed between the monarchy of Great Britain and the newly formed United States in September 1783.*

9

After winning independence from Great Britain in 1783, a group of fifty-five Americans met at the State House in Philadelphia on May 25, 1787, to draw up the plans for the new government. Called the Constitutional Convention, this meeting lasted for about four months. The Framers, as the men who attended would be later known, brought with them many ideas for what the new government should look like. They also had other documents to help guide them.

*The Framers of the Constitution met for four months in Philadelphia while drafting the Constitution.*

11

One of these documents was the Articles of Confederation, which some of these same men had drafted in 1781. Having fought the American Revolution to be free of Great Britain's king, the Framers were afraid to give too much power to any one person or branch of government. The Articles of Confederation created a very loose union between the thirteen colonies. But very soon, as the colonies grew in population and economic power, it became necessary to establish a stronger national, central government. This central government could speak for the whole country in matters such as trade with other countries and national defense.

*Colonists from England began arriving in the New World in 1585. The first permanent settlement was founded in Jamestown, Virginia, in 1607. The last of the original thirteen colonies was established in what is now Georgia in 1732.*

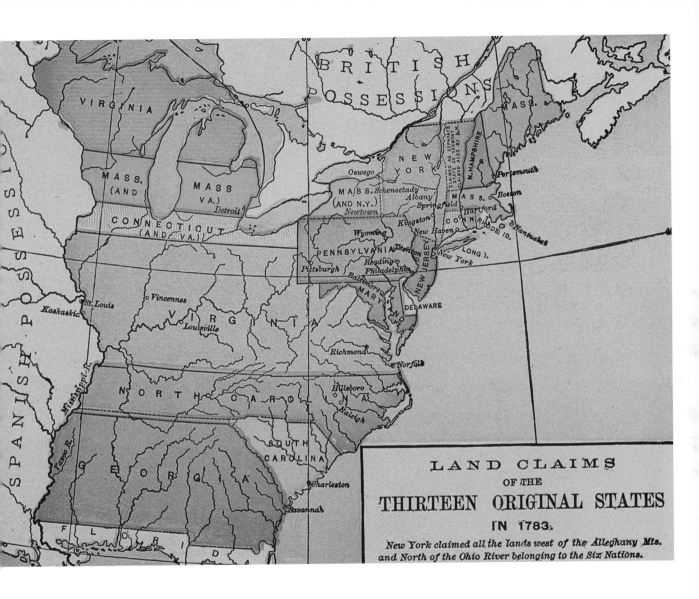

LAND CLAIMS
OF THE
THIRTEEN ORIGINAL STATES
IN 1783.

*New York claimed all the lands west of the Alleghany Mts.
and North of the Ohio River belonging to the Six Nations.*

13

14

Instead of trying to change the Articles of Confederation, the Framers decided to create a brand new document, called the Constitution. In it, they gave important duties and responsibilities to a central government and a chief executive called the president of the United States. Individual states and individual citizens also have power under this document, but they are unified by the national government.

*On April 30, 1789, George Washington stood on the balcony of Federal Hall in New York City and took the oath of office to become the first president of the United States. New York served as the nation's capital until 1800, when it was moved to Washington, D.C.*

The system of government created by the Constitution is a representative democracy. A democracy is a system in which the people govern themselves. Representative democracy means that the citizens do not actually handle the day-to-day affairs of the country themselves, but instead elect representatives to carry out the duties of the government. The president of the United States and the members of Congress (the House of Representatives and the Senate) are our representatives at the national level, while the governors, state representatives, and mayors handle governmental duties at the state and local level.

*James Madison, Benjamin Franklin, and George Washington—It was their vision that created the system of government Americans enjoy today.*

17

# Congress OF THE United States

begun and held at the City of New-York, on

Wednesday the fourth of March, one thousand seven hundred and eighty nine

THE Conventions of a number of the States, having at the time of their adopting the Constitution, expressed a desire, in order to prevent misconstruction or abuse of its powers, that further declaratory and restrictive clauses should be added: And as extending the ground of public confidence in the Government, will best insure the beneficent ends of its institution

RESOLVED by the Senate and House of Representatives of the United States of America, in Congress assembled, two thirds of both Houses concurring, that the following Articles be proposed to the Legislatures of the several States, as amendments to the Constitution of the United States, all, or any of which Articles, when ratified by three fourths of the said Legislatures, to be valid to all intents and purposes, as part of the said Constitution; viz.

ARTICLES in addition to, and Amendment of the Constitution of the United States of America, proposed by Congress, and ratified by the Legislatures of the several States, pursuant to the fifth Article of the original Constitution

Article the first ... After the first enumeration required by the first article of the Constitution, there shall be one Representative for every thirty thousand, until the number shall amount to one hundred, after which, the proportion shall be so regulated by Congress, that there shall be not less than one hundred Representatives, nor less than one Representative for every forty thousand persons, until the number of Representatives shall amount to two hundred, after which the proportion shall be so regulated by Congress, that there shall not be less than two hundred Representatives, nor more than one Representative for every fifty thousand persons.

Article the second ... No law, varying the compensation for the services of the Senators and Representatives, shall take effect, until an election of Representatives shall have intervened.

Article the third ... Congress shall make no law respecting an establishment of religion, or prohibiting the free exercise thereof; or abridging the freedom of speech, or of the press, or the right of the people peaceably to assemble, and to petition the Government for a redress of grievances.

Article the fourth ... A well regulated militia, being necessary to the security of a free State, the right of the people to keep and bear Arms, shall not be infringed.

Article the fifth ... No Soldier shall, in time of peace be quartered in any house, without the consent of the owner, nor in time of war, but in a manner to be prescribed by law.

Article the sixth ... The right of the people to be secure in their persons, houses, papers, and effects, against unreasonable searches and seizures, shall not be violated, and no Warrants shall issue, but upon probable cause, supported by oath or affirmation, and particularly describing the place to be searched, and the persons or things to be seized.

Article the seventh ... No person shall be held to answer for a capital, or otherwise infamous crime, unless on a presentment or indictment of a Grand Jury, except in cases arising in the land or naval forces, or in the Militia, when in actual service in time of War or public danger; nor shall any person be subject for the same offence to be twice put in jeopardy of life or limb; nor shall be compelled in any criminal case to be a witness against himself, nor be deprived of life, liberty, or property, without due process of law; nor shall private property be taken for public use, without just compensation.

Article the eighth ... In all criminal prosecutions, the accused shall enjoy the right to a speedy and public trial, by an impartial jury of the State and district wherein the crime shall have been committed, which district shall have been previously ascertained by law, and to be informed of the nature and cause of the accusation; to be confronted with the witnesses against him; to have compulsory process for obtaining witnesses in his favor, and to have the assistance of counsel for his defence.

Article the ninth ... In suits at common law, where the value in controversy shall exceed twenty dollars, the right of trial by jury shall be preserved, and no fact tried by a jury, shall be otherwise re-examined in any court of the United States, than according to the rules of the common law.

Article the tenth ... Excessive bail shall not be required, nor excessive fines imposed, nor cruel and unusual punishments inflicted.

Article the eleventh ... The enumeration in the Constitution, of certain rights, shall not be construed to deny or disparage others retained by the people.

Article the twelfth ... The powers not delegated to the United States by the Constitution, nor prohibited by it to the States, are reserved to the States respectively, or to the people.

ATTEST,

Frederick Augustus Muhlenberg, Speaker of the House of Representatives.

John Adams, Vice-President of the United States, and President of the Senate

# THE PRINCIPLES OF THE CONSTITUTION

The U.S. Constitution outlines a system of national and state government that has very specific and limited powers. It consists of the Preamble or introduction, seven articles or sections, and twenty-seven Amendments or additions. Its first ten amendments are called the Bill of Rights. The Bill of Rights protects the rights of individual citizens.

*In order to provide for freedom of religion and freedom of the press, among other individual liberties, the U.S. Congress ratified the first ten amendments to the Constitution. Collectively, these ten amendments—pictured here—are called the Bill of Rights.*

The first three articles of the Constitution set up the three branches of government: Congress (legislative, or lawmaking), the presidency (the executive), and the federal courts, including the Supreme Court (the judiciary). This division of authority sets up a system of checks and balances that ensures that no branch of government can dominate the others.

*The Constitution creates a system of separate branches (the executive, the legislative, and the judicial) that share powers. Because the three branches share power, each can check the powers of the others. This is the system of checks and balances.*

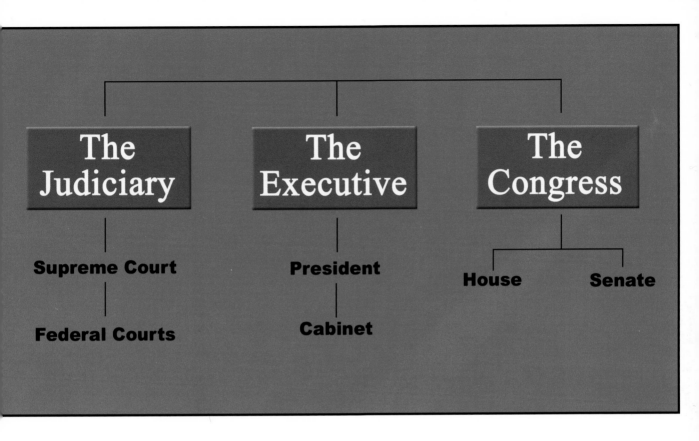

Article 1 of the Constitution gives all lawmaking powers to Congress. Article 2 gives executive power to the president, including responsibility as commander in chief of the military forces and the power to appoint individuals to positions within the federal government, with the approval of the Senate. Article 3 puts judicial power into the hands of the federal courts, with the Supreme Court as the final court. Article 4 outlines the relationships between the state and federal governments and among the states themselves.

*The nation's first president, Washington, was also the first commander-in-chief of its armed services. Here, he leads the colonial forces during the Revolutionary War.*

The Framers also recognized the need to include a method for making changes to the Constitution itself. Article 5 spells out how to do this. Changes to the Constitution, called amendments, can take place in two ways. Amendments to the Constitution require either approval by two-thirds of the members of both the House and Senate, or a request by two-thirds of the state legislatures for a Constitutional Convention.

*"The rights of citizens of the United States to vote shall not be denied or abridged by the United States or by any state on account of race, color, or previous condition of servitude." So reads the Fifteenth Amendment, enacted in 1870. The drawing here depicts citizens celebrating their right to vote.*

## THE FIFTEENTH AMENDMENT

PUBLISHED & PRINTED BY

Entered according to act of Congress in the year 1870 by Th. Kelly in the Office of the Librarian of Congress at Washington D.C.

THOMAS KELLY 17 BARCLAY ST. N.Y.

1. Reading Emancipation Proclamation
2. Life Liberty and Independence
3. We Unite the Bonds of Fellowship.
4. Our Charter of Rights the Holy Scriptures.

5. Education will prove the Equality the Races.
6. Liberty Protects the Mariage Alter.
7. Celebration of Fifteenth Amendment May 19th 1870
8. The Ballot Box is open to us.

9. Our representive Sits in the National Legislature
10. The Holy Ordinances of Religion are free
11. Freedom unites the Family Circle.
12. We will protect our Country as it defends our Rights.

13. We till our own Fields.
14. The Right of Citizens of the U.S. to vote shall not
be denied or abridged by the U.S. or any State on account
of Race, Color or Condition of Servitude 15th Amendment

# Thirty-Eighth Congress of the United States of America;

At the Second Session,

Begun and held at the City of Washington, on Monday, the fifth day of December, one thousand eight hundred and sixty-four

## A RESOLUTION

Submitting to the legislatures of the several States a proposition to amend the Constitution of the United States.

Resolved by the Senate and House of Representatives of the United States of America in Congress assembled, (two-thirds of both houses concurring), that the following article be proposed to the legislatures of the several states as an amendment to the Constitution of the United States, which, when ratified by three-fourths of said Legislatures shall be valid, to all intents and purposes, as a part of the said Constitution, namely: Article XIII. Section 1. Neither slavery nor involuntary servitude, except as a punishment for crime whereof the party shall have been duly convicted, shall exist within the United States, or any place subject to their jurisdiction. Section 2. Congress shall have power to enforce this article by appropriate legislation.

Schuyler Colfax
Speaker of the House of Representatives.

H. Hamlin
Vice President of the United States
and President of the Senate.

26

Approved, February 1. 1865.

Abraham Lincoln

The Constitution has been amended only twenty-seven times in its history. The last amendment to be ratified was the Twenty-seventh Amendment, which was first proposed in 1791 but not ratified until 1992. The amendment prohibits senators and representatives from receiving a pay increase for which they voted until after a federal election.

*The Thirteenth Amendment, enacted in 1865, abolished the system of slavery in the United States.*

# PROVIDING CHECKS AND BALANCES

The Framers designed the government so that the powers and responsibilities of different branches of government would often overlap. This system allows each branch to check the power of the other branches and to balance that power with its own. For example, Congress has the authority to enact laws, but the president can veto, or overturn, a law. However, if two-thirds of both houses of Congress votes to overrule the veto, the law is enacted despite the president's disapproval. The president serves as commander in chief of the armed forces, but only Congress has the power to declare war.

*As commander in chief and president of the United States, Franklin Delano Roosevelt signed a declaration of war against Japan on December 8, 1941, signaling the United States' entry into World War II.*

Although the president has the power to appoint all federal judges, ambassadors, and other high government officials, the Senate must confirm all appointments. As the head of the judicial branch, the Supreme Court has the final authority to strike down both legislative and presidential acts as unconstitutional.

Another form of checks and balances involves the sharing of power between the individual states and the federal government. Called federalism, this sharing of power allows the nation to speak in one voice in such matters as foreign affairs and trade, but allows the people of each state to have more of a say in the way their state and local governments run.

*The first Monday of every October, members of the nation's highest court meet here, in the Supreme Court Building in Washington, D.C., to start a new term. By reviewing cases brought before it, the Supreme Court helps ensure that the laws of the United States and of individual states correspond to the rights and rules embodied in the U.S. Constitution.*

# THE RULE OF LAW

The Framers considered the rule of law essential to keeping social order and protecting individual rights. They believed that if our relationships with each other and with the state were governed by a set of rules, rather than by a group of individuals, it would be less likely that the country would fall victim to the tyranny, or harsh rule, of any one person or branch of government. The rule of law calls for both individuals and the government to submit to the laws as enacted by the Congress and enforced by the president and the rest of the executive branch.

*The two houses of Congress—the Senate and the House of Representatives—form the legislative branch. This branch is responsible for drafting and enacting new laws. Here, the fifty-ninth session of Congress meets in 1905.*

# THE BILL OF RIGHTS

When the Constitution was first drafted, it did not mention any rights that individual citizens would have under the government. The Framers thought that by limiting the power of government to interfere in the lives of citizens, they were protecting individual rights. But many people thought that it was important to spell out these rights very clearly. James Madison, one of the chief Framers of the Constitution, prepared twelve amendments that provided for individual rights. Ten of them were ratified in 1791 and became known as the Bill of Rights.

*The son of a wealthy Virginia planter, James Madison led a long and active career as one of this country's Founding Fathers. He served as a member of the Constitutional Convention from Virginia, a U.S. congressman, U.S. secretary of state, and president of the United States.*

The Bill of Rights prevents the government from interfering with certain individual liberties, including freedom of speech, press, assembly, and religion. Almost two-thirds of the Bill of Rights help safeguard the rights of people suspected or accused of crimes. These rights include the right to a fair trial by a jury of one's peers and protection against cruel and unusual punishment.

*Guaranteed by the Sixth Amendment, the right to a trial by a jury of one's peers is an essential part of the criminal justice system. Here, a jury listens to evidence.*

# HARPER'S WEEKLY
### A
## JOURNAL OF CIVILIZATION

VOL. XI.—No. 568.]    NEW YORK, SATURDAY, NOVEMBER 16, 1867.    [ SINGLE COPIES TEN CENTS.
                                                                 $4.00 PER YEAR IN ADVANCE.

Entered according to Act of Congress, in the Year 1867, by Harper & Brothers, in the Clerk's Office of the District Court for the Southern District of New York.

38

A series of new amendments were written after the Civil War. The Thirteenth Amendment (1865) abolished slavery, and the Fifteenth Amendment (1870) granted newly freed male slaves the right to vote. The Fourteenth Amendment, ratified in 1868, guaranteed due process and equal protection under the law to every American. Since then, thirteen other amendments have been added, including the Nineteenth Amendment, which gave women the right to vote in 1920, and the Twenty-second Amendment (1951), which prevents a person from serving as president of the United States for more than two terms, or eight years.

*In 1870, Congress enacted the Fifteenth Amendment—depicted here—which says that no man can be denied the right to vote on the basis of race, color, or previous condition of servitude. Women were not allowed to vote until 1920, after the passage of the Nineteenth Amendment.*

# THE CONSTITUTION AS A LIVING DOCUMENT

All laws made by Congress must conform to the rules set forth by the Constitution. The Supreme Court decides whether these laws are constitutional or not. If a citizen challenges a law because he thinks it is unconstitutional, the Supreme Court may review that law to see whether it conflicts with any provision of the Constitution. In a famous 1954 court case called *Brown v. Board of Education of Topeka*, for instance, a citizen challenged a Kansas law that required black and white children to go to different schools. The Court declared that the law was unconstitutional under the Fourteenth Amendment because it denied blacks and whites equal protection under the law.

*In 1954, the Supreme Court struck down laws that separated blacks and whites in schools and other public institutions. Here, black children enter an all-white school for the first time.*

More than 215 years ago, the Framers created a governing document that continues to define what it means to be an American living under the rule of law. At the time the Constitution was signed, the population of the United States was just four million. Today, more than 280 million people call themselves Americans, but the same Constitution continues to provide meaning and force to such basic issues as individual freedom and justice. It remains a strong and vital document that reflects the faith that most Americans place in the enduring traditions of the United States government.

*The U.S. Constitution created one of the strongest and most flexible forms of government in the world, one that guarantees equal protection under the law to all of its citizens, regardless of race, color, gender, or ethnic origin—a principle certainly worth celebrating!*

**American Revolution** the war between the American colonies and the British government from 1775 to 1783

**Articles of Confederation** one of the first documents that created a national government for the newly independent colonies

**Bill of Rights** the first ten amendments to the United States Constitution designed to protect individual rights

**Congress** the House of Representatives and the Senate, responsible for creating the nation's laws

**The Constitution** the document establishing the government of the United States and describing its parts and processes

**Constitutional Convention** the meeting of lawyers and statesmen that created a new government after the American Revolution won independence for the colonies

**Federalism** the division of power between the national government and the individual state governments

**The Framers**  the statesmen who drafted the United States Constitution.

**Judicial Branch**  the branch of government responsible for interpreting the laws of the nations, headed by the Supreme Court.

**Legislative Branch**  the branch of government responsible for creating the laws of the nation, made up of the two houses of Congress, the Senate and the House of Representatives

**Monarchy**  a system of government led by a king

**The Preamble**  an introduction to a text such as the Constitution

**Ratify**  to approve or enact

**Representative democracy**  a form of government in which the people elect representatives to make the laws for the country

# FIND OUT MORE

BOOKS

Agel, Jerome. *The U.S. Constitution for Everyone*. New York: Perigree, 1991

Fritz, Jean. *Shh! We're Writing the Constitution*. New York: Paper Star, 1998.

Patrick, John J. *The Supreme Court of the United States: A Student Companion*. New York:
      Oxford University Children's Books, 2001.

ORGANIZATIONS & WEB SITES

If you want to see copies of the original Constitution, Bill of Rights, and other documents
of national importance, this is the site to check out:

National Archives

700 Pennsylvania Avenue, N.W.

Washington, D.C. 20408

http://www.nara.gov


The PBS Democracy Project

http://www.pbs.org/democracy/


To Form a More Perfect Union

The Work of the Continental Congress and the Constitutional Convention

http://lcweb2.loc.gov/ammen/bdsds/bdexhome.html

Suzanne LeVert is the author of nearly a dozen books for young readers on a host of different topics, including biographies of the former governor of Louisiana, Huey Long, and author Edgar Allan Poe.  Most recently, she wrote four books in Benchmark Books' Kaleidoscope series on the human body, *The Brain*, *The Heart*, *The Lungs*, and *Bones and Muscles*.

# INDEX

*Page numbers for illustrations are in boldface.*